PAS DE TROIS

BRYNN FORD

More from the Author
www.brynnford.com
brynnfordauthor@gmail.com

For Sara.

Thank you for inspiring me
to be bold and brave.

CONTENT WARNING

This is a dark romance series involving many triggering elements which may be upsetting for some readers. A complete list of tropes and triggers can be found on the author's website at brynnford.com/triggers.

SERIES NOTE

Pas de Trois is book 3 of 3 in a complete trilogy. It is not a standalone, and the books must be read in order.

BOOKS BY BRYNN FORD

THE FOUR FAMILIES
Counts of Eight

Dance with Death

Pas de Trois

THE FOUR FAMILIES SPIN-OFF
King of Masters

EMBER GLEN
Spark of Madness

Blaze of Misery

Embers of Mercy

STANDALONES
Sugar Wood

Jagged Line Paradise

LAWLESS
Coming Soon!

The Darkness We Hide

PAS DE TROIS [French pahduh **trwah**]
noun, plural pas de trois. Ballet.
1. a dance for three dancers.

(www.dictionary.com)

PROLOGUE
Ezra

BLOOD TAKEN REQUIRES *blood given.*

That's what Renata had said to Anya as we drove away from the Vittori mansion. My girl had left no room for doubt when she'd admitted that she'd been the one to pull the trigger on Vigo Vittori.

I would have lied for her.

I would have told them that I'd been the one to kill him.

But Anya—either with bravery and pride or resentment and stupidity—had revealed the truth clearly. The wrath of the four families will fall on us and my only hope is keeping Nikolai alive long enough to…I don't even know what.

I just know that we need him.

Nikolai's pilot was on standby because of the quarterly meeting, and with his help, the three of us were able to board a helicopter and take off from the Vittoris' island in record time.

No one followed us.

They didn't need to.

They know who killed Vigo, they know where we'll be, and they will come after us in their own damn time.

That's what has me wondering about whether we might be able to escape everyone's grasp when our helicopter lands on the private airstrip in Palermo. When we'd landed there before—on our way to the quarterly meeting—the airstrip had seemed mostly deserted and hidden away. It's located in a valley beneath a rocky mountain cliffside which conceals it from the populated areas beyond.

"We could run." Anya leans toward me, raising her voice over the whir of the rotors, though I can hear her fine through the headsets we're wearing. "When we land at the airstrip, we could run. We don't have to go back with him to Russia."

Anya's thoughts reflect my own. But having her say it out loud forces the deliberation necessary to ensure the best possible outcome for us. It's the photographs that give me hesitation—the pictures I'd been so carefully studying in the green and pink floral box in Anya's room at Mikhailov Manor.

Her sister, Lidia.

My ex-girlfriend, Emma.

Would they be killed if we ran?

That was what we'd always been promised.

It was what kept us from running in the first place.

I bend over in my seat and tap the back of my fingers against Nikolai's cheek. He's prone on the fuselage floor, lying on his back, his body stretched out sideways in front of our feet. He's bled quite a bit and he fades in and out of consciousness, but he responds to my touch, turning his head toward us.

I point across the cabin. "Give me that headset." Anya reaches for it. I put the headset over Nikolai's ears so I can talk to him. His gray eyes flicker toward mine and I can see the intensity of his stare has lessened considerably. "What happens to Lidia and Emma?" I ask him. "Tell me the truth. Will they die if we run in Palermo?"

I feel Anya eyeing me skeptically. Surely, she's wondering why I would bother to ask because Nikolai can't be trusted.

We have no allies in this war we've created, but Nikolai is the closest thing we can get right now. He stole Anya away from Vigo. He gave me the opportunity to save her life. He had shown something resembling concern, even if he only meant to bring us both back into his servitude.

Perhaps this monster is capable of human emotions, after all.

"If I die…" Nikolai struggles with his breaths. "If I die, *they* die."

Anya looks back and forth between us, fear clouding her features. I know she hasn't seen her sister in years—not since she was taken by Nikolai—and I know how much she loves her. I sense the conflict she feels, knowing that if there were ever an opportunity to run, *this* would be it. No one would stop us from leaving the airstrip. We could abandon Nikolai and run.

But how far would we get?

Given the reach of the four families—and the fact that they know where to find Emma and Lidia—means that they can find us. And they *would* find us. It was clear in Renata's voice on that phone call.

Blood taken requires blood given.

Christ.

I run a shaking hand through my hair.

Nikolai lifts a hand at us, only just barely able to move it above the floor. "I can keep them safe. I can keep Anya safe. But she must…" he pants, "Anya must come back with me to Mikhailov Manor."

Anya and I look at each other with strain painting our expressions. We both know our options—and we both know the consequences—but the truth is that there isn't really a choice.

If we flee, they will only hunt us down.

If we go back to Mikhailov Manor, we may never leave again. But maybe Nikolai can keep Anya safe from them. The contradiction of everything I thought I was certain about is a total mind fuck.

Anya sighs, her eyes falling as her chest sinks. She turns her head to look down at Nikolai. "It's not enough to keep me safe. Can you keep us both safe? Can you promise that, Nikolai?"

"No. I can't promise that. But I do promise I can keep *you* safe." Nikolai holds her gaze as he pauses, taking a few haggard breaths. "I have things you'll need to show them. Hidden away. Come back with me and I'll help you. I can't do anything if you run, Anya. Get on the plane back to Russia with me and I'll call off the watch on your sister."

A tear slips down her cheek and I reach out to brush it away. She looks at me and the sadness I see in her eyes physically hurts me. "You can still run. You can run when we land. They won't need to come after you. I'm the one who killed Vigo…I'm the one they want. I can…I'll find a way to keep Emma safe. You can run and be free."

She's giving me permission to run without her.

She wants me to run without her?

Fuck, no.

I grab her face with both hands and lean close. "I'm not leaving you. I'm not running without you. If the only way to keep you safe is to take you back, then we're going back to Russia together. I don't care what they do to me, but I'm not leaving you on your own. It's you and me, okay? I'm gonna make sure Nikolai keeps his promise."

"But you could be free, Ezra. I—"

"Don't argue with me. We're going back together. It's already been decided. I told you before, my life is nothing without you." She's fucking crazy if she thinks I'm gonna leave her.

She presses her eyes shut and with a sigh of acceptance, nods. Her hands come up to grip my wrists, holding my hands in place against her cheeks.

"Mine?" she asks.

"Always fucking yours," I reply.

If we're going back, if the four families are coming after us seeking vengeance and blood, I will make damn fucking sure that the blood they spill isn't my blue-eyed girl's.

CHAPTER 1
Anya

MY HEAD IS swirling with too many emotions, the range and depth of which brings aching confusion.

Nikolai spills a trail of blood along the black pavement as Ezra and the pilot carry him across the airstrip from the helicopter to the private jet. I've never seen so much blood as I have tonight—I'm still covered in the splatter from Vigo.

I drag myself up the airstair steps onto Nikolai's jet, stepping carefully with my legs wide, straddling the red trail up the staircase to avoid stepping in Nikolai's blood with my bare feet. I step onboard the luxury plane just in time to watch Ezra and the pilot lay Nikolai on the couch—he just barely fits on it.

I watch him as he lays on his back, bleeding, with one arm on his chest while the other flops off the side of the couch. I can't help but think how frail and weak he looks—two words I would have never thought to call him before.

He took a bullet for me.

Did he save my life?

The pilot rushes off to the cockpit with Ezra's insistence that we hurry. In mere minutes, the plane takes off, carrying us into the night, away from one master's homeland to another's.

The cabin is silent as the plane reaches its cruising altitude and levels out—silent, except for Nikolai's heavy breaths. He was shot in the stomach nearly an hour ago. He's bled a lot, and I don't know what's going to happen to him. I don't know if he'll live or die. My mind splinters as it tries to grapple with the strange mix of emotions that simple fact inspires.

Nikolai may die.

There's relief in that possibility, but there's fear, too. Nikolai stole me back from Vigo. He was angry for Vigo's treatment of me, which is odd to think about, but clearly, it's true. I don't know how to feel about any of this. And the fact that Nikolai first tried to buy me back at a sum of ten million—I know my worth as a slave and it's nowhere near that sum. If the families dealt in rubles instead of euros, that would've been reasonable. But they all deal in euros, even the Leblancs.

It was an outrageous offer.

Ten million.

Then again, I suppose the worth of anything can only be determined by the amount someone is willing to pay for it. Tonight, Nikolai had determined that I was worth ten million.

I don't know whether to feel good or bad about that.

So, while I could—and probably should—stay in my seat, close my eyes, and rest up for the battles to come, I can't think of doing anything other than getting answers from him.

I unbuckle and rise, stepping around Ezra in the seat beside me to move into the aisleway. I cross the small space to Nikolai where he lays helpless on the couch. His eyes are open, looking above him, but they turn my way as I approach.

I stand still at his side. I'm not entirely sure what I want to ask him, what I want to tell him, what I want to do to him. But I just have to stand still for a moment as it happens—as the power that he always held over me pours from him with each breath, mingling with the air between us.

With each uneven breath I take, some of his power seeps into my lungs, swirling like a storm and punching my heart with lightning bursts that fortify me, strengthen me, embolden me. Our eyes remain locked as I willingly and gratefully take that power from him. "Why?"

"Why…what?"

Why did you choose me when I was eleven?

Why did you bring me partners you hated?

Why did you choose Ezra?

Why did you sell me?

Why did you risk everything to steal me back?

I take a step closer, knowing that he can hardly move, knowing that he can't hurt me right now. "Why me? Why did you choose me to live this life of torment?"

I feel Ezra approach before I see him appear at my side. I hold up my hand to stop him because I *need* this exchange with Nikolai without interference, without the distracting pulse of Ezra's pure goodness.

Nikolai lets a smirk curl up the corner of his lips. "You wouldn't believe me if I told you."

I scoff, "I've become fairly open-minded to nonsense over the years, Nikolai." I feel a rush when I say his name rather than call him *master.* "I'm a talent slave serving the four families with dance. An entirely unbelievable and unnecessary tradition of four slave trafficking families, spread across the globe, who descended from murderers. So, please, indulge me with the truth you think I won't believe."

I feel Ezra take a step back and I see him cross his arms over his chest from the corner of my eye. I don't tear my eyes away from Nikolai, but I sense the look on Ezra's face shows something resembling pride and encouragement.

Nikolai's eyes turn to the ceiling again. "I struggled to

select a beneficiary before I found you." He sounds breathless and weary. "I was twenty-six and I knew what I wanted. I wanted to find a boy. But I couldn't bring myself to tell my father. He judged me rather harshly for my...ambivalence. I selected your studio at random, showed up that day on a whim. I took one look into the studio and I saw you dancing." He shifts and flinches and I'm glad for his pain. "Anya," his eyes fall on me again, "I felt something deep for you. I was drawn to you. Instantly obsessed. I thought it felt like falling in love."

Oh, fuck no.

"Don't feed me lies," I hiss. "Tell me the truth."

"That's the truth."

"I was a *child.* You don't fall in love with a child!" I step closer, looming above him in the way he always loomed over me.

"It wasn't like that. Not then. I saw..." his breath stutters, "I saw another little girl who kept bumping into you. You gave her that fierce look of yours and when your teacher wasn't looking, you marched over to her, waved your finger in her face, and told her something that made her cheeks go white. She moved as far away from you as she could, and you took center stage. But you were obedient, too, and you followed your dance teacher's instructions perfectly. There was no one else in that room worth looking at. I fell in love with your spirit. I knew someday you'd make the perfect slave."

I reach down and I slap him. "You're *disgusting.* Lusting after a child."

His face contorts in pain. "Lust came later." He closes his eyes. "But I always cared deeply for you, Anya. If I didn't, you would have died a hundred deaths at my hands by now. I made you stronger."

"You made me a *slave.*"

"I gave you *everything.* I gave you the life of a Mikhailov."

Ezra makes a derisive sound but doesn't interrupt.

I drop to my knees, just so I can lean over Nikolai and show him the rage on my face. "I would rather *die* than have the life of a Mikhailov."

He chuckles, but it cuts off abruptly with a stuttering breath. "*Rabynya*, that is the exact choice you must make. And you must make it in a hurry. I think I might be dying."

I glance at Ezra and we share a look of confusion. "What are you saying?"

"How have you been feeling?" Nikolai asks.

"What?"

"Have you seen a doctor? Have any blood tests been done?"

"What are you *talking* about?"

"We make our money stealing and selling human lives... but we control each other with lies and secrets."

Ezra steps closer. "What are you trying to say?"

"I put a lie in Vigo's contract," Nikolai groans, crow's feet wrinkling at the corners of his eyes as he squeezes them shut in pain.

Good.

I want him to feel pain.

"What was the lie?" I demand.

"I'm sure if you think about it enough," Nikolai coughs, "you'll figure it out. Maybe in time the truth will grow on you."

What the hell does that even mean?

I shoot to my feet, enraged, indignant, fucking tired of him and the games he plays with my head. But I'm so tired and weak, so hungry, so thirsty, so out of my mind with suffering that I feel immediately light-headed and I stumble to catch my balance. I veer sideways. Ezra's at my side in an instant, catching me around the waist, and righting me.

I look up at him and a green spark catches fire in his eyes.

It lights my skin in flames that refuse to be ignored. In the mad rush from Ezra saving my life to fleeing the Vittoris, I hadn't taken a moment to let it hit me that Ezra is with me.

We're together and alive and safe for the moment.

He swallows as he ignites me with his fire and the heat is almost too much to bear. My mind is already overloaded, and my body can't take much more stress. Nikolai is talking in riddles that only induce further frustration. I want answers, yet I don't. I feel jittery and anxious and completely overwhelmed. The touch of Ezra's hands on the small of my back makes me tremble.

It's too much.

It's too fucking much.

I gently push Ezra's hands from me and scoot around him, storming off to the back of the plane. I slide open the door to the small bedroom, marching past the bed Nikolai has fucked me on more times than I can count, and enter the bathroom just beyond it. I slide the accordion door shut behind me. The bathroom is small, but not tiny like a commercial airline bathroom. There's enough space in here to pace three small steps from one end to the other.

I bend over the sink, gripping the rounded counter's edge as I breathe heavily, trying to get control of my rising panic before it grips me. I slowly lift my head and take in my appearance in the mirror above the small sink. I've never looked so awful. My cheeks are hollow, skin sallow, hair wet and matted from being trapped in Vigo's tub.

But worst of all is the red.

Vigo's blood coats my skin and stains the white shirt.

I look down at the buttons and suddenly remember that this is Vigo's shirt.

I'm wearing Vigo's shirt and it's covered in his blood because I killed him.

I shot him.

I killed him.

Oh, God…

My skin is suddenly crawling for me to get it off, and my fingers fumble, trembling as I reach to unbutton the shirt.

Get it off.

Get. It. Off.

The bathroom door slides open and shuts again, but I don't even look up.

"Anya." I hear Ezra's voice.

"Get it off me." One button comes free and I fumble for the next, trying and trying, but my fingers keep slipping. "Get it *off* me. Get his shirt off me!"

"Anya, stop."

Ezra reaches for the buttons to help me, but I'm out of my mind. It only feels as though he's trying to interfere, and I push his hands away as I keep struggling to unbutton this godforsaken shirt.

Are there a hundred fucking buttons on this shirt?!

"Anya." He snatches my wrists. "Stop. Let me help you."

I don't hear him trying to help me; I only feel him stopping me. I yank free from his grip and slap his hands away, then reach for another button. My whole body shakes as this overwhelming agitation takes over and I can't stop it.

I can't stop it.

I need Ezra to stop it.

"Fuck. *Please,*" I beg, words failing me.

In a rush, he's in my space, hands grasping the hem of the shirt that reaches halfway down my thighs. His fingers brush my skin and the jolt of lightning startles me into stillness. He lifts the oversized shirt, peeling it up my body.

"Arms up," he says to me.

In this sudden stillness that he's sparked with his touch, my mind can listen, and I obey.

I raise my arms and he peels the shirt from my body, tossing it behind him on the floor. I would feel stupid for not thinking to do that myself if it weren't for the fact that I'm so acutely aware of his presence, his heat, his power that poses no threat but only exists to care for me.

He pulls several paper towels from the dispenser beside the sink and wets them in the slow-running faucet. Without being asked, he wipes the blood from my skin. He cleanses me without command because he loves me.

I stand still as he wipes my face clean. His movements are gentle, though the paper is rough against my skin. My panicked breaths begin to slow as I watch him work. His brows slant inward, wrinkling his forehead with a look that's focused and caring and worried.

He's worried about me.

He *should* be worried about me.

I'm worried about me.

I let out a breath as my heartbeat wills itself to steady, to calm, to slow. I sigh as he moves from cleaning my cheeks, drawing the towel down to my neck. He scrubs across the hollow of my throat and I swallow hard. His eyes flick upward and meet mine, and we catch on a beat of nothingness.

It's that beautiful nothingness where no mental or physical anguish exists—it's only the two of us and everything is perfect because there is nothing else.

"I'm sorry," I tell him as he curves around to the side of my neck.

"For what?"

"For…being crazy."

He smiles as he gently tosses my hair back over my

shoulder. "You've never been crazy. The four families...? Fucking nuts. You? Never."

The edges of the towel flutter across my earlobe as he scrubs the side of my neck. I find that my head naturally falls to the side, opening the curve of my neck to him. Ezra's lips fall open as he looks at me and his hand stills.

My heart skips a beat.

Though I'm blood-covered down my neck and chest, I'm otherwise standing bare and exposed in front of him. It's been six months since I've been naked with Ezra. Yes, we'd had sex in that dungeon at the Leblancs' the night I tried to kill myself three months ago, but it was quick, and we'd remained in our clothing.

But now my chest heaves with a heavy breath as something deep within me stirs, remembering what it was like to be touched gently, to be loved and given pleasure instead of pain.

His breath hitches as if he responds naturally to the coiling tension in my belly—which, of course, he does because our souls are linked beyond reason. His hand lowers, scrubbing over the dried blood on my chest, though his eyes don't leave mine. The blood streaks across the mound of my right breast and his towel doesn't neglect. I gasp as the rough ends of the paper graze my nipple while he scrubs. He's diligent, finishing his work, cleansing me thoroughly of the stains of this awful night.

His eyes burn into mine and air catches in my lungs.

Before he's done, we're both panting, huffing together in an unsteady but shared rhythm—a shared rhythm we'd lost when we were apart.

Nothing else in the world exists.

It's just Ezra and me and heat.

Heat.

"Ezra..." I whisper on a breath.

The paper towel drops to the floor and his hand clamps

around my breast. We both exhale heavily on cue, and then we crash. He bends to meet me, and our lips collide, ramming together with bruising, desperate force.

I need him.

I need him more than water, more than food, more than rest. I need him to love me in the way only Ezra can. I need him to flood my senses and take over my emotions and drown me in his endless hope and possibilities.

He pushes back until I hit the wall and he presses into me so impossibly close that I can hardly breathe. But it doesn't matter because I take in air through his kiss. His tongue swirls with mine as he absolutely devours me. I'm trapped by him and it doesn't scare me, it doesn't lead me to panic or fear—it excites my senses.

And I need more.

My arms latch around his neck, yanking him down to hold his face to mine, silently begging him not to stop. His hands fall to my waist and he squeezes, digging in his fingertips. He starts to lift and I jump in frantic determination, tightly wrapping my legs around him.

He holds me against the wall, kissing me with more urgency than I've ever felt before. He feeds me a growl, a groan of need that vibrates his entire body, and it pulls a tight knot in my stomach that only he can unravel.

"Inside me. Please," I manage against his lips.

He groans again, shaking with need. I know how much he wants to sink inside me—-one I'd ever want to take me fiercely, passionately, without restraint. But he's just such a damn good man.

Too damn good for me.

He doesn't want to be like all the rest who take and take from me without care or concern. But he could never be like them. I have no fear with him, no shame, no guilt. I *want* him to have me, to love me, to enjoy my body because he's earned it. Ezra has earned my heart and soul, and with it, my body.

I grip his face in my palms, pulling him away from our kiss by hardly an inch. I give him the full force of my gaze. "I need you inside me."

The feral, masculine part of him roars internally—I see the flash fire of it explode behind his eyes. Inexplicably, it makes my stomach clench and wetness rush between my legs with need. Still, he restrains that beast within him.

"You need rest. I don't want to hurt you."

I'm already rocking and rubbing myself against Ezra's waist because he just does something to me that I can't explain. "I can't rest until you come inside me."

He groans and his hips buck up against me. I feel his erection against my bare skin and I've never needed him as much as I do right now.

"Please, Ezra," I beg. "Make me forget everything but you."

He presses me harder against the wall, his hips working. "Jesus Christ, Anya."

He's holding back and it's killing me. I feel like I have to seduce him, and it's such an odd role reversal for me. It makes me feel powerful to know he won't take advantage of me, to know that he *can't* take advantage of me. He's too determined to protect me, to care for me, to keep me safe. He gives me power over him. In a world where I have been powerless and abused for so long, it's a rush to know that he's mine.

And it's the biggest fucking turn-on.

I lean forward, biting his lower lip and sucking on it. I release it and he shudders. "Lay me down and fuck me, Ezra Bell."

CHAPTER 2
Ezra

LAY ME DOWN *and fuck me.*

Anya demanded it and I was compelled to give it.

I hadn't come after her with the intention to do this. I just wanted to make sure she was okay, maybe hold her, comfort her, put her to bed to rest while I went back to get all the answers we still need from Nikolai before he bleeds out and dies—or before I strangle him myself. But it's impossible to be near Anya and not feel the chemistry—that natural draw to be closer to her—and it's been so fucking long since I've seen her.

It feels like an urgent and necessary *need.*

I don't know if her body can handle this right now. She nearly died tonight and had already seemed in such precarious health before Vigo trapped her in that fucking tub. Sex is probably the worst thing she can do to her body right now.

I know that.

But how can I deny her when she commands me so insistently?

She wouldn't encourage it if she didn't want it, though. I know that much is true. I refuse to be another man in her life who tells her what she can and can't do. So, even though giving her what she wants might actually kill her from exhaustion alone, I'm not gonna deny her. I'm not gonna deny either of us when we both need this so much.

Moving one of my hands up between her shoulder blades, I step backward before turning us around. I fumble to slide open the small accordion-style door behind her back, but once it's open, I rush straight to the almost queen-sized bed just beyond it. My knees hit the mattress and I bend forward, laying her down on her back and moving with her.

I can't let go of her; I can't move away.

Her fingers find my hair and she keeps our faces close as we both pant with need, heating the air between us with unsteady breath. My cheek rests against hers as I reach down between us to unbuckle my pants. I don't get up until they're unlatched, and when I do, I slip them off quickly, eagerly climbing back on top of her.

She doesn't need words to tell me how much she needs me to fill her or how she needs me to make the empty feeling of being apart from each other go away. There's a pause as I grab my cock and angle toward her, brushing the tip against her slick folds that beg me to push in deep. She gasps and moans as I let the pause linger, let it heat and catch on fire. There's just breath between us—breath and the aching need to be lost in our love together.

I press delicate, sensual kisses to her cheek. "I've missed you so much."

Her hips wiggle beneath my weight and it only makes me feel heavier, weighted down, like my body and hers need to fuse entirely for us to feel complete. When I finally push inside her—too desperate to drag out the anticipation any longer, too needy for foreplay—I sink in deep.

We both moan with sounds of pure satisfaction when we're finally connected again. This isn't just sex. And if I was honest, it was never just sex with Anya. It's spiritual. It's prayer.

It's fucking worship at the altar of our souls. I slip my arms around behind her back and move my hips slowly, with long, full strokes that reach deep inside her as I hold her close.

She moans through a long exhale as she grips my hair, angling my head to kiss me with parted, gasping lips. "I missed you, Ezra. I missed you." Her lips find my ear. "Tell me you missed me. Tell me you love me. Tell me how much you need this with me."

"Anya…" I kiss her cheek, along her jawline, down her neck, but never stop moving inside her. "I was dying without you."

She stays close to me, nuzzling her cheek against mine. "You're mine."

"I'm yours."

"Say it again." Her spread knees squeeze my hips and I thrust faster, with more force and depth, making sure she feels every inch of me.

"Christ," I groan. "I'm yours."

I drive my cock inside her, pushing deep. Each stroke feels like the strike of a match to my insides, heating me, setting me on fire, and I know the only way to put out the flame is to douse it in the wetness of her desire.

She pants beneath me, gasping for breath. "Please… *please*," she whispers against my ear.

"Come for me, baby. Please. I need to feel it." I angle my thrusts upward, faster, rubbing along her most sensitive spot until she squeezes her eyes shut, grasping my hips firmly between her knees.

"Oh…*oh*," she whimpers and with two more thrusts, she explodes, her pussy pulsing around my cock as her stomach clenches and she coils around her center.

She's still coming as her clenching climax drags me along with her. It takes me by surprise the way her pleasure links with mine, twisting around me and pulling me into orgasm. I spill deep inside her with a satisfied groan, the swell of my cock somehow dragging out her orgasm a few perfect seconds longer.

The tip of her nose brushes along my cheek as breath rushes in and out. I turn my head to kiss her with gentle lips and a languid tongue. She wraps her arms around me, holding me close as our bodies slow to stillness.

She opens her eyes and looks at me, catching me fully with her brightness. "I love you." Her blue eyes are vibrant, sparkling, though I can see the exhaustion behind the luster of her love.

"I love you, too." I kiss her once more, slow and wet and lovingly.

Gradually, I pull out and I hate it because it feels so right to be inside her. I roll slowly onto my side next to her and she turns with me, shrinking and curling against my chest. I wrap my arms around her and cherish the feeling of being able to hold her and keep her safe.

"I know hell is coming," she says quietly, "but right now, I feel safe with you." She sighs. "Why can't we always feel this way?"

I run my hand down her side. "Someday we will."

She kisses the center of my chest and it makes my heart skip a beat. "You are hope incarnate. I don't know how you keep the faith." Anya yawns through the final word.

I brush my hand down her hair before kissing the top of her head. "You need to sleep."

"Shit." She starts to sit up. "I need to talk to Nikolai. I need to know what's going on; what we do when they come after us. I need to know that Lidia will be safe…Emma, too. We need so many answers from him and he's—"

"Let me handle it." I pull her back down beside me. "I want you to sleep. You *need* to sleep, Anya. I'll get all of the answers from him."

"I need to know everything."

"And you will."

She tilts her head up to look at me with those piercing blue eyes. "Ezra. It's important."

"I know it's important. It's critical. And I'll get all the answers to all the questions. But we only have a couple of hours before we arrive, and I need you to sleep before then. I need you to get your strength back. Okay? I'm worried about you." I tuck a strand of hair behind her ear. "I shouldn't have been so rough with you. Probably shouldn't have fucked you at all." I grin. "I just couldn't help myself."

She smiles at me. I see her desire to fight me flash across her eyes. But then she yawns again as she's trying to give me her commanding stare and I can't help but laugh. She does, too. I pull her closer, hugging her and kissing her forehead.

"So, are you gonna rest? Or are you gonna argue with another yawn that you're not tired?" I joke.

She giggles and I feel the vibration of it against my chest, over my heart.

Fuck.

This woman is everything.

"Okay," she concedes with a sigh. "I trust you."

I lift her chin so she has to look up at me and I grin. "Say that again, baby. Slowly."

"What? I trust you?" She bites her lip through a smile. "I trust you, Ezra."

I groan. "Yes, that. That's so hot."

She makes a sexy face in good humor. "I. Trust. *You.*"

I lift my eyebrows. Though it was said humorously, it actually is kind of turning me on again.

"Shit. I've gotta get out of here before you make me hard again."

She captures my lips, taking me off-guard with the passionate force behind her kiss as she pushes me onto my back and rolls on top of me. She pulls back and smiles, looking down at me, her eyes flickering across my features, taking in every inch of my face. She tilts her head regarding me. "I really do trust you."

It's a somber and precious moment when I catch her eyes. Our souls stare and our hearts beat in time. I know there's hell all around us, but I can't believe how lucky I am to be the man she loves. She kisses me again before I roll her back onto the bed and get up. I lift the covers for her and she crawls beneath. For the first time ever, I see peace in her features as she watches me dress. Anya deserves that peace, even if it's only for a few hours. We're safe here together on this plane…for now.

I put my pants back on and finally remove my shirt, leaving it behind on the bed as something for Anya to wear later. Then I leave her to sleep peacefully as I return to Nikolai in the main cabin.

Blood trickles from his side, soaking the side of the leather couch and pooling on the carpet beneath, staining it crimson. My heart thumps an extra beat when I notice his eyes are closed.

Fuck.

Did we miss our opportunity for answers and assurances because we couldn't keep our hands to ourselves?

My hands land on top of my head, fingers locking together as I force out a steadying breath. I drop my hands against my sides with a slap before crossing to him. His head turns toward me and his eyes open slowly. I never thought I would be relieved to see that Nikolai Mikhailov still lives and breathes.

"I'm still alive, in case you cared," he murmurs. "You might have been quieter fucking my slave," he pauses to draw in a ragged breath, "just in case I live." He chuckles darkly.

"She's no more your slave than I am right now. You're weak, Nikolai. You're dying."

"If you came to ask something of me, you're doing a very poor job of it."

I move beside him, kneeling on the carpet next to the pooling blood. "You said you would keep Lidia and Emma safe. I want you to make that happen."

He sighs. "Give me my cell phone."

My head tilts with surprise. His concession without taunting is jarring, but I won't squander the opportunity. I pull his phone from my back pocket where I stored it for safe-keeping and hold it out for him. He unlocks it with his fingerprint, then drops his hand, too weak and too tired to hold it up. He directs me through his contact list, and I scroll until I find *Contractors, NY*—his hired mercenaries on contract in New York City, where both Emma and Lidia happen to reside.

With a pinch of anxiety, I tap the contact and put it on speakerphone for him. It only rings once before the other line picks up, but no one says hello.

Instead, Nikolai asks, "Is the weather better today?"

I squint my eyes in confusion.

"The weather is better than yesterday. What can I do for you, sir?" Comes the reply from the other end of the line.

Was that some sort of verbal code?

"Remove the trace and threat on Antonov and Mayfield."

"You're certain, sir?"

"Yes."

"Consider it done. They'll be left alone and unharmed."

"Thank you."

That's it? This whole time…It was that fucking easy?

I have a sudden feeling of terror that he's joking, that he's about to say he's kidding and order the contractor to murder Emma and Lidia immediately, just as a final *fuck you* to me and Anya. So, I quickly tap to end the call before he can say anything else and set the phone aside where he can't reach it.

"Now, tell me how you can keep Anya safe from the four families."

"I'll tell you, but I want you to promise me something. "

"You're not in a position to ask for favors."

"Neither are you, *mal'chik*. You can let me die without ever knowing," he takes a shuddering breath, "what I've done for her."

Goddammit.

I need answers.

I swallow my pride and force down the tick of righteousness that swells in my chest. "Fine."

"Promise me you won't tell her anything until we're back at Mikhailov Manor. If I die before then, you can tell her what you want."

"What does it matter if I tell her now or wait?"

"I don't know…it doesn't. I suppose I'm hoping for a final dramatic revelation of how I've changed her life and saved her. And I'd like that to happen in my own home." He gasps another ragged breath. "But I don't know if I'll make it until then." His eyes meet mine dead on and pierce me in his gray stare. "I almost don't care if I die. But if I do, I'd like it to be in my own home, Ezra."

Ezra, not mal'chik.

Shit.

The use of my name in his plea reminds me that he's human—a fucking shitty one, but a human, nonetheless. The words spill out before I can think better of them. "You have a private doctor, don't you?"

Why did I even say that?

I don't want this bastard to get medical treatment.

I want him to die.

Still, the human part of me insists that help be offered, if only for the sake of proving to myself that I'm a better man than he is.

"Don't call him. I don't think I can be saved."

It's like he's already given up. It's possible his wounds could be healed with proper medical treatment, but without… he'll continue to bleed until he dies.

He knows that.

And he doesn't care.

I sigh. "Okay. I promise. I won't say a word to Anya until we get back."

"Good. Thank you."

His stare softens before he presses his eyes shut, sucking in a breath through his nose to steady himself. When he opens them again, he looks somehow…haunted. But there's no more time to delay in decoding his expression.

"Tell me everything."

CHAPTER 3

Anya

I'M THANKFUL EZRA encouraged me to rest on the plane. I'm surprised by the fact that I was able to sleep at all, let alone the remainder of the flight. For the first time in a long time, I felt safe aboard that plane, even when I knew it was only temporary. I knew Ezra would watch over me, and Nikolai was incapacitated, leaving all threats to my life behind on the ground.

We'd transferred to a helicopter after we landed at the Mikhailovs' private airstrip in Russia. Ezra and the pilot dragged a bleeding Nikolai yet again from one aircraft to the other. We took off silently into the night, not a word from any of us as we approached the Mikhailovs' vast landscape.

When we finally landed on the helipad in the middle of the dark forest, the pilot left us after assisting Nikolai once more, helping Ezra place him into the back of the car that had been left there. The three of us were alone to make the solemn, silent drive back to Mikhailov Manor.

We could have found his private doctor's number on his cell phone and arranged for him to come and treat Nikolai at the manor, but we didn't.

Nikolai had told Ezra not to and when I asked Nikolai myself, he insisted that we don't call. He said there was no point, and I can't for the life of me imagine why he seems to have given up. It's as if he *wants* to die.

I think we all know logically that he *is* dying without treatment. He was shot hours ago, and the blood loss has been… overwhelming. I think he's only survived this long to make the trip back to his homeland so he could die on his own terms. If I let myself think about it for too long, tears well behind my eyes, burning liquid that has no reason to exist because I won't mourn his loss.

My captor, my master, my tormentor—he's dying and I'm glad.

But then why does it hurt to think about?

I help as much as I can, but it's Ezra who does the work to get Nikolai from the car across the threshold into Mikhailov Manor.

"Take me to the dance studio," Nikolai manages before huffing out heavy breaths.

His face is pale, and blood continues to leak from his injury as Ezra drags him through the main entrance. Mikhailov Manor is large and empty, just as I remembered it being. But the atmosphere is particularly haunting now. My eyes follow the grand staircase up to the second floor. I feel as though the ghosts of Mikhailovs past watch as we bring the last of their line home to die.

The last Mikhailov is going to die.

My pulse kickstarts.

I follow Nikolai's trail of blood to the dance studio, wrapped only in Ezra's dress shirt since we'd left Vigo's bloodied shirt on the plane. Ezra drags him with his arms hooked beneath Nikolai's armpits, sweat glistening across his bare torso from the exertion of moving a body over and over again. Ezra pulls him across the threshold of the dance studio, finally setting him down in the center of the brightly-lit space.

"Okay." Ezra takes a few deep breaths. "We're here. Now tell her where the box is, or I will."

The box?

"What box?"

Ezra talked to Nikolai on the plane while I rested. But all Ezra told me was that he'd promised Nikolai the opportunity to tell me everything himself when we arrived. I don't know why it mattered to Nikolai or why Ezra agreed to it. I only know that Ezra is a better man than he gives himself credit for. I can imagine his heart wouldn't allow him to deny a dying man's last request—even when that man is vile and undeserving of sympathy.

"In Nobility Hall," Nikolai says on a whisper. "The box is under my seat. You know my seat." He's gasping, struggling for air. "Hurry."

Nikolai's seat.

He always sat in the same spot for my performances in Nobility Hall. He'd chosen a favorite spot, and I'd always wondered why he picked it because I knew it wasn't the best seat in the house. But it makes sense now. If he's hiding something so important there—something that he claims will save me from the four families' fury—then it serves to reason he would always sit there and remain in that very spot until everyone else had left after my performances.

"Keys," I say, suddenly urgent to find this box and learn his secrets. "I need the keys."

Ezra pulls the set of keys that he collected from Nikolai's pocket and hands them to me.

"Stay with him," I tell Ezra.

He gives me a nod and I take off on a jog, thankful for the burst of adrenaline that comes from the urgency of it all.

I jog past the main entrance, dash down the garden corridor, and rush to the locked door in the alcove. I find myself fumbling with the keys, my hands shaking. There may as well be someone behind me holding a gun to my head for the way I tremble.

Once the door is open, I move through the short hallway, quickly finding my way to the lobby of Nobility Hall. I take a breath as I stand before the two sets of double doors and slowly, I step forward. I pull one of the doors open wide and move into the darkness.

I head to the light booth to turn on the house lights and take no more than a moment to revel in the twinge of excitement that being in this space always gives me. The twinge has nothing to do with this theater and everything to do with my love of performing.

I make my way down the aisle on the left. I find Nikolai's seat easily enough, but I don't know what to do now that I'm here. It's an aisle seat, so I stand beside it, looking and waiting for something special to reveal itself to me.

I drop to my knees on the plush red carpeting and examine the area. I lift the hinged seat up and down, looking beneath it, trying to find a latch or a lock—something, *anything* that looks out of the ordinary. With a huff of exasperation, I slap my hands on the veneered wood flooring under the seat.

Did I imagine that hollow sound?

I run my hands across the floor, covering every inch until I feel a gap with the pads of my fingers—a miniscule crevice that cuts across the floor in the wrong direction. I claw at it, digging my fingernails into the edge and pulling, but nothing happens.

If it were truly important, Nikolai wouldn't leave it unlocked.

I practically crawl beneath the seat, inspecting the chair, the legs, the floor…but there's nothing.

Nothing.

But then…Nikolai wouldn't get down on his hands and knees to retrieve a secret box, that would be rather undignified of him.

I climb back out and inspect the back rest. My hands roam along the flat back, finding nothing and moving on to the armrests. My fingers slowly graze down the sides, sliding along the outside of the armrests, then the inside.

That's when I feel it—another unusual ridge on the inside of the aisle armrest. When I dig my fingernails into this one, it clicks. A tiny wooden door carved into the intricately-etched pattern at the end of the armrest pops open.

I bend, moving my head closer to look inside it, and sure enough, there's a keyhole. "What on Earth?" I whisper in the empty room.

I already know which of Nikolai's keys will fit this. It's a small keyhole and there's only one tiny brass key on his keyring that appears as though it will fit. I insert the key, turn it, and jump back when I hear something click beneath the seat. I crouch down to look and see that the floor is now uneven—a piece of it has sprung upward on a hinged spring.

I scramble to pull the piece all the way back and find myself looking into a black hole in the ground, at least a foot deep. Other than the gray box sitting inside it, it looks like a void, a place where perhaps all my hopes and dreams and possible futures went to die.

I don't know what's in this box that Nikolai thinks will save me. But Ezra already knows and that knowledge took away some of his brightness.

I feel nauseous.

Time is wasting. The four families could arrive at any moment, and I need to know what's in this gray box that will spare me from harm. I lift it from the black cavern and carefully set it on the carpet. I close the hinged door in the floor, remove the key, and cover the keyhole on the armrest.

Though my curiosity threatens to kill me, I don't dare look inside the box—not here, not alone. Whatever is in this box is going to change my life. I know it. I can feel it. And I can't find out alone.

I pick up the box and carry it all the way across the manor and back to the dance studio, holding it delicately, as if it were a bomb that would explode should I drop it. I hurry inside the studio only to be welcomed by the sound of Nikolai's gasping breaths. They're heavier and shorter than they were before, and it halts me in the doorway.

Ezra is on his knees beside him, grasping his hand, almost comfortingly. Nikolai deserves no comfort…

Then why do I feel thankful that Ezra gives it?

Something inside me feels torn to see Nikolai this way—weak and helpless. He's finally getting what he's always deserved, yet I feel a prickling confusion from my head down to my toes.

Ezra catches my gaze and I lower to my knees on the opposite side of Nikolai. Ezra's expression is mixed with urgency and concern. "He doesn't have much time."

"I know," I reply.

Nikolai's head falls to the side and he looks at me. "Open the box."

I nod and sit back on my heels, bringing the box onto my lap. I inhale deeply, steeling myself against Nikolai's unpredictability one last time.

One last time?

The last time.

I remove the lid and set it aside.

Nikolai speaks, as quiet as a whisper, his voice weak and strained. "Everything is official. Legal."

Inside, there's a letter-sized envelope and a small black box. I reach for the envelope, lifting it with care, my fingers delicate on the paper that holds untold secrets. I quickly glance up at Ezra and he nods. I swallow down my anxiety and open it.

I pull out the pages.

I unfold them.

My hands tremble as I read the words.

Certificate of Marriage.

My heart stops beating.

Anya Antonov and Nikolai Mikhailov were joined in marriage on the twenty-first of September in the year…

Oh, God.

I remember.

This is what happened that day.

That's what he was trying to remind me of when I was forced to spend the night with him three months ago as my punishment for trying to commit suicide.

Nearly a year into my captivity—when I was tired of fighting him, when I was lonely, lost, and desperate—I'd come to his room willingly for the first and only time and he'd made me come with his fingers. He never showed me compassion or caring after. He used the knowledge he gained that day against me, knowing how to use my body to coax me into compliance. I went back to hating him after that, though I suppose that was the time when I stopped fighting and gave him my submission to avoid pain.

But this, this *Certificate of Marriage,* was from the day after that. I remember Nikolai's brother making me drink beyond intoxication. I remember him bringing me into Nikolai's home office. I remember seeing another man who I didn't recognize.

A clergyman.

And Kostya, whose name is here as a witness on the

certificate, along with Nikolai's brother.

Then it's true?

"We're married?" I stare at the certificate in my hands. "We're married. Is this true, Nikolai?"

"Yes," he whispers. "I told you, I fell for you." He gasps. "I was going to tell the board when I turned forty."

Forty?

He would be forty in a couple of months.

I look at Ezra, hoping for some sort of clarification and thankfully, he's able to provide it since Nikolai's breaths are becoming erratic. "Heads of House choose a bride when they're forty…to bear children and carry on the family name," Ezra explains solemnly. "He was going to tell them he'd already married you, but he wasn't supposed to marry anyone without their agreement. That certificate would've forced their approval."

With insistence and no warning at all, a bubble of rage rises into my chest and bursts explosively. "Why would you do this to me?" I shout at Nikolai. "Why did you do this?"

"To keep you," Nikolai says. "To make you worthy of me."

"You bastard," I snarl. "*Worthy* of you? I'm worth more than your sick soul could ever afford."

"I know." He's shaking, pale as a ghost, eyes shadowed with his oncoming death. "I know that now. That's why I tried to buy you back. To save you." His eyes flicker toward the box again. "Look."

I pull out the only other item I see in the gray box—a small, square, black jewelry box.

No.

Please, no.

I flip open the hinged top.

Sparkling bright is a large, square-cut diamond ring and a wedding band to go with it.

Hot tears spring to my eyes.

I don't know whether I'm livid or hurt or heartbroken. Probably all three. He took my future from me. He has well and truly stolen my life and this ring is a symbol of my slavery. He tied me to his family. Forever.

"Am I," my voice cracks, "am I a Mikhailov?"

"Yes. Since our wedding."

There's a page behind the marriage certificate proving that it's true. He had my name legally changed—legal in the sense that he paid off corrupt officials, no doubt.

My name is Anya Mikhailov.

I drop the jewelry box and dig my fingers into my hair at the scalp. "No. No, no, no. I'm not. I can't be. I *won't* be."

"You're the last Mikhailov," Nikolai says and I scream.

I scream and I sob and I don't stop until I hear Ezra softly say my name.

"Anya. There…there might be more."

I turn my head to look at him, my vision blurred by the tears that form a sheen across my eyes. "More? What more could there be?"

"I lied," Nikolai breathes out hard. "On Vigo's contract of sale…I lied."

"You lied?" My eyebrows lift, my hands fall hard onto my lap, and I nearly laugh. "Shocking."

"Tell her," Nikolai says to Ezra, panting, suffering.

Good.

Let the bastard suffer.

Ezra closes his eyes for a beat. He doesn't look at me when he speaks. "Nikolai wrote in the contract that you were infertile. That you couldn't get pregnant."

"He *what?*"

"He lied to Vigo. The last birth control shot Nikolai had

the doctor give you was three months before he sold you. You've been…" Ezra hesitates. "You've been off birth control for the past six months. The last shot would've worn off just before Vigo took you."

My nervous systems stutters and every muscle in my body freezes. I'm stuck in place for what feels like hours, though I know it's only moments. Suddenly I feel trapped inside my mind because what I've just heard is outrageous.

Absurd.

Laughable, really, though it's not funny at all.

I blink and my eyelids linger shut for beats longer than normal. When I open them again, I look down at Nikolai, my mouth open wide in misunderstanding and confusion.

When I speak, my words are measured, slow, so there is no possible way they can be misunderstood. "Did you *want* me to get pregnant with that monster's child? Is that what you *wanted*, Nikolai? Tell me. Tell me!" I shout.

"I wanted to punish you, *rabynya*."

I slap him.

Then I slap him again.

I punch his shoulder, his chest, his stomach, and he groans in pain when I do.

"I'm sorry," he grunts. "I'm sorry, Anya. It was a mistake. I tried to make it right."

"Oh, you tried? Tried how?" I laugh. "Tell me, Nikolai, how did you try to make it right?"

"At the Leblancs'."

I tried to kill myself at their last quarterly meeting three months ago. I'd been caught by Vigo before I could do it and they went to the board to decide my punishment. Ezra and I had been locked together while our fate was decided. Ezra and I had made love there.

But then Nikolai took me for the night to serve my punishment by giving me pleasure that I didn't want. He fucked me over and over again that night.

That's how he tried to make it right?

I don't understand…

I don't….

Oh, God.

"I've been sick." I lift my head and meet Ezra's solemn green eyes. "I thought it was from malnourishment. I don't remember having a period…Oh, God. Ezra."

"Hey, it's okay," Ezra says to me. "It's all gonna be okay."

I feel composed and frantic all at once, my brain faltering and restarting again and again.

"Am I pregnant? I can't be pregnant. There's no way. With the stress my body's been through? No. *No.* It's not possible."

"Letter," Nikolai hardly gets the word out. "Lid."

"What?"

Ezra nods toward the lid of the box beside me on the floor and I reach for it, flipping it over. On the underside is a small envelope taped to the lid. I pull it free and tear it open. My hands shake as I look at the handwritten letter. The date at the top tells me it was written last week.

It's Nikolai's handwriting, all in Russian.

It's a letter he wrote to me.

> *Dear Anya,*
>
> *I don't know if I will ever give you this letter. But if you're reading it, then please know that I do feel regret—not for making you mine, but for selling you out of anger.*
>
> *I gave you everything you could have ever needed. But I'm starting to understand now that I never gave*

you what you wanted. I wanted you to have your pet. I would have let you love each other if only you had both loved me.

Ezra was the perfect fit. The pet that would have given you the happiness you deserved while I was away. If only you had both obeyed. If only you had both recognized your true master. We all could have found our happiness together.

There's emptiness in this home without you. I know I hurt you. I wanted to hurt you. I've become obsessed with hurting you. But when you hurt me by bringing Ezra into your bed against my orders, I couldn't stand to look at you.

But I missed you only hours after you had gone.

It was a mistake to sell you to Vigo.

If the gods see fit to bless me with your child, I will take you back, claim you forever, and try to be better.

I suppose I never learned how to show it, but I do love you, Anya. Please forgive me.

Yours,
Nikolai

The paper crumples in my hand and it forms creases on my heart.

CHAPTER 4
NIKOLAI

I AM THE devil.

Destroyer of destinies.

Keeper of souls.

Lord of chaos and king of torment.

But if I'm to go down in my own hellfire—in the flames I willed to burn around me—then I'm glad that this is the way it had to happen. Ezra was the spark that ignited Anya in a white-hot blaze, and I was the one who poured the fuel that fed their fire.

I did this to them, and it ruined me.

There is no redemption for me.

I may have stolen Anya back from the Vittoris, but she's no longer mine. She gave her heart to Ezra, and I have no one to blame for that but myself. They don't know that they each hold half of my heart in their hands, and I feel them squeezing the life force out of me with their love for each other. They grow stronger together while I burn to ashes at their feet.

I'm tired of the ache, the longing, the inability to master them and make them honor me the way they were meant to. My whole life has been a carefully crafted series of lies and manipulations, and I'm sick of the fight, the fear, the loneliness.

I'm ready to burn for them.

I'm ready to burn because of them.

It's time for me to go down in a blaze and return to hell where I belong.

CHAPTER 5
Ezra

NIKOLAI'S PULSE IS fading. I could feel it pulsing when I gripped his hand, but now it's unrecognizable. With my free hand, I press two fingers to his wrist. I think I feel something there, but it's faint and slow.

I glance up at Anya, who is reading the letter, and though I don't know what it says, her emotions are precisely etched into her expression. One of her hands rises from the crumpled letter and she covers her mouth, fresh tears spilling from her wide blue eyes.

Nikolai gasps, stealing attention from both of us. His gray eyes widen for a moment, flicking to look at me, then at her. He holds her gaze and I watch her closely. More emotions than I can name dance across her glassy eyes. I can't look away from her. This hurt and pain and shock she's feeling sits like a heavy weight in my stomach. It's a weight that begs me to carry it so she doesn't have to. But whatever it is she's feeling in this moment…it belongs to her.

Her emotion, her burden, her weight.

Her hand falls heavily on his chest, almost as though she wants to hit him but stops herself at the last possible second. His head slowly rolls toward her and I look at him expectantly, waiting for his final words.

But they never come.

The light has gone from his eyes.

No breath or sound comes.

His pulse is gone.

I look at Anya and have the misfortune of having to watch as she comes to the realization that his heart is no longer beating

"Nikolai," she whispers, looking at him expectantly. She lifts her hand and lets it fall on his chest. "Nikolai?"

I shake my head, though she doesn't look at me. "I think he's—"

"Don't say it!" she shouts at me.

Her words hit me with such force that it pushes me backward as they echo through the studio. I sit on my heels, letting go of his hand and setting it on the floor by his side.

Anya bends over him, putting her hands on his cheeks. She smacks her right hand against his cheek, but he doesn't flinch.

He doesn't blink.

He doesn't breathe.

He doesn't move.

My blue-eyed girl's face is a dreadful mixture of all the worst emotions she could ever possibly express. I rub my palm over my chest, recognizing how my heart aches to see anything but happiness on her face.

This shouldn't be a sad moment…but it is.

She smacks his face again. "Don't you *dare*." Her voice is low, deep, full of fury and pain. "Look at me!" she screams and I watch helplessly as she slips into emotional overload, climbing on top of him, straddling his waist with her knees on either side. "*Look* at me!"

She lets go of his cheeks and his head falls limply to the

side. She pounds a fist against his chest and waits.

She pounds again.

She slaps his cheek.

Then again.

She screams and beats on his chest with both fists, over and over. "I hate you! I detest you! You ruined me! You ruined my *life!*"

I rub my palms over my thighs, watching her with wide eyes. I don't really know what to do here; whether I should stop her or let her blaze in the fire of her emotions and wait for her to burn out on her own.

She grabs his face again and leans down over him, her voice shifting from anger to softness with one jarring beat.

"Nikolai. Nikolai, wake up. Look at me." Her entire body trembles. "If you really love me, you'll open your goddamn eyes and look at me…"

Anya presses her lips to his, lingering with a kiss, and I freeze. She has stunned me into silence, and I can't move.

What is she doing?

Why did she do that?

"Nikolai?" she says, her voice hardly a whisper as she stares at him, the tips of their noses practically touching. "Nikolai?"

Her voice catches and tears stream down her cheeks like waterfalls. She sobs, letting her cry echo through the open space of the dance studio, the sound of her sadness bouncing off the walls and slamming into my heart.

"It hurts. I hate him." Her sobs take over everything and nothing else is happening in the world right now. "I hate him so much. Why does this hurt? Why does it *hurt?*"

I latch my arms around her waist and drag her from Nikolai's dead body. She reaches for me as I pull her closer, her small limbs wrapping around me as I hold her tight. She squeezes me harder than ever before and sobs into the side of my neck, drenching me in her pain.

My own tears fall.

Not for Nikolai, but for my girl.

As far as I'm concerned, this is just one more awful thing that Nikolai has done to her. He tried to redeem himself at the final hour, only to go and die on her.

"Why does it hurt?" she repeats softly.

I rub my hands over her back, trying to comfort her when I have no idea how. I give her silence, letting her have her emotional purge. The longer we sit here with each other, the more she cries and hurts, the more my own pain washes over me. Before long I'm crying with her, and I can't even say why.

Nikolai stole us.

He enslaved us, he hurt us, he *brutalized* us.

He sold Anya to someone more sadistic than himself.

And then he helped us.

He helped us.

There are so many questions left unanswered and they're all rushing around in my head, scrambling my brain. But the questions tumble down our cheeks as tears because we will never get those answers.

The *whys*, the *what ifs*, the *how could he possibly...*

They all just died with Nikolai.

Anya's crying slows and her sobs fade into small hiccups of hurt. All her tears have been shed and she goes quiet and still in my arms. I reach up behind her, cradling the back of her head before stroking my hand down her long, dark hair. She pulls her head back so she can look at me and lets her forehead fall against mine.

"I'm sorry for being crazy again," she whispers.

"Nothing to apologize for."

"I kissed him." Her eyes glass over again with fresh tears as she looks at me. "I'm so sorry. I kissed him." She shakes her head. "I don't know why I kissed him."

"Hey. It's okay. It's okay, baby." I stroke her hair again. "It's all okay. I promise."

I take a deep breath, holding her gaze with hope that I can feed her strength from within me. It forces me to swallow my own pain—it *does* hurt that she willingly put her lips to his, but I don't feel justified judging her for that. I know my only choice is to get over it.

Somehow.

But that's not her concern.

This whole damn thing is the cluster fuck to end all cluster fucks.

I tuck her hair behind her ear. "The four families could be coming at any time."

She lifts her head from mine and nods. "I know."

"We're gonna have to drive out there to the helipad when they get here. We took the car. There's no way for them to get here once they land."

Anya's voice is quiet. "We could just leave them there to rot."

The corners of my lips curl up. "I would love nothing more. But we both know they would find a way to get to us."

She nods somberly. "I know."

I rub her back slowly before I speak, hoping my touch calms her. "Nikolai told me we should text a picture of the marriage certificate to Renata…to keep them from killing you on sight." Those words feel so vile as they break from my lips.

"It won't stop them from hurting you, Ezra." She looks at me so sadly, it feels like my heart is in a vice.

"I know that. But I stand a better chance if they know that you're…" I hesitate to say it, "Nikolai's wife.

She pinches her eyes shut. When she opens them again, she slides from my lap, crawling slowly around Nikolai's dead body to retrieve the box he left for her. She pulls out the marriage certificate and lays it on the floor beside her. I pull Nikolai's cell phone from my pocket.

And I realize it's locked.

"I'm gonna have to…use his fingerprint," I warn Anya—knowing the idea of lifting a dead man's hand to use his fingerprint to unlock his phone is morbid.

Her head bobs in something resembling a nod and she turns her attention away. I'd be lying to say I'm not bothered by her reaction to his death. This would all be so much easier if the death of her two sadistic masters brought her relief instead of agony. Vigo and Nikolai are both dead, and I don't entirely understand why she seems so upset by the loss. I just want to know what's going on inside her mind.

I get access to the phone and the first thing I do is change the fingerprint unlocking access so I don't have to use a dead man's finger ever again. Anya has smoothed the certificate out on the floor and I go to her, holding the phone above to take a clear picture of it—I do the same with the document showing the official name change. I find Renata's number and send her the pics, followed by a quick text message.

NIKOLAI: Nikolai is dead, but not the last Mikhailov. Anya is his wife.

Anya comes up next to me as I press send. We watch the phone silently as we wait for a reply. Within minutes, the phone rings. Renata's name flashes across the screen with her call.

"Let me talk," she says, taking the phone from me and tapping to answer. "This is Anya."

"I want proof that Nikolai is dead." Renata's voice is

smooth on the other end of the line.

"I will send you a video of his lifeless body if that would satisfy you," Anya says with an unusual edge to her voice.

"It would," Renata replies. "We'll be arriving in six hours. Have someone meet us at the helipad."

"Why? So you can kill us on sight? I want a guarantee that our fate will be considered judiciously."

"We consider all matters of the four families judiciously." There's a pause. "Though I wish to cut out your heart and keep it as a trophy for what you've done to my brother. You're lucky that I care more for my home and family than I care for your pathetic life. My family needs my leadership…now more than ever. And I'll be damned if I let my hatred for you get in the way of doing what must be done."

Anya's eyes show panic, fear, and a hint of curiosity, but she speaks with smoothness and determination. "I want confirmation from a Head of House. From Murphy O'Shea. If I'm not afforded the courtesy of the board to determine my fate fairly, then you can walk from the helipad to Mikhailov Manor for all I care. And knowing you, Renata, I imagine your current footwear is inappropriate for such a journey through the wilderness."

There's silence from Renata's end and fuck, I want to cheer for my girl. For all she's been through—all the pain, humiliation, for all the near-death experiences—she is still one brilliant, beautiful, powerhouse of a woman.

"Fine," Renata finally concedes. "I will have him call."

The phone beeps and the call ends from Renata's end of the line. We wait for a few minutes for Murphy to call, but I think we both realize they're going to make us wait for it. They want to keep the upper hand, as if Anya and I could ever hope to have a hand-up on them.

With a sigh, she holds out the phone for me to take and I put it in my back pocket for safe keeping. I hesitate in the quiet between us for a few moments before working up the nerve to ask the question that feels heavy in this space.

"Do you think we should find out if you're…" I trail off, wondering if I should even have brought it up right now.

She looks over at me, concern flashing off the sapphire blue of her eyes. She clears her throat and swallows nervously. "You're right. We should find a pregnancy test. I think Nikolai keeps them in his bathroom. He'd have me take one every so often…just to be sure." She shakes her head as if trying to shake away all of her worries.

I grab her cheeks and hold her face still, giving her the intensity of my stare. "Hey. It changes nothing between us if you're pregnant. Do you understand me? You didn't ask for any of this. You didn't choose this. Tell me you know that."

She hesitates. "I know. I do. It'll probably be negative anyway, right? What are the odds of a pregnancy surviving everything my body's been through…right?"

I don't have a fucking clue.

"Right," I agree, knowing that she's seeking assurance and that's all I can give her right now—even if it ends up being false assurance.

Fuck.

"Come on." I stand and hold out my hands for her, pulling her up when her palms land on mine.

We walk hand-in-hand out of the dance studio, though she pauses once at the door, turning to look back at Nikolai. He's a still, dead body in the middle of the room where we found each other—a lifeless corpse in the center of the space where my blue-eyed girl and I danced together and fell in love. I'm not sure if that's hauntingly poetic or morbidly gut-wrenching.

We follow the trail of blood Nikolai left as he bled out all the way from the dance studio back to the grand staircase. We ascend and Anya takes me to Nikolai's bedroom. She goes straight for his bathroom and I wait beside his bed, listening as she pulls open drawers and flings open cabinets. A minute or two later, she comes out with a small pink box in her hands.

"Found one," she says with a wry smile. "This one hasn't expired." She sucks in a harsh breath. "I don't want to do this here, though…not in his room."

I nod. "I know. Come on."

I take her by the hand and lead her back to her room…*my* room…*our* room. It's a part of Mikhailov Manor, but somehow, this room still feels like *our* space. She stops at the threshold.

"It…it looks the same as when I left it." She glances toward the bed. "My dress."

My gaze follows hers to the bright fuchsia gown she wore to the reception the night before she was sold to Vigo—the night of our performance.

"It never leaves the bed," I tell her. "I always sleep next to it."

She looks up at me with love and sadness in her eyes. I want to bend and kiss her, but then she sighs and turns away, looking down at the pink box hopelessly.

All the fucking boxes and secrets tonight.

"I just need to get this over with," she tells me, melancholy ripe in her tone.

She turns and wanders away without another word, her eyes glued to the box in her hands. I step after her, thinking I should hug her, kiss her, tell her again that everything will be okay. But before I can reach her, she closes the bathroom door behind her, transfixed on whatever words are printed on the back of the box.

I pace for a minute or so.

The toilet flushes.

The faucet runs.

The door clicks open.

She comes out empty-handed, arms crossed tightly over her chest. "It…it says to wait two minutes."

"Okay."

"Two pink lines is positive. One line is negative."

"Okay."

"I took both tests in the box. There were two. I left them on the sink."

"Okay."

Her eyebrows slant toward her nose. "Okay? Is that all you have to say? *Okay?*"

I toss up my hands. "I don't know what the fuck else to say, Anya. I'm at a loss here. Just a few hours ago, the only thing I had to worry about was saving your life. I never in a million fucking years would've thought pregnancy was even on the table."

Her jaw sets and ticks as she shakes her head. She's pissed and she's directing all that angry energy at me. I step closer, putting my hands on her biceps to comfort her. She tenses against my touch and I don't know what to do with that so I drop my arms and back away, lifting my palms as if I need to surrender.

Her forehead wrinkles, frustration with me peaking. "What are you doing? Don't back away from me, I just—" Her breath catches in her throat and she suddenly starts to cry. Her arms slip from their hold and slowly fall to her sides. "I don't know how to deal with all of this."

Fuck.

I feel like I'm handling everything wrong.

I dash to her, throwing my arms around her, pulling her close, impossibly close. I press one hand to the small of her back and hold her against me, the other traveling to the back of her head, guiding her to press her cheek to my chest.

"I'm sorry, Anya. I'm sorry. I know it's shit. It's all shit. I just…I don't know how to deal with this, either."

She cries into my chest and I hold her.

I just hold her.

I don't let go until her sobs have calmed and she pulls back. She lifts her head to look at me with those goddamn bewitching eyes of hers. "I think it's time."

I nod at her, give her a small smile, and place a kiss on the center of her forehead. "You want to look alone or together?"

"Together. Always together."

I release her from my hold and slip my hand down her arm. I catch her palm in mine and lock our fingers together. I let her lead us to the bathroom. Her fingers squeeze mine tighter and she puts her free hand over her heart, freezing in the doorway and pressing her eyes shut. She takes a deep breath, then another. I watch as she centers herself, finding her courage to face the truth, whatever it may be.

She steps past the threshold as she opens her eyes, going straight for the sink. I step with her but keep my eyes on her face. I don't want to see what the tests say—I don't *need* to. I just need to see her, know what she feels, and be ready to open my arms for her.

Standing squarely in front of the sink, she looks down to her right where two pregnancy tests lay side by side. Her eyes flicker, registering what she sees.

She stills.

She sucks in a sharp breath.

Her lips fall apart when she exhales and her forehead wrinkles as her eyebrows knit together.

Then her face falls.

The hand over her heart lifts to cover her mouth and her

eyes catch her reflection in the mirror. She sways in my hold and her eyelids flutter, as if they want to force their way shut. She tilts away from me, her hand loosening from my grip.

"Anya!"

"I'm—" Her eyes roll back in her head and she starts to fall sideways, away from me.

I wrap my hand around her wrist and yank her upright, pulling her to fall into my arms instead. She's limp in my hold—she *fainted*. I bend and scoop my arms beneath her legs, lifting her and carrying her back to the bedroom. I carefully set her on her bed and check that she's breathing and that her heart is still beating.

She's alive, just exhausted, overwhelmed, and malnourished.

Fuck. I need to get her something to eat.

I leave her on the bed to dash back down to the kitchen. I grab juice from the fridge, some bread from the cabinet, and snatch a banana from the fruit bowl on the counter. I rush it all back to the bedroom, wondering on the way if we're completely alone in this mansion. I didn't see any signs of the chef or either of the people who clean the home. Of course, Nikolai probably dismissed them to return to their families while he was away for the quarterly meeting.

I get back to Anya just as she's opening her eyes. She pushes up to her elbows as I kick the door shut behind me. Rushing toward her, I set everything on the floor beside her bed and kneel.

"Take it easy," I murmur. "You passed out."

"Ezra, I'm...did you look at the tests?"

I shake my head. "No. You passed out. I set you down here and went to get you some food." I grab the single-serve juice bottle and open it before handing it to her. "Here, drink this."

She takes it from me and drinks slowly, taking several

small sips before handing it back. I start to peel the banana for her. "I'll make you a proper meal as soon as I can, but I'm guessing your blood sugar is ridiculous right now. Eat this."

I hold out the fruit for her, but she doesn't take it. Instead, she gives me unflinching, soul-shattering eye contact.

"I'm pregnant."

No, she's not.

She can't be.

Fuck. She is.

I let out a heavy breath, sinking back to sit on my heels. "Well. Fuck."

"I'm so sorry."

My gaze jerks to hers. "What?"

"I'm sorry." She falls back to lay on her pillow, her hands coming up to cover her eyes.

"Hold on. What in the actual fuck are you *sorry* for? Anya," I take her wrists gently in my palms and pull her hands away from her face, "you didn't do this. You didn't *choose* this. You have nothing to apologize for."

My blue-eyed girl is pregnant.

My heart starts beating a quicker rhythm as reality starts to grip me. Anya is pregnant, and we don't know who the father is.

Anya is pregnant.

Pregnant.

"Ezra?" she says softly.

I shake my head, dragging myself out of this pit of worry I seem to have fallen into. I lean over her, pressing a soft kiss to her lips. "I love you. I love you forever. No matter what. We're gonna figure this out together."

Her blue irises flash from side to side as she looks deep into my eyes. "You promise you're mine? Still mine? Always mine?"

I lift her wrists and kiss her knuckles. "Still yours. *Always* yours."

"No matter what?"

"No matter what." I shove the banana into her hand and smile at her. "Now eat this so you can start getting your strength back. I have a feeling you're going to need it."

I think we're going to need all the strength in the universe to cope with this shit. I feel like I could break down over this. The woman I love is a Mikhailov by marriage and she's pregnant with *someone's* child—a child who very well could belong to either of the two sadist, slave-owning fathers…or a child who could belong to *me*.

It could be mine.

I could crumble under the weight of these unknowns.

I feel that weight settling on my shoulders and it's fucking heavy. But I have no choice other than to carry it. I have to carry my weight, and *hers,* because I can't stand the thought of her lifting a finger to shoulder this burden.

This is my time to step up.

This is my time to figure out how to be a fucking man— how to be *her* man. She needs me more than ever and I'm not going to fail her.

CHAPTER 6
Anya

EZRA HAS BEEN urging me to sleep since I regained consciousness. He's so worried about me and it shows. I don't want him to worry so much about me, but there's nothing I can do about it. Sometimes I think he loves me too much, so much that he would sacrifice his own well-being for mine. But I can't blame him for feeling that way.

Because I love him that much, too.

About an hour has gone by since I passed out from the devastation of the two pink lines. Nikolai's phone begins to ring in Ezra's back pocket. He reaches behind him, interrupting our prone embrace on my bed, and pulls out the phone. We both sit up slowly and he hands it over to me with a reassuring nod—his encouragement gives me confidence. He strokes my hair and somehow, that gives me strength.

I tap to answer the call. "This is Anya."

"Murphy O'Shea." His familiar Irish accent croons through the phone.

I open my mouth to speak again, but Murphy starts talking before I have the chance.

"Listen here, lass. You must have the luck of the Irish on your side. Fucking rainbows and four-leaf clovers. If that wanker old man of yours hadn't done his due diligence and made you a Mikhailov, we'd be busting arse to put a bullet between your eyes the moment we touch down. So, here's the good news for you. There are no other Mikhailov descendants, and *you* are the only person with his goddamn name. So, welcome to the fucking board. When we arrive, I expect you to be there to meet our helicopter. You and that slave boy bring two cars to accommodate all of us. We'll convene with you in the boardroom at Mikhailov Manor and decide what the fuck to do with the two of you *judiciously*, as you requested. We're all en route to you now. We'll be there in less than five hours. See you then."

The call ends.

I look at Ezra. "Five hours." I feel like ice is scraping over my bones as I realize time is ticking.

He nods, then curls his hand around the side of my head and pulls me close. I rest my head on his shoulder as he strokes my hair.

"Let's sleep for three. Then we'll get ready and drive back to the helipad to meet them."

"Ezra, I'm scared. What will they do to you?"

"Don't worry about me. As long as they don't hurt you, I'll be okay. No matter what. As long as you're okay, then I'm okay. Now stop talking about it and let's worry about getting our heads in the game. We need to be sharp, clear-headed, prepared for anything, right?"

I nod against his shoulder, turning my head to press my face into the side of his neck. I inhale the sweetness of his scent before placing a kiss to his skin. He inhales and exhales sharply.

"How do you do that?" he whispers, his fingers snaking into my hair, his nails softly scratching my scalp.

I lift my head to look up at him. "Do what?"

"Make me forget about everything but the way you make me want you, even in the face of death?"

The green of his eyes appears to melt as the lighter vibrant color drains slowly, letting the darker shade of emerald wash over. It's a color that's urgent, greedy, hungry, and his hunger only sparks mine.

"I don't know," I say softly. "But I feel it with you, too."

His grip on my hair tightens, and though the possessiveness of it should alarm me, I find that it doesn't.

Not even a little bit.

Not at all.

Ezra's possession is wanted, *needed*. If I am his, then he is mine and I want nothing else.

"Ezra…" I say his name on a sigh and the spark in his eyes tells me he knows what I need.

How is this intense lust even possible from my abused, exhausted body?

He holds my head still and bends to kiss me recklessly. I moan against his lips as every bit of my body prickles to life with a hum of awareness. I part my lips for him, inviting him to taste me because I desperately need to taste him. He devours me with a fervor unlike anything I've felt from him before.

The way he claims his possession of me is desperate, needy, protective. This ferocity should scare me, but it doesn't because I'm as ferociously needy as he is. My fingers claw at his chest, madly trying to cling to his skin and hold him against me. Everything inside me collapses and clenches, coiling tightly, painfully, low in my belly. It transforms me into a body with lust so frantic that it demands to be released.

Now.

I climb onto his lap, straddling his hips. "Make me come," I beg between hectic kisses. "Make me come right now."

Something resembling a growl shudders his entire body and it shakes mine, too. His hands fall to my hips, gripping me tightly. Then he rolls me off him, slamming my back into the mattress, and lays down heavily on top of me.

There's hesitation in his eyes for the briefest moment. He doesn't want to be like them—like the monsters who raped me. But he could never be that. He can fuck me any way he wants to because he does it with such love for me. If I tell him to stop, he will…and because of that, I won't.

I want to see him lost in this, lost in me, lost in us.

I reach between us, working his buckle. I undo the button and zipper and slip my fingers beneath the elastic of his boxer briefs. I shove them down, unsheathing his hard cock. He groans, placing his forehead against mine as my fingers graze along his shaft.

I feel as possessive as he does as I run my fingers along the part of him that needs me so insistently. I wrap my hand around the base and tug gently.

"Mine?" I ask, sucking my bottom lip between my teeth.

"It's yours," he says and I melt, sinking deeper into the mattress, letting him smother me with his love. "Every part of me is yours."

"I want you inside me. *Please.*"

I'm still bare and exposed beneath Ezra's button-down shirt. His green eyes sparkle as he reaches down to position himself against my opening and his fingers find me already wet for him—it's true and honest arousal, and the slickness of it makes me feel powerful. I'm not dry and waiting to take the pain; I'm soaked and anxious for the pleasure.

He groans, letting his hand linger, his fingers playing with me—they slip along my folds, dip inside me, drag, and swirl and spread my wetness until I'm squirming beneath him.

I never thought I'd know such desire.

I never thought I'd want a man this way.

Ezra worships me with his touch and it makes me want to give him everything I have.

I gasp and moan as he circles my clit with his thumb, slowly pressing the tip of his cock inside me. "*Please*," I beg, and he gives me what I need.

His hips thrust forward, and I feel every perfectly agonizing inch of him as he sinks inside me, stretching my pussy to accept his pulsing length. He rears back, sitting up on his knees as my legs encircle him.

He grabs my hips as he rises on his knees, dragging my body closer, burying his cock deep. He looks down at me as though he could consume my very soul with nothing more than a groan, a deep thrust, and a perfectly-timed kiss to devour me. I gasp at the feel of him, at the look on his face as he watches mine. When he starts to move, I feel as though I might die from this intensity.

He leans forward, his fists landing on the mattress, holding him up as he fucks me with a rocking motion that sets my insides on fire.

I can't speak.

I can hardly breathe.

My lungs beg for the release that will set them free from my panting and gasping need.

"You're pussy feels like heaven. Fuck. You feel incredible."

His words that worship me tighten in my chest. Not a painful tightening—it's more like a warm embrace around my heart. He watches me as his hips roll, his eyes flickering across my expression, and I know how he sees me.

He sees the way my face changes when he angles just right. He sees the tension in my jaw, the slant in my brow that forms with the creasing of my forehead. He sees my teeth tug on my bottom lip, then the way they part with a gasp in pleasure-filled surprise

"There," I gasp. "Right there. Oh, God. Make me come. Make me come, Ezra." I lift my head from the mattress, pressing up onto my elbows to look between us to see where we're joined.

Given all I've been through, the sight of a man thrusting inside me should be abhorrent. But with Ezra, it's anything but. Seeing the way we connect so perfectly, so beautifully at the end of his chiseled, sculpted, perfectly toned abs—beneath the patch of dirty blond hair that leads the trail to his cock— turns me on. He's so strong, so powerful with his lean muscle; a dream of a man brought to life that heaven sent to me.

Oh, God.

He looks so good.

I exhale harshly as the start of my climax tugs through my body, stretching from head to toe in a tight string of tingling tension. "*Oh. Ohh…*"

Ezra snatches my wrist, yanking my elbow out from beneath me, and I land flat on my back. He brings my hand down between us, encouraging my fingers to dance over my clit. I watch him while I rub, while his gaze falls down to observe carefully as I rapidly circle over my sensitive flesh.

It only takes moments like this and a groan from deep within his chest to ignite me. My heart stops as the string that pulls tension through my body stretches tighter and snaps in two, bursting all the tingling pressure right in my core. The soul-crushing climax bursts and ripples through my entire body.

I go limp on the mattress, but Ezra keeps fucking me. Thrust after thrust after thrust and…

Oh, God.

Oh, my fucking God.

His cock swells just before his orgasm spills inside me and the pressure only lifts me higher. Then I fall hard and fast into a second, unexpected orgasm.

That's never happened to me before.

Ezra could feel it. He could feel the way my walls clenched and pulsed around him, and I watch his face as a grin of pure satisfaction touches every feature. He brings such brightness to his face that you could fool me into thinking that the light haloing around him radiated from his soul, though I know it's only from the light fixture above him.

"Anya," he says with a sated chuckle. "*Fuck.*"

I lick my suddenly dry lips as I look up at him with half-hooded eyes. I feel so wet. The mess of him and me coming together drips from my sensitive pussy and the mere thought of it sends a tiny, clenching aftershock of pleasure—just a quick lightning bolt of bliss that strikes straight through to my clit.

He bends with a proud smile, kissing the corner of my lips sensually, kissing my cheek and along my jawline, nuzzling his nose over my earlobe. I reach for him, wrapping my arms around him and running my hands over his back.

"I've never felt so completely…" I struggle for words.

"Undone?" he offers.

"Fulfilled," I counter.

"Unhinged?"

"Satisfied."

"Content?" he asks.

I grab his face in both of my hands. "Complete. I feel so *complete* with you inside me."

He sighs, his brow slanting to form a V. "You're complete on your own without me."

What does he mean by that?

"No," I tell him. "I hate that. I feel complete with *you.*"

"I know, baby." He brushes the sweat-stuck hair from my face. "I know what you mean. I feel it, too. But I don't ever want you to forget how perfect and amazing and complete you are as you. Just you."

"Stop that." My eyes narrow at him. "Just stop it. I don't want to be perfect and amazing and complete on my own. I want to be as complete as I feel with you. A part of me is missing without you." I feel strange, angry tears start to well up and I hate it. I hate it so much. "What are you even trying to say to me?"

"Hey, it's okay. I'm sorry. I'm not saying anything at all. I'm just saying that if…if something were to happen to me…you don't need me to—"

"Stop!" I shout, shoving at his chest and pushing him off me. I scoot to the edge of the bed and climb off as he rolls to sit up. "I hate what you're saying. You're saying I can live without you if they kill you. But I can't. I *can't*, Ezra. I can't live without you. I will die without you. I don't want to *exist* without you." My breaths turn shallow and rapid, and I find I'm pacing beside the bed. "I'm only complete when I'm with you. Don't tell me I'm complete on my own. Are *you* complete on your own?" I stop and turn to face where he sits at the edge of the bed. My voice lowers to a whisper. "*Are* you complete on your own? Without me? Is that what you're telling me?"

What is happening to me?

I've gone down a rabbit hole of insanity. Every thought and emotion buried within my soul is bursting to the surface and I can't seem to control it. I don't want to hear his response because I fear the worst. I fear he'll tell me that he *can* live without me. That he doesn't need me to be complete. I don't know how I'll survive if he tells me that.

I turn on my heel and storm off to the bathroom before he

can respond, slamming the door shut. I stand still for a second and in moments, he's pounding on the door, begging to be let in.

"I have to pee. Leave me alone," I shout through the door before I realize I actually do have to pee.

"Fuck," he says through the door. "*Fine.*"

I wait a few seconds for quiet before heading to the toilet to handle my business. As I sit there, my eyes fall on the two pregnancy tests on the counter and I reach for one. I carefully pick it up, studying it as I sit.

Two pink lines.

Two pink lines that tell me my life has irrevocably changed.

"This is real," I whisper to myself. "This is really real."

I finish up and wash my hands before opening the door again, my cheeks flushing in embarrassment over my tirade. I bring the test out with me. Ezra is sitting on the edge of my bed—beautiful, naked, though sadness shines in his posture with his elbows on his knees and head in his hands.

I stand there in the doorway. "I'm sorry."

He looks up at me, pushing to stand and striding toward me as I speak.

"Just hours ago, I thought I was dead. I was under the water, trapped in that bathtub, and I was *dying.* I'd said goodbye to life, Ezra. I thought it was all over and then suddenly…it wasn't. And all of this? Nikolai dying, finding out that I'm his wife, that I'm pregnant with *someone's* baby…I feel like my mind is snapping and I'm sorry. I'm so sorry for fighting with you. I don't want to fight. I love you and I just need to hear that you love me, too."

His shoulders slump and he closes the space between us, slipping his arms around my waist and holding me tight. His body is warm against mine and it melts the iciness inside that makes me cold and hard.

"I love you, Anya. I love you forever. And I'm not complete without you. I never was. Every minute we were apart was agony for me. I need you. And I'll remind you of that every minute of every day if that's what you need."

"That's insane." I chuckle through glassy eyes. "Every five minutes will be fine."

We both laugh, pulling apart just enough to look at each other, to watch each other, to love each other with silence and simple togetherness.

"Come on. We need to get some rest. I'll set the alarm on the phone. Come lay down with me and let me keep you safe while you sleep."

He takes my hand in his and leads me to the bed. I'm so grateful for him and the way he loves me.

Lying down side by side, comforted and protected in each other's arms, we somehow manage to fall into a quick, deep, dreamless slumber.

Nikolai once told me that I looked like a queen.

It was the night of my second annual performance in Nobility Hall. I wore a beautiful black evening gown that night. It had a boat neckline formed by sheer black fabric that stretched down to the smallest part of my waist—the sheerness was embroidered with decorative flowers and flourishes that hid my breasts and made the dress more modest.

I remember the way the gown cinched around my waist, flowing down to the floor in sweeping layers of black and gray tulle that dusted gracefully over the marble floor as I walked. I might've felt like a queen in that dress if I hadn't been in mourning.

After my performance, Nikolai had taken my second partner from me. His name was Erik, and though we were only just okay together as dancers, he was a friend.

And the loss of him hurt all the same.

With the four families' impending arrival, I do my best to steel myself, to harden myself, to freeze my soul in a protective layer of ice. I know I have to transform before they arrive. I can no longer remain the emotional, broken slave girl they'd seen me as before—that won't be tolerated as a Mikhailov and I won't be taken seriously.

I have to become like them.

I have to become regal, god-like.

I have to become a queen.

I need to make them see me as the bereaved wife, the strong and persevering goddess, the determined woman who would meet their force with force of her own as the sole surviving matriarch in the Mikhailov line.

It's what I have to become, without any time or preparation for such a role. But with Ezra by my side, I know I can do it. His presence emboldens me, empowers me, and inspires me to find the strength within myself to be who I need to be.

It's like any other performance—it's just playing a part. And to play a part successfully, I have to be convincing. I have to convince them, but more so, I must convince myself that I *am* who I pretend to be.

If I need to convince us all that I am a queen, then I must dress the part. I put on the same black gown that convinced Nikolai all those years ago that I could look like a ruler in his world.

Before I put on my costume, I use Renata as inspiration for my role, spending some time perfecting my appearance. I style my hair into perfect, long waves that softly curl over my shoulders and down to the middle of my back.

I paint my face with color, shading my eyes with a light shade of pink that makes the blue of my irises pop. I outline my lids with brushes of dark gray shadow and black eyeliner. I curl and plump my eyelashes, brushing them with black mascara to make them thick and sultry. I add a hint of bronze to my cheeks and draw dark pink gloss over my lips.

I put on my dress and stare at my reflection in the bathroom mirror. The small, ominous black box—the box that holds the diamond rings Nikolai purchased for me—sits on the counter, resting forebodingly beside the two positive pregnancy tests that I just can't seem to bring myself to throw away.

Not yet.

With a steeling breath, I reach over and pluck the box from the countertop, flipping open the lid. I'm met with a bright sparkle from the diamond rings within. It strikes an unresolved ache in my chest because I still don't know what to make of all this.

If Nikolai wanted to marry me, why did he treat me as his slave?

These rings symbolize how Nikolai has controlled my life, even now from beyond the grave. It's a symbol of my oppression, but it still stirs some strange feeling within me that I can't place. It's something I can only vaguely describe as gratitude, though I know that's not the right word.

I feel no gratitude toward that man.

Then why do my eyes well with tears at the reminder that he's gone?

I hear my bedroom door click open as Ezra returns to me. I sniffle back my sorrow and dab beneath my eyes to catch any tears that might ruin my makeup. I look at him as he crosses to me and the twinge of sadness fades away, and in its place, tremendous pride for the fact that I can call him mine.

He's so ridiculously handsome wearing a black suit. He's chosen a plain white shirt and a black necktie. He looks professional, in charge, prominent, and proud.

"You look perfect," I tell him as I set the jewelry box down on the marble counter.

Ezra moves behind me, his hands skimming down my sides as we both regard our reflection in the mirror. "You look spectacular. Stunning."

"Do I look like one of them?" I ask, hoping he'll say yes but also hoping he'll say no.

He nods before pressing his lips to my shoulder. "You look better than them. You *are* better than them. You look exactly as you should."

"Queen Mikhailov?" I say jokingly with a small, twisted smile.

"Just a queen. You don't have to be ruled by his name."

I spin to face him and trap him in my gaze for a beat. Any gratitude I might've felt toward Nikolai slips away entirely, because there's no room left for it when I'm filled to the brim with gratitude for Ezra.

He pulls away from my stare as his eyes draw to the sparkling diamonds on the countertop and he plucks the rings from the box. "I think you need to wear these." He swallows hard and pinches his eyes shut, then opens them again. "They need to see you wearing these rings."

I nod, though he doesn't see it. His eyes are transfixed on the diamonds between us and I wonder what he's thinking. I wait for him to tell me and eventually, he does, starting slowly.

"Nikolai owes me," he says. "He owes me a life for the life he's taken from me. He owes you a life, too. These rings… He wanted them to be a symbol of the life he took from you; a symbol that you belong to him. But I don't want them to mean you belong to him because you don't."

I sigh, closing my eyes. "I belong to *you*, Ezra." I open my eyes again just in time to see the corners of his lips curl up and

I smile, too. He's just so relentlessly sexy, especially when he smiles at me like that.

"You only belong to me if you want to."

"You're the only man I ever want to belong to."

"If that's true, then…maybe these rings are mine. Maybe yours is the life he owes to me and mine is what he owes to you."

Oh, God.

That makes my heart beat wildly and my pulse thrums. "Ezra…"

"Maybe you can wear these and think of me. Maybe someday you can…marry me. And we can belong to each other forever. If we're ever lucky enough to get that chance."

I grab his face and kiss him. I kiss him with love and passion and gratitude. "You're my forever. I already know it… however long our forever might be."

He lets out a slow breath. "Then you'll wear these for me? Not for him."

"I'll wear them for you," I promise.

He takes my hand and slips both the wedding band and engagement ring onto my left ring finger. He doesn't know that in Russia, women wear their rings on the right hand. And I'm glad he doesn't know because wearing it on my right hand *would* feel like wearing them for Nikolai.

To wear them on the left makes it more special somehow.

It's for Ezra.

I wear them for *him*.

I reach up with one hand to caress his cheek, my thumb brushing over his skin.

"We can do this, Anya. You and me. We can face this."

"Mine?" I ask even though I already know the answer.

"Baby, I'm yours."

CHAPTER 7
Ezra

MY BLUE-EYED GIRL and I stand side-by-side on the gravel surrounding the helipad as an oversized helicopter gradually descends. My heart is thumping like crazy against my rib cage. I reach out and snatch Anya's tiny hand in mine, tangling my fingers with hers and locking us together.

I don't know what will happen and the uncertainty makes every muscle in my body seize with tension. I glance over at Anya as the chopper lands, the blades gradually slowing in their rotation.

She takes in a heavy breath and lifts her chin a little higher, pulling her shoulders back. I watch her face as she lets the coldness freeze her in determination—the same coldness she possessed when I first met her. She needs that now; she needs the fierceness that allows her to do what needs to be done.

I know all of that, but it still stings when her shields come up and she pulls her fingers free from mine. Still, she glances over at me appraisingly, asking me with her eyes if I understand and I nod in reassurance.

She needs to stand on her own as the regal, worthy queen of Mikhailov Manor.

The doors open and Murphy O'Shea is the first person out

of the helicopter. He jumps out with intention, lands heavily on the asphalt, and pauses just long enough to straighten his waistcoat. His white shirt sleeves are already rolled up to his elbows, exposing his tattoo-covered forearms.

His eyes fall on us as Leo Leblanc climbs out behind him, looking svelte in comparison to Murphy's broad, muscular frame. Murphy charges toward us, long fast strides bringing him swiftly to where we stand. I start to move, to sidestep in front of Anya to protect her against his onrushing force, but she stops me, placing her hand on the crease of my arm.

She steps forward.

Fuck.

She steps forward and I've never been so terrified in my life. My pulse thrums, my fists clench, my muscles ache to fight for her, to protect her, to keep her safe. But her life depends on negotiation, not fists and blood and violence.

But then I realize she never needed me to stand in front of her for protection…because he's not going after her.

He's coming straight for *me.*

Murphy's jaw is set, eyes determined, and I'm overwhelmed by the surge of adrenaline inside me. But my instinct still pulls me toward Anya because I'd jump in front of a bullet for her without a second thought. I glance at her, and because my attention is on her, Murphy catches me off-guard with a sucker punch to my cheek.

The rings that he wears mar my face, adding an extra oomph to the shooting pain that bursts across my cheek. His other fist collides with my gut, doubling me over. When he hits me in the stomach a second time, I slump to my knees with a grunt and a groan.

The fucker packs a killer punch.

I lift my head just as he moves his attention to Anya,

pointing a finger in her face. "You are proving to be far more trouble than your worth, lass."

She takes him on with a deadly stare. "I'm worth the entire fortune of the Mikhailov family," she says with the most convincing coldness.

Murphy chuckles, glancing back over his shoulder as Leo helps Renata off the aircraft, then his cousin Cordelia. "You sure have got a sizeable pair of balls, woman."

"Bigger than yours, I imagine," she returns with a lifted brow.

Murphy cocks his head to the side. "Get in the car. I'll drive."

Anya sets her jaw. "I have guests to greet first."

Murphy cracks his knuckles with another small laugh. "You're quite a proud little bitch for destroying two families, aren't you? If we didn't have to handle this as a board matter, I promise you, I'd have strangled you to death by now."

I plant one foot on the ground, ready to rise to my feet, practically trembling with rage, but Renata marches toward me with one long finger outstretched, pointed directly at me.

"Stay on your knees if you wish to live beyond this night, slave."

My jaw tenses. I open my mouth to retort, but Anya snaps at me, just like she used to in the beginning, "*Mal'chik.* Don't say a goddamn word."

Fuck, I want to fight.

I want to argue.

I want to shout.

I want to attack.

I force myself to dampen my natural urges because I know what has to happen here.

I'm not in control.

I don't have the power.

But Anya might just be able to take it for herself—for the

both of us—if I just shut up and do as I'm told for once.

So, I keep my shit under control, and I do it for her.

I settle there on my knees, sitting back on my heels. I throw my hands up momentarily in surrender before I let them flop down onto my thighs when Renata appears satisfied with my concession. She rounds on Anya next, and it takes everything within me to remain where I am.

"You vile little slut!" Renata shouts at her, her words clipped and precise. "You killed my brother!"

I see a venomous smile touch Anya's cheek. "He deserved it."

Renata forces her way around Murphy, slapping Anya with a thwack that echoes through the clearing. She wraps her fist around Anya's hair, tugging her head sideways. Anya yelps and my muscles twitch.

"Stop it," Murphy says coolly. "She may have killed your brother, but she's a fucking *wife*. You can't behave this way, Renata."

Renata grits her teeth, hesitating with her grip on Anya, but after moments, she finally lets go. "Fine," she says, stepping back. "I'll be civilized."

Murphy laughs. "Right, you will."

Cordelia quickly finds her way to Renata's side, her face red and eyes glossy with tears. She links her arm with Renata's and pets her hair as if she's some broken creature who requires comfort. It's almost comical to watch these heathens pretend to be human, as if they have actual emotions and give a shit about human life.

When all the passengers have gathered and the whir of the helicopter's engine shuts off entirely, silence washes over the dark clearing. The wind whispers through the trees surrounding the circular space, encircling the stand-off between Anya and the board of the four families.

She stands alone, proud—as cold and hard as she needs to be—and utterly fucking strong. The sheer power of her will is a supernatural force that could bring them all to their knees… and I have no doubt that in time, she will.

"Is this everyone?" Anya asks without a hint of wavering in her tone, though I sense her anxiety rushing beneath the surface. "If you're all ready, I'm happy to take you to the manor and welcome you to my home."

Cordelia shouts, "That is *Nikolai's* home, not yours! You're a talent slave, no better."

Anya raises her chin. "I *am* better than a talent slave. I'm a Mikhailov. I'm Nikolai's bereaved bride. Surely, you would grant me some kindness in my time of *grief*."

It's a total fuck-up on my part, but I just can't hold back my chuckle. Thankfully, they're all so high-strung that they don't seem to notice or care.

"Give me the keys and get in the backseat, lass. I'll drive that car," Murphy gestures to the car Anya drove here.

"Fine," she replies, holding out the keys for him.

She doesn't wait for anyone. She confidently strides away, turning her back on all of us, gliding away like a queen to her carriage.

I'm so fucking proud of her.

Head over fucking heels in love.

"Lorenzo, drive the other car," Murphy says to a man that must be a Vittori—he looks like a younger version of Vigo.

Lorenzo forces me into the backseat of the second car—separating me from my girl—and I'm forced to make the entire thirty-minute drive back to the manor with anxiety pricking pins and needles into my bones. I know she can handle her own, but I hate being apart from her.

I fear our separation, and not just for this relatively short car trip—it's deeper than that. I fear what will happen to her if they sell or kill me. I don't want to leave her behind to live this life alone.

We arrive at the manor and Anya is the first one out of the cars. She marches ahead to the main entryway, holding her long, layered skirt up with her hands near her hips. She moves with intent and grace. The rest of us get out and follow behind as she walks into Mikhailov Manor. She's leading this mission rather than falling in line and waiting for a command.

I love this side of her—this strong, take-no-shit, take-no-prisoners side of her. It's a part of her personality that's been repressed for far too long in captivity and it's shining now. She's playing a part, but she owns it, because it really is *her*.

No time is wasted as she heads straight for the staircase and the four families follow behind her. We cross the blood trail made by Nikolai and the throng pauses as Cordelia and Renata decide to trail off and follow it. Anya turns halfway up the grand staircase, her skirt twisting around and framing her as a worthy goddess, looming above them all. She's dignified and powerful, watching them as she waits for the two women to make their confirmation of Nikolai's passing.

They disappear inside the dance studio and I hear faint crying, as if either of these women might actually miss Nikolai. When they return, they look somber and it makes me fucking glad to see any form of hurt touch their features.

"It's true. He's dead." Renata confirms to the group in a solemn tone, then turns her head toward Anya. "She is the last Mikhailov."

A ripple of truth slithers through the air around us, coiling and wrapping around the board members. I can feel the buzz of awareness as they steal glances with one another, grappling to accept the new reality—two Heads of House murdered in one night, and only one member left of the Mikhailov family. Then, almost all at once, heads snap to Anya and I hold my breath as they look at her.

Silence descends and Anya stands taller.

"Well?" Renata asks.

"It's legitimate, all right. This marriage is legal. As is the name change," Murphy says.

I've been ordered to kneel in the far corner of the boardroom as this conversation carries on. My jacket is off and my wrists are zip-tied tightly in front of me. I sit back on my heels and struggle against my instinct to fight and shout and interject every other sentence with a sarcastic comment.

"This is unprecedented." Renata's eyebrows furrow.

"Oh?" Anya says from her spot at the head of the table. She took that spot the moment we walked in here, refusing to be told where to sit—and she looks fucking sexy as hell. "Didn't you just grant permission for Lorenzo to marry your talent slave?"

"Yes," Renata replies, "but Lorenzo is not a Vittori. He's a Fiore. Nor is he Head of House."

"But that has happened before, hasn't it? I recall Vigo saying something to that effect when Lorenzo first asked the family for permission to marry Olivia. I was there, Renata. We sat and listened to her practice her talent on the piano, and I remember *every* word of the exchange when they asked for permission to marry. I suppose you must have forgotten about me while I was a broken doll." Anya sits a little taller in her seat. "But I can assure you won't forget me now."

Renata smiles at her slowly, but there's no joy in it. "That's correct. But it doesn't matter in this scenario. You killed a Head of House, which in turn resulted in the fatal shooting of a second Head of House in the aftermath. Mikhailov or not, you will be punished severely. Blood taken requires blood given."

"I'm aware of your family's bloodlust, Renata." Anya speaks with a commanding voice. "But there is another item of information you'll want to be aware of before delivering any such punishment."

"And what is that?" Murphy asks.

I see the way Anya's throat contracts as she swallows. "I'm pregnant."

A stale silence falls over the room.

"Come again, lass?"

"I'm pregnant." Anya whips her head to meet Murphy's eyes. "I don't know how far along. But depending on the timing, it could belong to Nikolai or Vigo." She conveniently leaves out that it could also be mine. "If you recall, the board decided I should be given to Nikolai as punishment for my attempted suicide at the Leblancs' last quarter. We had unprotected sex several times that night."

"You're a damn, rotten liar," Cordelia sneers. "I went through your contract of sale with a fine-toothed comb that very night with Vigo. It plainly states that you are infertile… incapable of becoming pregnant."

"Nikolai *lied*," Anya replies. "I assure you, I am capable of becoming pregnant because I *am* pregnant. There are positive tests on my bathroom sink right now to prove it."

"I don't believe it. How could a pregnancy possibly survive all your body has been through?" Renata questions with a tilt of her head.

"I don't know," Anya replies. "I honestly don't know. What I *do* know is that this child is the descendant of Nikolai or Vigo."

Or me.

Cordelia fails at her attempt to hold back a sob, her hand coming up to cover her mouth as she pushes back from the table and practically runs from the room.

Murphy leans back from the table, running a hand over his beard. "Well, fuck all. If this is true, it changes everything."

"It changes *nothing*," Renata practically spits with fury. "She is responsible for the deaths of two Heads of House. She must be punished."

"And she will be, in due time. But we can't afford another change in family line if it can be avoided. The Leblancs' rise to take over the Campbells caused enough disruption in our distribution lines. We can't afford more this year. If the child is a boy, he can ascend to Head of House when he comes of age, whether he's a Mikhailov or a Vittori." Murphy pauses. "I propose Lorenzo take on temporary leadership of the Vittori family under Renata's advisement."

Renata's hands slaps the table as she leans forward. "*I* will lead our family.

Murphy leans forward on his elbows, raising an eyebrow at Renata. "We've been around and around this point of contention with you. You can't be Head of House. But you will bear some of the responsibility under Lorenzo. He's been part of the board long enough to know the ins and outs of the business. You're gonna need to focus your attention elsewhere."

"Oh?"

"I'm proposing Anya be sent to live at the Vittori home. Renata, you will provide her with the medical care she requires until she delivers."

Renata hisses, buzzing with fury. "You want me to take care of the woman who killed my brother?"

"Yes," Murphy replies, unaffected. "It will keep your

grieving mind occupied with a more important task. She may very well be carrying your niece or nephew…remember that."

Anya struggles. I see the way her jaw ticks and her muscles flinch as she takes in the reality of that statement. The baby could be Vigo's and that's a hard fucking truth. But then, she adjusts her body and sits a little taller than before, her cold strength freezing her over again.

Renata turns her head slowly to look at Anya, scrutinizing her features with her narrowed eyes. Then, subtly, her face relaxes. Her eyes tell me that she's making the connection of her potential relation to the baby growing in Anya's belly.

I hang my head as the connection hits me all the same.

"I suppose that's true," Renata says. "But who will run the Mikhailov sector? Who will make decisions? Say the baby is a Mikhailov boy and can become Head of House when he comes of age, who will serve in his stead until that time comes?"

Murphy drums his fingers against the tabletop, considering a solution with squinted eyes. He jerks his head to look at Leo. "Any suggestions?"

"Kostya knows the sector well, doesn't he?" Leo suggests.

"Kostya?" Anya whips her head around to look at them. "Is he alive?"

"Yes," Murphy replies. "He's being treated and held prisoner at the Vittoris while his wound is tended to. He was shot in his right shoulder…nothing life-threatening." He sighs. "The problem with Kostya is that I don't know whether he can be trusted. I've always known him to be a loyal guard to the Mikhailov family…It could serve to reason that he was blindly following Nikolai's orders—like a good servant would—when he fired back during your escape. But, perhaps, he was more inclined to fire back because of his relationship with you and with Nikolai. How could I possibly know if he cares whether you live or die?"

"I can assure you," Anya begins and I can sense the lie coming, "Kostya was only following orders. He is fiercely loyal to the Mikhailov name. He followed Nikolai's orders blindly, even to his own detriment. You see where it got him…injured in gunfire."

"See, that's where I have a problem, lass. How am I to know if his loyalty now shifts to you? Perhaps he will blindly follow your orders now. I don't trust you as far as I can throw you."

"My only interest is in self-preservation," Anya says.

Murphy jabs his finger in her direction. "Don't test me, woman. I know better than that. You care about more than just self-preservation." He points his finger in my direction next. "*Him*, for one."

"So, what if I do?" she says, leaning forward on her elbows and folding her hands.

"It means we can leverage him against you when you start making stupid decisions. Notice my use of the word *when*, not *if*." Murphy grins sarcastically. "So, here's what's going to happen. I have a Vittori and I have a Mikhailov." He gestures to Renata and Anya, respectively. "I have two men aligned with each family, Lorenzo and Kostya, capable of making joint business decisions. If Leo agrees, let's say we create a temporary joint family board for overseeing the Vittori and Mikhailov sectors. Renata, Anya, Lorenzo, and Kostya will be the members of this joint board, and we'll require you to convene weekly to make any and all business decisions for either family sector. All decisions must be made with a three-fourths majority. Once we find out the gender and paternity of Anya's child, we'll re-evaluate how to proceed."

Anya's voice is quiet, but strong, "And what if the child is a girl?"

"We will re-evaluate your…value when the time comes."

Murphy's tone is full of threats and warnings that make my stomach flip. He turns to Renata. "Until that time, Anya will be treated as a Mikhailov guest in your home. Do you understand?"

Begrudgingly, Renata replies, "Yes. I understand. But what is to become of the slave boy?" Her head nods toward me and I pull my shoulders back.

"He's still the Mikhailov talent slave, but I suppose the decision rests with your joint family board. We can kill him and require Anya to find another."

Shit.

"I don't think that will be necessary. I have an interest in him," Renata replies smoothly.

Murphy chuckles. "Of course, you do. But are you equipped to handle such an unruly slave in your home? One who pines for Anya? Can you manage him *and* your duty to provide care for her during her pregnancy?"

"Managing him will ensure I can provide for her care. You said it yourself, he's leverage. I can slowly take the blood she owes to my family from his veins. Drop by drop. I can use him against her when she thinks of doing something foolish. She can use him as her talent, but I want unilateral authority over him while he's in my home."

My fingers twitch with my sight set on wrapping them around her throat.

"Well," Murphy leans back, crossing his arms over his chest, "seems fair enough to me. Three-fourths of your family board is here now, so you can make that decision jointly. Kill him now and Anya finds new talent. Or let Renata take him on as her slave until his talent is needed. We know Renata's vote. Lorenzo?"

Lorenzo's eyes dart in my direction, then look to Anya. His expression twists as his eyes narrow in consideration. I watch as Anya lifts her chin and meets his gaze directly, waiting for his response. Her nostrils flare in fearful anticipation as she breathes deeply.

Lorenzo holds the power—right now in this moment—and his choice will determine whether I live or die. Obviously, Anya will vote for my life, even if it is to make me a slave to Renata Vittori. Lorenzo holds my fate in his hands.

His head tilts to the side and his expression softens as he states his vote, turning his eyes to Murphy. "Renata can keep him."

Anya's lips part as she tries to control the breath of relief that forces its way out. I clench my fists, wishing I could wrap my arms around her and hold her, wishing I could give her a safe space to break apart her icy shield and relax after this fucking awful meeting is done.

But I know I won't be given the opportunity to be there for her when she needs me most, and I fucking hate it.

"Do I even need to ask your vote?" Murphy says to Anya.

Anya clears her throat, turning her head toward him. "Renata may have him as her slave."

Hearing her say those words—in the cold, detached way that she has to—sucker punches me in the gut. I hate that she has to be this way…that she has to be like them to survive.

But she has no choice in the matter. Agree to let me be Renata's slave or see me die. It's no choice at all for her, just like it would be no choice for me.

How bad can Renata really be, anyway?

Murphy slaps his hands on the table, pushing himself up to stand roughly, his chair sliding away from the table. "Pack your bags, lass. We're all leaving here tonight. I don't have time to deal with this anymore. Everyone good?" He looks at each person pointedly, but quickly, as if he doesn't really care. "Good. I'll be downstairs dealing with the body in the dance studio."

CHAPTER 8
Anya

ANOTHER NIGHT HAS fallen upon us by the time we arrive at the Vittori mansion off the coast of Italy. It requires a feat of strength beyond measure for me to cross the threshold to enter the home we only just escaped from. I can no longer behave like a slave if I want to remain in the family's good graces—though to say the graces are good is an exaggeration.

I stay frozen behind my icy shield. I have to hide my panic, my fear, my absolute horror at coming back into this house, and it takes everything I've got to put on that brave face.

But I do it.

Somehow, I steel myself and walk inside, knowing that there is no other choice. To save my life—Ezra's life, my *baby's* life—I have to live here in this house like one of them.

I have to *be* one of them.

I can no longer be Anya Antonov, stolen and captive talent slave to the Mikhailov family. I have to be Anya Mikhailov, bereaved wife of the Mikhailov Head of House.

An entire houseful of Vittoris and extended relatives go from quiet chatter to utter silence as we enter. They stop and stare at us in the foyer. I didn't expect their quarterly meeting guests to be here when we arrived, but I suppose it makes sense.

Family surrounds family when there's a loss, and I took away their most revered Head of House.

I killed Vigo.

And though I feel a brief rush of pride knowing that I ended the life of my vile abuser, I also know that these people regard me as his murderer.

I'm the killer of their brother, their cousin…their *family.*

I need Ezra's strength to bolster me as I face them, but I can't allow myself to connect with him. Though he's only steps behind me—his wrists bound in front of his body with a cable tie—there may as well be a mountain between us. I hate this emotional separation that I've had to force. I have to freeze him out, shield myself behind a glacial fortress to protect myself from feeling.

Because if I feel everything that's happened to me, my weakness and vulnerability will seep through the cracks—and these people will smell it on me.

I can't be weak here.

Renata stops in the open foyer, turning to face me, Ezra, and Lorenzo behind her, just as her loyal slave Luca comes through the throng of guests to be at her side. "Luca, would you be so kind as to show Ezra to his new quarters? Anya's box in the basement is vacant; he can stay there until he's trained."

My mouth automatically opens to protest, but I stop myself, sucking in a sharp breath through my nose. Somehow, I manage to force myself to swallow my rising panic as my heart hammers out of control. I'd rather go back into that box than think that Ezra might be put through the same tortures I suffered here at Vigo's hands.

Vigo is dead.

I killed him.

He can't hurt me anymore.

Renata tilts her head as she regards me with an undercurrent of fury and retribution on her mind. "Did you have some objection to that, Anya?"

She knows I care too much about Ezra. It's why she wants him to stay in the box in the basement. She wants him there to punish me. It's the only reason she wants him here at all, rather than dead…to torment me. I'm untouchable—for the time being—but Ezra is fair game.

I reason with myself that I need to appear detached and distant when it comes to matters involving Ezra and his treatment. If she thinks it doesn't bother me, perhaps she won't torture him in all the ways my abused mind imagines.

Wishful thinking?

I bolster my pride, forcing calm resignation into my expression, though I feel as though I could crumple in fear for the man I love. "Where will I be staying?" I ask.

Her face falls at my lack of reaction. She looks at Luca. His white button-down shirt is open in the front, baring his torso, and he's wearing his black leather collar as usual. I don't think he ever takes it off. Renata jerks her head in the direction of the kitchen, and he acts immediately. He grabs Ezra's arm, tugs him forward, and drags him toward the kitchen where the basement entrance hides behind a normal-looking wall.

Renata's nostrils flare in frustration as she returns her attention to me. "I'll show you to your room upstairs. Lorenzo, please tell our family that we'll join them for dinner tomorrow night to discuss Vigo's funeral and the new…structure of our business." Her eyes snap to mine. "Follow me."

She moves toward the staircase, expecting me to follow her, and there's a sort of snap inside my soul that tugs my attention to Ezra as he's dragged away, struggling against Luca. My skin prickles with goosebumps—knowing he's being taken to that god-awful box—and my heart demands that I let him in, just for a moment, so he can feel that I'm still here with him. My soul demands that he know I haven't abandoned him, that my spirit remains strong and true behind my shields.

Our eyes connect and mine tell him how much I love him, how much I want him, *need* him. How I'll do everything in my power to stay alive and to keep him alive, too. His fight against Luca stops and he nods, the slightest movement of acknowledgment and acceptance, and it unburdens my troubled mind...for now. His eyes tell me to do what I have to do, and he knows I will. Then, he disappears beyond the arched entryway to the kitchen.

His unwavering faith in me is disarming, nearly dismantling my protective walls altogether.

My pulse kicks into overdrive knowing where he's going, knowing that my love is going to suffer the same as I did being trapped in that transparent box in the basement. With my heart racing, I have to work twice as hard to build my walls back up, but I manage to do it somehow.

Renata snaps her fingers to get my attention—literally *snaps* her fingers. I jerk to look at her and I know my expression is filled with the indignation I feel toward her. Her expression nearly mirrors my own.

Malice reflecting malice.

"This way," she says, leading me up the staircase. "Leave your suitcase. It will be brought up shortly."

I wonder what happened to the silver hard-shell suitcase that was packed for me when Vigo first took me away from Nikolai. I never got to peek inside it to see what Nikolai had packed for me. Nearly all my belongings—at least my most treasured items—had remained in my room at Mikhailov Manor, and they're in the suitcase I brought with me today.

Maybe Nikolai hadn't packed me anything at all when he sold me.

Vigo had my silver suitcase discarded when I first arrived, so now I have Ezra's black suitcase full to the brim with everything I treasure and anything I thought might be important to Ezra. I have my box of photos of my sister, my most recent worn-in pair of ballet pointe shoes, and clothes for the both of us.

I have my underwear—such a simple thing that I never would've thought twice about before. Since that luxury had been stripped from me while I served as one of Vigo's broken dolls, it was comforting to know I had a way to cover myself now…to protect myself.

Vigo's dead.

He's gone.

I have to remind myself frequently that I killed him because it still feels like a dream, a nightmare. The ghost of him still haunts me.

As I carefully ascend the steps behind Renata, we pass Olivia—their former talent slave and now Lorenzo's fiancée—coming down the stairs. Her forehead wrinkles in confusion as she sees me with Renata who is, by all accounts, unnaturally calm for escorting the woman who murdered her brother.

I murdered him.

I'm a murderer.

We reach the balcony landing and we turn right—in the direction of Vigo's room, where I was tortured, humiliated, left to die a slow and horrible death, and down the hallway where I killed him.

My breath catches in my throat.

My steps slow as faint, distant voices from a memory leap to the surface of my mind.

Nikolai demanding that we leave.

Ezra urging me along.

Vigo threatening to come after us, to torture and kill Ezra and force me to watch.

The phantom pull of my hand as it covered Kostya's on the gun, my finger curling over his, aiming, and squeezing the trigger.

"Anya," Renata snaps at me again and my head jerks up to look at her.

I'm standing in the same spot, looking down at the dark stain on the carpet where Vigo's blood was spilled by my hand. When I look up, the voices in my mind fade and drift away, and I come back into reality. It takes me that long to realize we're standing in front of Vigo's bedroom door.

"You'll be staying here."

"No." I shake my head. "No, I'm not staying in Vigo's bedroom. Find me another room," I demand.

I feel uneasy being so bold. Nikolai spent years grooming it out of me, and taking it back is proving to be intensely challenging.

"There is no other room, Anya. You've seen our extended family is here and all the guest rooms are occupied. Unless, of course, you'd like a box in the basement."

Truthfully, I consider it. At least then I wouldn't be living in the space where I'd been tormented endlessly, forced to live with the ghost of the man who brought me to the brink of death so viciously. But I can only imagine what Ezra would have to say about that.

A twinge of pain pulls through my side. I place my palm over the ache and that motion alone reminds me that I'm pregnant.

I'm pregnant.

Oh, God. I'm pregnant.

I have to think about the baby. I don't even know how it survived everything I've been through—perhaps it won't survive much longer. It's a real-life miracle, though it's also a real-life nightmare. But its very existence offers me protection and want it or not, I have to take care of it, which also means taking care of myself.

It physically hurts me to consider having the child of a Vittori or Mikhailov. There's a small chance that it could be Ezra's because we'd had sex the same night Nikolai took me as punishment for trying to kill myself. But the most likely outcome is that it belongs to Vigo. He raped me more times than I care to count over the past six months.

Renata has already typed in the code on the keypad lock and the door clicks open. She sniffles, then clears her throat. "The code is 7-4-2-5. Both to get in and out." She pushes the door open and I follow her inside. "I'll send someone tomorrow morning to…to clear things out while our family doctor evaluates you."

A quick glance toward the bathroom shows that nothing has been touched since we escaped. The tiled floor is glossy with the water that spilled from the tub. The oversized mirror that trapped me inside still rests cockeyed on the tub. My heart pounds furiously and I take a step backward.

"Could you…could you close t-the bathroom door?" I stammer, nerves clawing at my confidence.

My eyes are fixed on the cold tiled floor as my panic is triggered. I think Renata's watching me discerningly, but I don't know for sure. All I can see is water—above me, around me, encapsulating me.

The noise she makes sounds pleased. "I'm not your servant, Anya. You may have risen in status on a technicality, but you're no better than I am. You and I, my dear, are on equal footing. Close the door yourself."

I only realize she's left when I hear the door click shut behind her. My head turns and I look at the doorknob with the keypad above it.

"Shit…shit."

Did it lock automatically?

What did she say the code was?

7-4-4-5…No.

7-4-5-…Shit, shit, shit.

I reach for the handle and pull down. It opens. The weight of my relief-filled sigh threatens to drag me down to my knees. My pulse sounds like an internal thunderstorm as it thrums behind my ears.

I should've known the door would open. Vigo always entered his code on the keypad once we were inside the room to lock me in.

I need to know that code.

I peek my head out into the hallway to see Renata walking away. I open my mouth to ask her, but I never even get a chance to. She must've heard the door click open. She halts, turns her head back toward me, and even from this far away, I think I can see a tear rolling slowly down her cheek.

"7-4-2-5," she says before I even ask.

Then, she disappears around the corner.

I can't bring myself to lie on the bed.

I won't sit on the small stool in front of the vanity.

I've been brutalized in every part of this room and I'm haunted by my memories. They cling to me like a virus for which there is no cure. But I'm exhausted—physically and emotionally—and I can hardly stand on my own two feet anymore. Without conscious thought, my body slumps and I sit on the carpet, right here where I'm standing in the middle of the room.

The sound of a running faucet ghosts across my mind and the phantom noise grips me, the sound gradually increasing until I find myself covering my ears to block it out.

It's not real.

The faucet is off.

Vigo is dead.

I'm safe for the moment.

Vigo is dead.

I close my eyes and all I can see is his face rippling above me as I look up at him from beneath water. My eyes snap open again immediately and I half expect to see him standing in front of me. I breathe in and out, in and out, willing my hammering heartbeat to settle, but it only beats faster. My lungs strain as my breaths quicken and shorten until I'm panting, desperate for a decent breath…as if I'm under water again.

I'm hyperventilating.

I'm panicking.

"Stop it," I say to myself. "Stop it, stop it, stop it."

I need Ezra.

I need to…to breathe.

I can't breathe.

I gasp with no success.

I topple sideways to the floor.

Consciousness slips away.

Crying.

I hear crying.

I open my eyes to see that I've fallen asleep in the rocking chair. I look down, though the baby isn't in my arms. I glance around the room until my eyes fall on the beautiful wooden crib in the corner. I'm humming an unfamiliar tune as I rise from my seat and slowly move toward it.

I look down over the side of it to see a tiny baby lying on his back, arms and legs stiffly pawing at the air as he reaches for his mother with uncoordinated movements.

He's brand-new to the world.

I want to keep him safe.

His eyes are closed as he cries out and I'm drawn to him. His one-piece pajamas have a pattern of tiny rainbows printed on them. At least, I think they're rainbows. I don't see any color. I blink, glancing around the room again and realize that nothing is in color.

Everything is black and white.

I'm still humming the tune I don't recognize.

The baby boy screams harder and I can't ignore the instinctual pull to lift him, to hold him, to comfort him in my arms. I reach over the edge of the crib and place my hand on his belly, rubbing a gentle, soft circle to comfort him with my touch.

That's when he opens his eyes.

That's when color returns to my world.

Bright green light sparkles in his familiar gaze and from it, color ripples throughout the room.

Green eyes.

Enchanting green eyes and sandy blond hair.

Ezra.

He looks like Ezra.

This is my baby...our baby.

I smile so wide it makes my cheeks ache and I lift the tiny squirming boy from his crib. I hold him closely to my chest, still humming that tune. Perhaps it's a lullaby I heard somewhere before.

My baby boy calms in my arms, his cries gently change to soft coos of happiness. He's where he belongs, right here in my arms.

"I'm so lucky to be yours." Ezra's voice comes from behind me and I turn to see him in the doorway to the nursery.

His eyes and our baby's look the same. Perfect, green, filled with light and goodness.

We smile at each other.

But then Ezra's eyebrows raise in shock and he gasps. He looks down and my eyes follow. Blood soaks his white T-shirt, circling outward, the spot growing larger as moments pass. And then he falls to the floor. I jump back, holding our baby tighter against my chest.

Ezra is dead and I didn't even see it coming.

Oh, God.

Why is he bleeding?

What caused the wound?

There was no gunshot, and I didn't see a knife. I don't understand how he's dead.

He's dead.

No. No!

I back away until my backside bumps into the edge of the crib. I don't know what to do. I want to help him, I want to save him, but I can't let go of our baby.

I have to protect our baby.

I'm still humming that song.

What song is this?

Where have I heard it before?

"Give me the child." Nikolai's voice booms from the doorway and my body goes rigid.

Nikolai is dead; he is death standing in my doorway. He still bleeds from his gunshot wound and it drips down to the carpet beneath his feet. His face is pale, expressionless, lifeless. He steps forward and I shout, but then he falls to his knees before dropping lifelessly onto the floor beside Ezra.

I'm humming the song.

I hum it louder as unseen voices swirl around me.

"Give me the baby."

"That baby is mine."

"He's a Mikhailov."

"He's a Vittori."

"He's mine."

"Kill him. Kill them both."

"Stop!" I scream and the voices fall silent.

But then the song comes again, only I'm no longer humming.

It's....it's Vigo.

His sound carries from the hallway outside the nursery. The humming becomes whistling, growing louder and louder until he finally appears in the doorway. Blood pours from him, from every part of his body, spilling like morbid waterfalls and pooling on the carpet. He bleeds so much and so fast that it cascades into the room like a flash flood. It spills and spills, filling the space.

And the pool rises.

Slowly, it rises.

The song.

The one he's whistling, the one that I was humming.

It's the tune he whistled when he left me to die in his bathtub, locked beneath the mirror and the running faucet.

The blood is to his knees when he stretches his arms out wide. He tilts his head back. As if he's willed it to happen, he explodes, bursting into crimson liquid that splatters the walls and drenches me and my baby in a thick coating.

I scream.

The baby cries and I look down, but he's no longer in my arms.

I dropped him.

He's sinking into the pool of blood that continues to rise.

I lunge after him, diving beneath the surface and reaching for him, but he's already gone. I can't find him. I don't know where he is. I rise to break the surface, to catch my breath, but my head hits something hard above me.

I open my eyes and immediately close them again.

I'm back in Vigo's bathtub, drowning beneath clear water, my reflection splintered in the cracked mirror that keeps me locked in my own watery grave.

Somewhere nearby, my baby cries again but I'm trapped. I can't get to him. But I have to get to him. I need to get to him. He needs me.

I hear....

Italian.

A woman's voice.

Renata.

Though I can't see her, I know she has my baby. He continues to cry and scream. He doesn't want her. He needs me.

"Sweet child. You were never meant for this world," she coos.

I try to scream for him but water fills my mouth.

"Your father is a slave. You never should have existed."

My baby screams louder and she only shushes him. His cries become muffled as if something smothers him.

"Go to sleep, baby. It'll all be over soon," she murmurs.

I scream as loud as I can, but the sound is swallowed by the water all around me. The air rushes out of me in bubbles as I scream and scream until I'm gasping for more air, but only taking in water. I'm drowning.

Drowning.

I hear the echo of Renata's voice somewhere above me.

My baby no longer cries.

I open my eyes beneath the water and see my reflection above me, but then it changes. With each ripple of water, it twists and morphs until it becomes Vigo above me.

He waves at me with a sadistic grin as I gulp in more water, my chest aching as it fills my lungs.

"It will be done soon," his reflection tells me. "Just a few more counts of eight. One. Two. Three. Four. Five. Six. Seven. Eight."

He counts.

He counts.

He counts.

And I fade away.

I awaken with a start, bolting upright as my eyes snap open. I look around me, quickly remembering that I'm in Vigo's room. I passed out on the floor in my panic-induced hyperventilation.

My hand falls to my stomach, a protective instinct to cover him and keep him safe.

Him.

The nightmare had been so vivid. I have to catch my breath because I feel like I truly had been drowning. Tears well, glassing over my vision before a sob forces them to fall down my cheeks.

My baby.

My baby was killed in my dream and it was the most horrifying thing I've ever experienced. More horrifying than anything Vigo or Nikolai had ever put me through. More horrifying than anything anyone could dream up to do to me. In my dream, my own life hardly mattered to me, but...

My baby.

My baby had to be protected at all costs.

Our baby.

It was just a dream, but I could feel it in my soul. The baby is a boy, and he belongs to Ezra.

This puts all our lives in grave danger. But oddly, this doesn't strike me with more fear. Instead, it injects me with more determination, with a fierce and powerful need to rise and become the queen that Nikolai granted me the ability to become with our marriage.

Our marriage is the only reason I'm not dead right now.

If it saves my life, Ezra's life, our baby's life, I will become ruthless, cold, and demanding. I will do what I have to do to save us.

CHAPTER 9
Anya

I SLEPT IN that same spot on the floor last night. It was uncomfortable…painful, actually. My back hurt, my neck hurt, my stomach felt stretched and achy. I know I was being stupid not to sleep on the bed, but I just couldn't.

The memories of what Vigo did to me on that bed when he had me drugged and paralyzed would flash across my mind each time I thought about going to lie down on it. So, the result was a painful night of unsatisfactory sleep on the floor.

Renata has just come to collect me for a visit with the family doctor this morning. She leads me downstairs to the first floor and I find myself constantly looking around me. My mind hasn't come to terms with the fact that Vigo is truly dead yet. I can just see him popping out from around a corner, grabbing me, dragging me into the nearest room, terrorizing me until night falls again. The thought of it appears like a crystal-clear vision in my mind, so clear that it makes me gasp and I stop dead in my tracks.

The vision of his torture won't let me go. It grips me like a rope coiling around my chest, squeezing my lungs, and crushing my heart. My heart explodes in a flurry of beats, pumping wildly as panic overtakes me again. One hand comes up to my chest as the other lands on the wall by my side to steady myself.

I feel like I can't catch a breath.

I feel like my lungs are being squeezed so tightly that they won't inflate, no matter how much I try.

I feel like I'm going to pass out again.

No, no.

Not here, not now.

I try to calm my mind and think of anything else, but the vision of Vigo in my mind keeps playing like a movie, an intrusion of a thought that I can't exorcise from within me, no matter what I do. So, I do the only thing my mind will let me do.

I count.

One. Two. Three. Four. Five. Six. Seven. Eight.

One. Two. Three. Four. Five. Six. Seven. Eight.

One. Two. Three. Four. Five. Six. Seven. Eight.

I count until the horror film plays out in my mind, until it fades away into non-existence and I can think of nothing but the numbers, the counts of eight, the basic structure of my dance steps, the dancing that makes me feel free.

Renata is at my side, as is another man. They speak in Italian with concern and their concern is directed at me. I realize that I'm on the floor, my back to the wall and my legs pulled up against my chest.

But I don't remember sitting.

The man puts a hand on my shoulder and I jolt at the sensation. He removes it as I turn my head to look up at him, as he crouches to his haunches beside me. I don't feel threatened by him—he doesn't give me the same creeping, prickling feeling down my arms that all the other Vittoris give me.

"I'm Doctor Lombardi," he says to me, his Italian accent thick but understandable. "I want to help you. Can you stand?"

I carefully study his face.

One. Two. Three. Four. Five. Six. Seven. Eight.

I believe he wants to help me. I nod and he holds out his hand to help me off the floor.

One. Two. Three. Four. Five. Six. Seven. Eight.

I take his hand and let him help me up. Renata says something in Italian, and though I don't know what she's saying, I do know what she's feeling. The anguish is written all over her face, and her rage and grief are all directed at me. Her feelings mix with mine in a tangled web of hopeless anxiety. There are dark circles beneath her eyes, the whites of which are tinged with red as if she's been crying.

Of course, she's been crying.

You killed her brother.

You're a murderer!

One. Two. Three. Four. Five. Six. Seven. Eight.

I can't let myself feel anything for her, for what I did to her brother. Because he wasn't just her brother; he was a demon spawned from hellfire—a monster in its truest form. He was a man who'd been born with the power, wealth, and privilege to do so much in this world, but he chose to burn it with his hate, his filth, his plague of darkness.

He deserved to die.

He deserved it and so did Nikolai.

Nikolai.

He's dead, too.

I look down at my hands to see myself unconsciously twist the diamond rings on my finger. The jewelry feels as heavy as the chain he used to clasp around my ankle. I hate Nikolai for these rings—these symbols of oppression and stolen freedom.

Yet, there's also a twinge of grief. It's an unwanted grief, like another fist squeezing my heart, though it doesn't hold on for too long. It lets go before I sink into another panic episode, as I recall that I made a promise to wear these rings for Ezra. The recognition of my choice to belong to Ezra calms my nerves.

Doctor Lombardi leads me into a nearby bedroom on the first floor. He stops at the door and turns to Renata. "Go eat, Renata. I will bring Anya directly to you after the exam."

Her eyes narrow at me, raking over my form as if I'm a dog who has pissed on her luxurious carpet. I don't feel badly about it—I feel the same way about her. She doesn't give me the benefit of speaking English in her response, but the way she jabs a finger in my direction as she talks to Doctor Lombardi gives me a good sense that she's told him to watch out for any bad behavior from me.

Good.

I want her to feel threatened by me.

The doctor closes the door behind her as she leaves. He turns to face me but stays where he stands, sensing my discomfort in being with an unknown person behind a closed door.

"I'm going to give you a physical. Is that okay, Anya?" His eyebrows lift in question and he waits for me to respond.

Wait…He's asking me?

Surprised, I nod, though I'm sure it's hardly perceptible, so I add, "Yes," with a quiet voice.

He holds his hand out toward the queen-sized bed behind me. "Please have a seat. I promise you, this will be very professional. I have no interest in harming you."

I swallow, skeptical by nature, though I still feel okay in his presence. Nothing is setting off any alarm bells in my mind, and I suppose I feel a bit calmer now that Renata is gone. I think I will always be skeptical of any man's intentions with me, except for Ezra. Ezra is my one great exception, my soul mate.

"Okay," I reply carefully, slowly lowering and perching on the very edge of the bed.

"Renata tells me you believe you're pregnant?"

"I *am* pregnant. I took two tests, and they were both positive."

He nods. "Good. Well, if you feel certain, then I'll give you an ultrasound so we can see how things are going."

"How will you do that? You have an ultrasound machine here?"

"Yes."

"Why?"

He clears his throat. "It's not my place to discuss. The equipment is here, so let us just feel fortunate for that."

He picks up a black laptop and pulls up an armchair from the corner to face me at a comfortable distance. He sits, then opens the laptop and starts typing as I sit in silence, waiting, twisting the rings around my finger.

"Just a few questions, Anya. When was your last period?"

My heads snaps toward him. "What?"

"Your last period."

My brow furrows and I glance down at the floor as I try to recall. But honestly, I don't know how he expects me to remember something like that. It's certainly been months, but I don't know how many. Vigo was practically starving me, so who knows if a skipped period was because of pregnancy or malnutrition. My body has gone through forced and brutal changes because of Vigo.

"I don't know," I tell him honestly. "Months."

He nods, though his eyes remain fixed on his computer screen and whatever it is he's typing. "Mm-hmm. Do you have any sense of when you conceived?"

I chuckle unintentionally. "I don't know. I've been raped with intense frequency over the past several years, doctor. My understanding is that my last owner stopped my birth control without my knowledge. I could've fallen pregnant anytime over the last six months."

"Mm-hmm. And do you think you are six months pregnant?" His eyes dip down over the laptop screen, scanning my relatively flat stomach.

Naturally, one of my hands float to rest over my belly button and I look down, too. I feel stupid now to think about it. I had noticed a slight difference in my shape before, but I wrote it off as being a result of my malnourishment and the fact that I couldn't care for myself properly.

"No," I finally respond to Doctor Lombardi's question.

"So, can you give me a guess as to when you might have become pregnant? It will help me to judge healthy development when we do your ultrasound."

I start to shake my head because I truthfully don't know when I conceived. But I know when I *hope* I conceived, so I tell him, "Three months."

We were at the Leblancs' three months ago. Three months ago, I had sex with Ezra and Nikolai on the same night. Three months is an estimate that gives me the hope that this baby might not belong to Vigo—even having Nikolai's baby feels somehow better than that.

I think I know the truth in my heart, or at least, I hope I do. I saw what I want to be the truth so vividly in my dream. That truth is that this baby belongs to Ezra by some absolute *miracle*, because the odds of that being true are poor at best.

Doctor Lombardi goes through an exhaustive list of health questions, only stopping when we both hear my stomach growl. I need to eat and I'm glad this man at least seems to have the understanding that we need to move this along.

He asks me to lay on the bed as he rolls a cart around with the ultrasound machine. I can't imagine that the Vittoris just happen to have an ultrasound machine sitting around. The doctor must have brought it here for some reason.

Perhaps she called him and he arrived with it last night. If not, someone else in this mansion must be pregnant, too.

Heaven forbid Renata should ever reproduce, though I wonder if that's even possible for her in her early forties. The only other women who live in this house are the elderly Vittori mother who I never did meet, children of Vittori cousins, and…the slaves.

I don't even want to think about what they would do if one of Vigo's broken dolls had become pregnant.

The same thing they would do to me if Nikolai hadn't made me a Mikhailov.

Oh, God.

Don't think about it.

Doctor Lombardi pulls me back to reality as he squirts a gel on my bare stomach—I hardly remember lifting my shirt. I watch the screen carefully, though I don't really understand what I'm seeing. I don't understand until…

I see the outline of the baby.

I see the outline of *my* baby.

"There it is," Doctor Lombardi says. "You see? Moving a lot."

I blink at the screen. It wasn't real until this moment. It was just two pink lines on a stick until just now. Now…now it's real…so, so real.

Doctor Lombardi tries to measure the baby, but the tiny squirming thing is moving around so much that he has to wait until he's still. Until then, it's just quiet, and we watch. Tiny limbs that look like arms wave and his legs kick as his body wriggles.

God, it looks like he's dancing.

My baby's dancing inside me.

Doctor Lombardi is clicking buttons on his machine

with one hand as he performs the ultrasound with the other. "Heartbeat is strong. Good. Baby is measuring about twelve weeks and five days. You were right, just about three months. A few more days and it will be your second trimester."

"Is it a boy?" I'm eager as I ask.

"It is a little too early to say with imaging alone. But I will do a blood test to find out. *Signora* Vittori would like an early gender result, as well. I don't know whether she'll share that information with you."

"It's my baby."

"Yes," he nods, "I understand. But I am…limited." He gives a sympathetic smile.

I understand what he means by limited, and though it makes me feel indignant, I can't fault him for those limitations. What I know for now is enough—the baby growing inside me is healthy and strong.

And apparently, a dancer.

He finishes his exam and starts talking to me about nutrition and exercise during the pregnancy, but I don't hear a word of it. The image of my baby dancing keeps swirling through my thoughts and the feeling it gives me is indescribably perfect.

A perfect image to chase away all the bad ones.

But even that perfect image can't keep them away forever because I know there's so much bad yet to come.

I'm not safe.

Ezra's not safe.

Our baby is not safe.

Even if they kill us and keep him, he will never be safe with them. This is not the life I want for my baby.

I'll lay down my own to make him free.

CHAPTER 10

Ezra

I'M CAGED LIKE a fucking animal and all I want to do is claw the life out of my jailer.

I'm out of my mind with worry over Anya and whether she's okay. They said she'd be treated like a Mikhailov wife, which I guess sounds okay in theory, but these fuckers think in such warped ways that it's impossible to know for sure.

Luca—Renata's current boy toy—told me that this is the same cell they kept Anya in when she belonged to Vigo. It makes my insides boil with rage, heartache, and guilt.

So much goddamn guilt.

I can't help but blame myself for the fact that she was ever sold to that creep in the first place. I'd been the one to suggest we have sex for the first time in her room at Mikhailov Manor after our performance together as talent slaves—it was the reason we'd been caught by Nikolai.

We could've done it in any room in that mansion. Or at the least, I could have gone right back to my room after the first time we did it in her bed. But I'd been selfish, refusing to leave until we were both fully satisfied and beyond aching for rest. Because of that, we fell asleep and got caught.

That's my fault.

It's my fault she was sold and my fault she was kept in this stupid transparent box.

I'm agitated, exhausted, frustrated, driving myself insane with worry. Not to mention the way adrenaline pulses through my veins with a steady thrum, insistent that I keep moving, keep fighting, *fighting* to get out of this small space. I fight and pace and fight and before long, I'm fighting just to stay awake... just to stay upright.

Eventually, I let myself sit on the mattress that rests on the floor. I realize that Anya slept here, night after night, trapped in this cage, only to be taken out and tortured in ways I can't even let myself imagine.

I'd witnessed her last horrific torture with my own eyes, and I consider us lucky that I was able to pull her out of that tub in time. It was the most horrifying thing I'd ever experienced. Vigo had tied the mirror so tightly to the top of the tub that I honestly thought I might not get it off in time. There was a moment where I thought she would drown and I wouldn't be able to save her, a moment where I feared pulling her lifeless body from the water.

I'd been so overwhelmed with fear and the chemical rush to keep fighting that it hadn't even occurred to me to drain the fucking tub until the moment the mirror started to budge. If she'd died because of my stupidity, I would never have forgiven myself.

Fuck.

I would've killed myself because nothing matters without her.

Nikolai told me once that my impulsivity would destroy me. Well, if impulsivity made me that fucking stupid, then I guess he was right.

If anything happens to Anya, it will destroy me.

The girl in the box next to mine has fallen asleep and

suddenly, I'm desperate to sleep, too. I let myself lay down, reasoning that it's okay for me to sleep, *good* for me to sleep. If I get the sleep I need and take care of myself, then I'll have the strength to keep fighting for her.

When I finally lay down, I swear I can smell her.

She always smells like fresh-cut roses.

Floral, fragrant, sweet, but heady.

Undeniably her.

The scent of my blue-eyed girl is all over this mattress and I revel in it.

It smells like home.

And because it smells like my home, I can feel her with me. We're apart, but at least we're in the same home…in the same *country*. At least I know she's not here, trapped in a box like me.

At least she's okay for now.

I close my eyes and fall asleep thinking about her blue eyes, her warm smile, and the electric touch of her skin.

"Ezra."

The sound of my name startles me awake and I bolt upright from the mattress on the floor. I glance around as I try to make sense of where I am. Reality comes crashing back into my mind as the dream I was pulled from swiftly fades, though I can still remember bits and pieces of it in flashes.

I dreamt that the four families took Anya from me, pinned her down, cut her stomach open, and took her baby as she screamed and bled. But the baby wasn't theirs to take. It didn't belong to them.

He belonged to us.

He was my baby boy.

My son.

Same green eyes and sandy blond hair.

He was undeniably, unquestionably mine.

But now, reality's back to bite me in the ass. Luca and Renata are opening the door to my cage.

"I have no intention to harm you right now, Ezra," Renata says as Luca pulls the transparent door all the way open, stepping back and allowing Renata to fill the space to stand in front of me. "But if you try to fight or run, you will regret it. There's simply no need for such incivility here."

I give Luca a once over as she speaks. He's shirtless, but he's wearing jeans and a black leather collar—a slave if I ever saw one. But he doesn't seem frightened of her. He doesn't even seem to show any hatred or disdain for simply being a captive and in her presence. My eyes narrow on him in my scrutiny because I don't understand what I'm seeing.

"I want to see Anya," I tell her.

She sighs. "You'll see her around. Although I don't have any reason to offer you assurance, I will tell you that she's fine if that troubles you. She's with our family doctor now."

"Where?" I climb to my feet, stepping toward her. "I *want* to see her."

She purses her lips. "You're in no place to make demands of me. If you cooperate and do as you're told, then you might get to see her this evening at dinner."

"What do you want from me?"

"You already know what I want from you," she says with a crooked smile. "Come with me. Don't keep me waiting." She turns on her heel and strides toward the staircase, high heels clicking along the cement floor.

Luca stands there, waiting for me to follow Renata, so I do. But not without glancing over my shoulder every few steps to keep an eye on him. I don't like having this guy behind me.

We arrive in the kitchen at the top of the basement steps.

Renata closes the door behind Luca and types in a code on the keypad to lock it shut, hiding it behind the drywall.

A secret basement to keep women captive.

These people are fucking nuts, and Vigo was a straight up psychopath. But when I remember that *my* girl killed him, a slight smile twitches in the corner of my lips and I have to hide it. He tried to end her, but she won that battle and ended *him* instead. It reminds me that she's strong enough to win the whole damn war if we can just figure out how to do it.

"I assume you're hungry," Renata says.

Is she asking or telling me?

I shrug.

She reaches into a cabinet and pulls out a small plate. It's stark white, just like the rest of the kitchen.

"Did Luca introduce himself?" she asks, nodding toward her collared slave. She reaches into the fridge and pulls out a large bowl covered in plastic wrap. "You should get to know each other. You'll be serving me as he does."

"And how exactly will that be?" I ask slowly.

She looks over her shoulder at me and smiles. "Have patience. The fun is yet to come." She pulls the plastic wrap off the bowl and grabs a serving spoon, scooping fresh fruit onto the small plate. "Luca, come. Eat."

She lifts the plate from the counter and bends, setting it down on the floor beside her.

What the fuck?

Luca circles the short side of the oversized kitchen island, going around to the other side where Renata stands. Then, he lowers, disappearing behind the island. I must be misunderstanding because I think he's down on the floor, eating fruit off a plate like a dog.

What in the actual fuck?

My eyes remain fixed on the edge of the counter near where she stands, in the place where Luca disappeared behind it. When she tells him, "Good boy," and bends down to pat him—on the ass or the head, I don't know which—my eyes flicker up to look at her.

She's staring at me.

"Come, Ezra."

I can't help the chuckle that escapes me. "You've got to be kidding me."

"Ezra," she chides. "I won't ask you again. If I have to ask you again, then perhaps..." She places her hands on the island counter's edge, leaning forward with her arms apart and elbows locked. "Perhaps Anya finds herself accidentally falling down the staircase. Perhaps she bumps her head and slips away in her sleep from complications. Perhaps she finally succumbs to her depression and succeeds in ending her life. Should I go on? I can think of a thousand ways to kill her without drawing suspicion."

God fucking damnit.

I move, walking to her slowly. Luca eats from his plate on the floor, just like I thought—like a dog, bending over to pluck each bite from the plate with his teeth.

"I'm *not* eating like that," I tell her, pointing my finger in Luca's direction.

She moves toward me and I press back against the edge of the island, my ass hitting the counter's edge. She moves closer and closer until her body is flush with mine. She's at eye level with her heels on, but she may as well be seven feet tall by the way she makes me feel without saying a damn word.

My hands grip the counter on either side of my hips as I try to lean away from her. She turns away for a moment, only to reach into the bowl of fruit from the counter behind her. She plucks a strawberry from the bowl and moves impossibly closer to me. She presses in so close that her body holds me in place, and I feel more trapped here than I did in the cage.

She lifts the strawberry between us and taps the tip of it against my lips. I keep them pressed shut.

"Eat," she says.

"I'm not that hungry," I lie.

I'm fucking starving.

"You won't be given another opportunity to eat until lunchtime, so I suggest you take the opportunity now. I intend to keep you healthy. I expect you to take care of my needs and that simply won't be possible if I don't keep you," she pauses, her eyes skimming across my chest and down my torso, "strong and healthy."

My jaw sets and my muscles clench. "Might have been nice if your brother had adopted that same philosophy for his girls."

Her face drops and she shoves the strawberry hard where my lips meet until I'm forced to open. I take a quick bite and slam my lips shut again so she doesn't choke me with it. "Don't *ever* speak about my brother again. He was more man than you could ever hope to become, Ezra."

Movement off to the left steals our attention. A man clears his throat. "I've completed Mrs. Mikhailov's health screening and ultrasound."

Mrs. Mikhailov. Jesus.

Renata takes a step back, walking around Luca to approach the man on the opposite side of the kitchen island. He's an older gentleman. His jet-black hair has touches of gray, hinting at his age, and his presence doesn't immediately put me off, which seems unusual here in the Vittori home.

Then, there's that punch to the gut awareness as Anya slowly moves into the room, looking lost yet hopeful at the same time. I stare her down until she registers that I'm there and her eyes meet mine. Her eyebrows bend to frame her beautiful blue eyes before she grants me a small, secret smile.

My heart leaps out of control. I forget how to breathe when she puts her hand on her stomach and looks at me with love in her eyes. For a moment, I forget where I am, who I am, why I'm here. For a moment, it's just me looking at my girl, dreaming about a future we might never get to have.

Renata starts to say something to the man in Italian, but he lifts a hand.

"Please, *Signora* Vittori. I've told you before. I'm very happy to care for your family and…the others, but we must speak in the language the patient understands."

Her nostrils flare and her chest rises as she takes in a sharp breath, but then she concedes, which is shocking. This man must have a long-standing relationship with the family to be able to speak so boldly.

Renata forces herself to calmness, then she switches to English. "Anything notable I need to be aware of?"

"The baby is measuring around twelve weeks, five days, so she's just about into her second trimester. A miracle if you ask me. She's malnourished and weak. Frankly, I'm shocked the baby's heartbeat is as strong as it is. I'm going to recommend a nutritionist—"

"That won't be necessary," Renata says. "I'll ensure she receives a healthy diet moving forward. Her life circumstances have recently changed. When can a DNA test be performed?"

"A DNA test?"

"To determine paternity. The board would like this done as soon as possible."

"Oh, well, it's possible to do now with blood samples from both parents."

"Both of the potential fathers are recently deceased."

The doctor's eyebrows slant in toward his nose in consideration. "If you have access to the deceased remains, I think it can still be done. I may need to consult with a geneticist. I know of one who can be discreet in this matter."

"Fine," Renata replies. "Lorenzo can put you in contact with Murphy O'Shea before you leave. Murphy has graciously made the arrangements to handle both of the deceased in our time of grief."

My eyes practically roll out of my head.

He nods. "Good. I'll go speak with Lorenzo. And please ensure Anya gets the rest she needs. Her body is overtaxed and it's not good for her or the baby."

Renata dismisses the doctor and turns, glancing from me to Anya to Luca on the floor. "Luca, serve Anya breakfast. Eggs, toast, and fruit. Make sure she eats it all and clean up after her when she's done. Ezra, come with me."

She brushes past Anya with a conflicted look of disdain and moves toward the open archway that leads back to the foyer. Luca rises from the floor, moving about the kitchen as if everything happening here is perfectly normal.

I look at Anya. She tilts her head toward Renata's retreating form, mouthing the word, "Go," with pleading eyes.

How can she be so strong after everything she's been through?

How can she be strong enough to still be ordering me around and making sure I don't make things worse?

I've said it before and it's still true now—she's a goddamn beautiful powerhouse.

I walk toward her. She's standing in the path I need to take to follow Renata, and she stays intentionally, knowing I'll have to pass by her on my way through. Our eyes are locked as I come closer.

I choose to walk between her and the island, even though the space is narrow. I should walk around her on the other side, but I can't help myself. I squeeze into the narrow space, brushing against her body as I move past. I catch her palm in my hand for the briefest moment, just for a quick squeeze of reassurance.

Fuck, that was a bad idea.

The small touch is a lightning strike, a shockwave of connection that sears through my skin and burns through my soul. She gasps and I know she feels it, too.

I'm forced to let go as I stride past, Renata looking back impatiently from the bottom step of the staircase in the foyer. But I dare to steal one last glance over my shoulder at my glowing girl. She covers her smile with a cold expression, but her eyes hide nothing from me.

I'm the man she melts for.

I'm the man who knows what lies beneath the surface.

I'm the man she loves.

CHAPTER 11
Ezra

RENATA'S BEDROOM IS like a luxury hotel suite. It's smaller than I expected it would be, but certainly not lacking in extravagance. The room is all shades of gold, ivory, and cream, and I wonder how the fuck she keeps it all so clean looking.

Probably slaves.

Maybe me.

She gestures toward an armchair in the far corner of the room, angled toward the end of her sleek, modern-looking bed. "Sit."

I cautiously cross the space, turning and walking backward because I don't trust her behind me. She moves to her cream-colored dresser beside the door, and I watch her carefully as she pulls something out of the top drawer. I fight the warning tension in my muscles and slowly sit on the chair. I've learned the importance of obedience in this life, but I don't think I'll ever stop having the immediate urge for defiance. I'm wary while waiting to find out which particular brand of demon spawn Renata will prove to be.

"It's been a long time since I've had a second slave," she says, working on something in front of her, though her back is turned to me and I can't see what. "Luca has been with me for four years, since he turned twenty-one." Her head turns to look at me and her dark brown eyes catch mine. "He wasn't taken, you know. He's a willing slave."

I scoff, "Yeah, right."

I see half of her smile from her profile before she turns away again. "Is that so hard to believe? Luca enjoys being my slave. It's a lifestyle choice for him. There are places to find people like Luca. We met at an establishment that caters to the wealthy and their very particular wants and needs. He wanted to find a master and I wanted a willing slave. Immediately, Luca and I knew we'd make a good match…instant chemistry." She gives me a knowing look. "He asked to be mine and I brought him home. I provide well for him, and I could do the same for you, Ezra. He's happy here."

"I don't believe you."

"Believe what you like. It's the truth." She turns, crossing the room to stand in front of me with a square box in her hands. "I'm going to keep close tabs on you. I don't trust you in Anya's presence."

"I don't trust you in anyone's presence."

"I expect you to cooperate during your training. Luca has been given permission to provide you with guidance on serving me."

"Serving you?"

She drops the box in my lap and bends over me, grasping my chin tightly between her fingers and forcing me to look up at her. The red silk blouse she wears drapes open as she bends, leaving nothing to the imagination, and she doesn't seem to care.

"You will serve me or you will die. If that's not incentive enough for you, then I will remind you of all the ways I could make Anya's life end without drawing suspicion from anyone in the four families. And I will do just that if you deny me."

"What do you want from me? What do you need me for if you already have Luca? I thought I was here to service your bloodlust."

"Blood taken requires blood given, yes. Don't be mistaken, I *will* take from you, drops at a time." She releases my chin and turns, moving to sit on the edge of the bed across from me. She exhales slowly and captures me with her stare. "I find the fire behind your eyes alluring."

Okay.

Really, how do I respond to something like that?

She goes on as if she's having a casual conversation with a friend. "I was a married woman not so long ago. Giovanni was the perfect husband for a woman like me. He was strong, capable, dominant." A half-smile twists her lips. "He was dominant enough to handle me, if you can imagine. I was in love with him. Giovanni was my everything. We'd been seeing each other for years before we married, but I only spent a few days as his wife." She pauses and I sense she only does it for dramatic effect. "He was murdered…gone before I even had a chance to legally change my name. It's been two years since his death and I still grieve him daily." Her expression melts into vengeful honesty. "Trust me when I tell you that I understand pain. I know how to use the woman you love to hurt you, and I will if you deny me what I need."

I swallow the raw truth I hear in her tone. "So, what do you what from me?"

She stands and moves slowly toward me. She pauses in front of me for a moment before she bends, placing her palms on my knees. I jerk backward, though my ass stays firmly planted in the seat. She pushes my knees apart, creating a V with my legs and she lowers until she's kneeling between them. I'm frozen in place, every muscle in my body hard and tense.

She tilts her head, giving me eye contact that I'd call uncomfortable at best. "Giovanni had eyes like yours…like a fire that refuses to stop burning. I miss that fire, that fervor, that all-consuming, reckless passion…the kind of passion you have for that awful girl." I clench my fists and pray I can keep myself from pounding them against her face. "Giovanni would share me with Luca, you know. We would play together. We'd command him and enjoy each other. It would be nice to have that again."

Ah, fuck.

Fucking heathens.

She grips my thighs and slowly slides her hands upward. I grab her wrists and forcefully remove them. "No," I say firmly.

"Yes." She yanks her arms from my grip and slaps her hands right back down on my thighs, digging her fingertips into my muscles.

I try to scoot back, but I'm already as far back as I can go. "Stop," I insist. Her fast fingers tug my shirt free from where it's still half tucked into my pants, and they quickly disappear beneath the hem. "Whoa. Fuck. *Stop* it." She starts undoing the button of my black slacks and I push through the armrests to stand. She leans back when I rise and sidestep free.

"Where do you think you're going?" she asks as I rush for the door.

I press down on the handle, but nothing clicks. It doesn't open. There's a keypad above it.

Fuck, I'm locked in.

I spin around just as she appears in front of me and I slam my back to the door. She comes in close, too close…*way* too fucking close.

"You seem uncomfortable, Ezra," she prods.

"I'm more than fucking uncomfortable. Knock it the fuck off."

She lets out a heavy sigh. "I don't want to do this the hard way, but I will."

I don't know if she's trying to sound threatening, but I'm not threatened by her. She makes me feel uneasy, not threatened. But then she turns and walks away, going to retrieve the box that fell from my lap when I got up, and she brings it over to me.

"Put this on," she says, lifting the lid of the box.

I laugh. It's a black leather collar, just like Luca's. "Fuck no."

"I didn't give you a choice. Put it on."

"Fucking *no*." She's really pissing me off now.

She picks up the collar, sets the empty box onto the dresser beside me, and boldly crushes her body against mine. I draw back, but there's nowhere for me to go. So, I do what I have to. I grab her by both shoulders and physically shove her back, pushing and walking her until her legs hit the bed and she sits to avoid falling.

I step backward, pointing a finger at her. "Stay the fuck away from me."

She just smiles from where she sits, placing a palm on the mattress and leaning on it with a suggestive tilt. "I'm surprised at you. You're being very forward with me considering how submissive you were with Nikolai."

I take another backward step. "I was submissive because I had to be, for Anya's sake."

She pushes to stand and I turn again, jiggling the door handle uselessly. I feel her presence behind me before her hand lands on my shoulder, gentle fingers dragging down my arm. I jolt from her touch and the warning prickle that creeps over my skin.

"And you still have to be submissive, for Anya's sake." She hugs me from behind and it's fucking weird. She kisses between my shoulder blades and my shoulders shrug against what feels like an attack. "I hardly gave her a second thought when she was nothing but a slave. But since she killed my brother..." She pauses and I feel both her hands on my back, her cheek pressed there, freezing me in place. "Since she killed him, I've spent every waking moment imagining her blood on my hands. Consider your submission a way to quench my bloodlust for her. I'll take yours as her penance. I would enjoy slicing her open and playing with her insides. But perhaps your service to me will fulfill that need. Do you understand me?"

Fuck.

Shit fucking cock-sucking motherfucker.

There aren't enough curse words in existence to express my fury as my pulse hums and my insides heat to boiling. My fists ache from clenching and I punch one against the door, the sound and force of it slamming against the hard wood startles her enough that she backs up.

My forehead drops against the door as I will my quickening breaths to slow. I'm a raging bull and she's a matador who taunts me, dangling Anya's safety in front of me like a red cape—I'll keep charging for it as long as she teases me with it. I may be stronger—brute and determined—but she holds the real power in this bullfight.

My mind winds through loops in my fury that tug on the intensity of my anger, allowing me enough rationality to submit for Anya's safety. My shoulders slump and I force myself to give up the fight because I understand her threat crystal fucking clear. I would do anything to protect Anya, even if that means giving Renata goddamn Vittori my submission.

I turn around to find her holding out the collar she wants me to wear. I'm still wearing the white button-down I had on when we met with the families back at Mikhailov Manor, though I removed the jacket and necktie and left them in the basement. The top two buttons of my shirt are already open, leaving her enough room to place the collar on my bare skin. I turn when she moves to my side and dip down to let her latch it in place at the back of my neck. I let her do it without fighting because I have no choice.

Renata is dangerous in the worst kind of way. She's the kind of dangerous you don't feel threatened by until you're fucking dead on the floor.

Once the collar is securely latched, she moves in front of me again. She reaches out and begins to unbutton my shirt with nimble fingers. I push her hands away, but she just starts again.

"You belong to me now. If you behave, I'll ensure you enjoy being mine."

Mine?

Fuck no.

She's not allowed to call me hers. No one is—no one except Anya. The word triggers a new adrenaline rush that I can't ignore. I step forward, crowding Renata, forcing her backward.

"I will submit to you, but don't you dare think for a *second* that I'm yours. I'm *hers*. I belong to Anya, and she is the *only* reason I'll obey you."

Renata huffs and pulls something from the pocket of her sleek black pants. She shows me a small black rectangle in her hand—something that looks like a tiny remote. She lifts an eyebrow and it tugs the corner of her mouth up into a wicked smirk. I watch her thumb press down on the remote and a lightning bolt strikes through the side of my neck. The shock of it makes me seize, every muscle in my body jerking to a rigid stop at the jolt of it for just a moment before the pain stops.

She put a shock collar on me.

My hands shoot up to grip the leather, fingers scrambling

to find the latch, and just as I do, another shock seizes my system. This one goes on for beat after beat before the searing pain stops.

I drop to my knees, and though it takes moments for my mind to shift back into focus, my fingers start moving again automatically, searching for the latch that will free me. But my hands are shaking and my fingers tremble as they clamber against the leather.

"Take this *off* me!"

"Be a good boy and I will help you. Come here," she says in such a deceptively cool way that I fully regret that I didn't just knock her on her ass when I had the chance.

Despite myself, I scoot on my knees to get to her because I need this *off*.

She looks down at me, pride on her face stolen from me. "Hold still."

She circles around behind me, dragging her hand from my shoulder, across my upper back until she reaches the latch at the base of my neck. I feel her pull on it, doing something I can't see, and in moments, I hear something metal *click*. My hands jump to touch it and I freeze. My fingers recognize the shape of a padlock at the back of my neck. It's hooked through the latch and locked in place.

The collar is padlocked around my neck.

A frenzy takes over and I'm desperate to get this thing off me. I pull and twist at the leather, somehow managing to spin it sideways, but it makes no difference. It's on and it's not coming off.

"You *bitch!*"

Her fingers slide into my hair, dig in, and grip the strands. She yanks my head back hard, stretching my throat until I'm looking up at her above me.

"You will call me *Signora* Vittori."

"*Bitch*," I insist and hate the way the word sounds coming out of my mouth—it feels wrong to be so rude and disrespectful to a woman, but this one has earned it.

She clicks her tongue. "Ah-ah-ah. Think of Anya and try again."

She pulls my head back a little farther and bends down over me, running her tongue across my throat. I jerk sideways, yanking free from her hold. She circles around in front of me, crossing one arm over her torso, the other dangling the remote in her fingers.

She speaks slowly, as if I'm fucking stupid. "*Signora*. Vittori."

I breathe heavy through my nose, nostrils flaring in fury. "*Signora* Vittori," I repeat.

She bends again, touching her nose to mine. "Good boy. Now take off your clothes." She steps away, moving to occupy the armchair in front of me, crossing one long leg over the other.

My jaw sets, my teeth grinding together. My fists clench at my sides and I feel as rigid as a stone statue. At this point, I shouldn't be shocked by that command. I shouldn't be shocked by anything at all, really. But having the foresight to guess how she wants to use me fills me with an uncomfortable kind of anger I've never felt before. It's a rage that I have to control to keep my girl safe, a rage I've felt before, but it's still....different.

I feel like I'm no longer human. And to Renata, I'm not. I'm a physical object for her to control and use for her own purposes, and it makes my blood burn.

She lifts the small black remote, twisting it in her hand to remind me of what she will do when I don't obey. "Take off your clothes. I won't tell you again."

My lips pull back from the tension I hold in my face and

I snarl. I feel nauseous. My fingers shake as I start to undo the buttons of my shirt. The way Renata ogles me as I do makes me feel small.

If my worth weren't already determined by the measure of Anya's love for me, Renata could make me feel like the most worthless piece of shit that ever existed. But I remind myself that I'm everything to Anya, so I'll be worthless to Renata if I have to be. I pull off my shirt and toss it aside as Renata drinks me in with her eyes.

"Kiss my feet," she says, running her tongue along her bottom lip.

"You're fucking ridiculous, you know that?" My eyes would literally roll out of my head if they weren't attached in there.

I can practically hear Anya in my head. *"Be quiet and do as you're told, mal'chik."* And I should have listened to that voice before my response because Renata sends a jolt of electricity through my neck. It goes on for longer this time, my muscles seizing, tightening beyond my control with the sharp pain of the shock burning my neck.

I immediately slump forward to the floor once the electricity finally stops. Luckily, I'm able to catch myself on my hands rather than face plant in front of her feet.

"I think I enjoy the look of you that way," she says as I balance on all fours, catching my breath. "Crawl to me and kiss my feet. Or disobey me, and I will find a way to destroy that girl. I promise you."

For her.

Do it for Anya.

Just do what you have to.

I crawl to her, fighting against every cell in my body that compels me to resist. I bend, resentfully placing a kiss on the top of her foot.

"Is that what you call a kiss?" she scoffs. "I'm certain you can do better than that. Wouldn't you do better than that for Anya?"

"Stop *fucking* saying her name." Renata isn't worthy enough to let a thought about my girl so much as cross her mind, let alone speak her name.

She kicks under my chin with the pointed toe of her bright red stiletto and my teeth slam together. "Shut your disrespectful mouth or I'll shut it for you." She wiggles her foot in front of me. "Now, do better."

Jesus fuck.

I press my lips to the top of Renata's delicate foot. I squeeze my eyes shut and because I'm thinking of her, my blue-eyed girl's perfect face steals space from all other conscious thought in my mind. I can see her so clearly when I let myself release all the tension of my fighting instinct.

It's only Anya behind my closed lids and she tells me to do what I have to for her. She tells me to imagine it's her that I kneel for and worship with my kiss. With her blue eyes sparkling in my mind, I can do just that.

Sitting back on my heels, I grip Renata's heel with one hand and slip the other behind her ankle. I cradle her foot as if it belongs to my girl, as if Anya has asked me to revere her this way.

And I would.

I would do it for her if she asked.

If she asked, I would run my tongue from her toes to her ankle, just like this. I would squeeze her in my grip and run my hand up her calf. I would scatter wet kisses over every inch of skin atop her foot. I would nip at her skin with my teeth, then sooth the sharpness with a flick of my tongue.

Just like I do it now.

My hand is just behind her knee when she finally stops me. She snatches my wrist and holds my hand in place. I open my eyes and look up at her and the spell immediately breaks—I meet dark brown eyes instead of vibrant sapphire blue.

But because I was thinking of Anya, I'm panting. Because I was thinking of her, I'm half fucking hard. I don't want to be. I don't fucking *want* to be, but I am, and I hate myself for it.

A memory from soon after my kidnapping—when I first met Anya—dashes across my mind. We were in my room at Mikhailov Manor. Nikolai had his arms wrapped around Anya from behind, his fingers shoved inside her, stroking. She didn't want it from him, but he took from her anyway.

He always took from her.

But when her eyes met mine, she sparked, igniting into pure need. He stopped before she came, but she was wet, panting, needy when she crumpled to the floor beside me— panting and needy the way I feel now, and it's the worst fucking thing I've ever felt.

I feel sick.

I feel like a bastard.

I feel like I'm cheating on her, even though I know I have no choice.

I feel now what Anya felt when Nikolai abused her. I could only imagine the pain of it before, but now I *understand* it.

And hell, that woman is strong for surviving it all.

Stronger than me.

Stronger than any other person I've ever known.

Renata uncrosses her legs and puts my hand on the inside of her thigh. "I've put Anya in Vigo's bedroom."

"You did *what?*"

"She's staying in Vigo's bedroom. She slept on the floor last night. That's how I found her this morning…passed out on the rug. She must have been too traumatized by all the things my brother did to her to sleep in his bed. She wouldn't even use his bathroom. It's impossible for me to see what you see in her. I see nothing but a weak little girl." Her hand slips over my fingers on her thigh, gripping them, drawing my hand up farther. "But if you do me this service, I'll consider moving her to a new room. Perhaps then she can rest and recover."

A frustrated groan vibrates through my chest. "You're cruel."

If I thought I felt sick before, my gut churns now with the thought that Anya is enduring such torment in Vigo's room. It makes my heart hurt, as though Renata has reached inside and plucked it from my chest herself. It's all the worse because I already know I'll do what she wants to get Anya out of that room.

"You're interested." Renata smiles as her gaze flicks down over my crotch.

"I'm not interested in you."

"But you'll obey me," she says with all the confidence in the world—she knows she has me trapped in this.

I nod in response, but it's so slight I don't even know if she sees it until she drags my hand a little higher. She lets go and raises an eyebrow at me, a silent command to keep going.

I hate this.

I hate this so much.

My stomach clenches when my fingers slip up her hip and under the hem of her red blouse. My spine prickles with a warning to stop this madness when I reach for the button of her pants. I start shaking as I lower the zipper. And my heart leaps with relief when she shoves my hands away and suddenly stands. I look up at her as she looks down at me and she grins with sick satisfaction spread all over her face.

She reaches down and pats my head with her hand. "Good boy."

"I fucking hate you," I seethe.

"I know you do. I like that energy from you, though. Hang onto it." She crosses her arms. "The collar has sensors. As long as you remain in the house, you'll hardly notice you're wearing it before long. There's a minimal perimeter around the house. You can go as far as the fountain in the front and into the garden out back. If you breach that perimeter, I can assure you that you'll die. There will be enough electricity in the shock to stop your heart in moments and I will send no one to revive you. Otherwise, you'll be mostly free to move about as you like. Though you'll stay far away from Anya if you know what's good for you."

I smirk, narrowing my eyes at her. "You shouldn't trust me to roam freely in your home."

She bends, lifting my chin and holding my gaze. I can feel her warm breath as it dusts across my lips. "I trust that you will do anything to protect that whore you call your lover. This is not Mikhailov Manor. There are always people in my home who won't hesitate to kill you on the spot if you step out of line. Consider this collar your fraction of freedom here."

Her eyes dance as they flicker over my face and the light reflected there can't hide her emotion. This woman is grieving, hurt, lonely, desperate. I take stock of that and store it in my mind, knowing I can use that information to exploit her with affection, obedience, and care.

If I have to, I will charm her, seduce her, make her love me enough to let her guard down. And then I will use her to find a way to save Anya.

CHAPTER 12
Anya

ACCORDING TO RENATA, I lack the appropriate attire for tonight's family dinner. She's left me a small pile of clothes from Olivia's wardrobe on the bed in Vigo's room. Olivia's clothes are a size larger than what I normally wear, but Renata assured me she'll purchase me new clothing soon...maternity clothing.

I still can't wrap my mind around being pregnant. There's hardly a bulge in my belly at three months. Doctor Lombardi said I'll start to show more in the coming weeks—once I start eating regularly again and regaining the weight I'd lost in Vigo's care. Still, I can't imagine myself with a pregnant belly.

I sort through Olivia's clothes and decide that I want to look as much like Renata as possible for this first family dinner. She's the model for my performance—I want to mirror her so I can find a way to *become* her and destroy them all from within. I have no plan for how to do that, but I know the first thing I have to do is convince them that I *am* a Mikhailov, and a damn strong force to be reckoned with at that.

I select a smart, black pencil skirt and a cream-colored silk blouse that I tuck in at the waist. I should wear flat shoes, but I know I'll be too short to posture against Renata if I do. So, even though I'm still weak in my recovery from Vigo's torments, even though I'm pregnant and understand that I should avoid the possibility of a fall, I choose impractical high heels—burgundy, peep toe, with a strap around the ankle.

Luca is waiting outside the door when I come out of Vigo's bedroom. He waits for me to lead the way, recognizing my newfound rank. He's been with me all day, attending to my every need at Renata's orders. I haven't seen Ezra since this morning, but I know he's been with her.

It sends my heart racing to think of him alone with her, which is the exact reason why I've fought with myself all day not to think of him.

I have to focus. My mind must be clear, and I must act with intention. Tonight is crucial for setting a tone on how I will behave with this newfound power.

Power.

It's something that's been beyond my reach for years, something I never dreamed I would have again. Now I have too much of it and it weighs on me. I'm terrified to make the wrong move.

Luca points me in the direction of the dining room on the first floor, a room I've never been in before. It's the size of a small ballroom, though there's only one large, wooden dining table at its center—it looks big enough to seat maybe fifteen people.

A flash of light draws my eyes down to my hand. Light bounces off the diamond rings on my finger from the crystalline chandelier above the table. I bring my hands in front of me and twist the shiny circles around my finger.

I'm a Mikhailov.

My breath catches. I could so easily slip into a panic with the reminder, but I know I can't. I can't do that here, not now. My diamond-decorated hand lands over my heart as I gasp in a sharp breath.

Just breathe and count.

One. Two. Three. Four. Five. Six. Seven. Eight.

One. Two. Three. Four—

"Sit here," Luca says, gesturing to a seat beside the head of the table. I'm thankful his instruction interrupted the anxiety building inside me.

Pull yourself together.

Lowering my hand to my side again, I look up at Luca and clear my throat. I know I must establish my place and I have to do it now. "No," I tell him bravely. "I'll sit here." I move toward the head of the table and pull out the chair with trembling hands.

"No, no." Luca reaches for the chair, but I sit before he can pull it away. "That is where *Signora* Vittori sits."

My heart stops, then starts again in a flurry. Sitting in a board member's seat would have gotten me killed when I was a slave. Though I know I'm one of them now and I can sit where I please, it doesn't stop me from feeling the fear of being disobedient to my master.

I wonder if I'll ever stop feeling like a slave.

Not until Ezra and I are free.

I feel like I can't breathe, but I will my body to stiffen, to straighten. I will myself to raise my chin and dismiss Luca as only a master would. "That will be all, Luca."

With my dismissal, he rushes from the room, probably running off to tell his mistress what I've done. I close my eyes, breathe in through my nose and out through my mouth.

One. Two. Three. Four. Five. Six. Seven. Eight.

My eyes snap open with a sudden flurry of noise. Lorenzo and Olivia enter the room, holding hands and chatting. Behind them is Bianca and my eyes widen. She's the girl who lived in the box next to mine in the basement—another of Vigo's broken dolls. I'm surprised that she's still alive, though I suppose I shouldn't be—no one would have had time to concern themselves with her life while chasing after me and Ezra.

Bianca's eyes catch mine and she stares at me with curiosity and something else in her expression, something resembling jealousy maybe. She and I never did get along, but I don't really feel anything toward her except for sadness. I feel sad for her because she's still a slave.

I was a slave a little more than a day ago.

There's a catch in my heartbeat that feels for her, for the fact that I'm only here and in this position because of sheer dumb luck—the same reason she's a slave. I wonder if they're going to take better care of her now that Vigo's gone. Perhaps they've brought her up to have dinner with the family.

My wondering is settled quickly as Lorenzo directs Bianca to the harp in the far corner of the room. She sits behind it and sighs as she stretches out her fingers.

"Play for us," Lorenzo tells her, "and don't fuck it up. Do well and you'll be our new talent slave."

Olivia was the talent slave before, a pianist. Olivia had the same turn of luck as I did. We each had a monster fall in love with us.

As Lorenzo turns toward the table to bring Olivia to sit, he sees me and I straighten in my seat. I feel my blood run cold with fear and I let it wash through my veins, an icy stream that slows my heartbeat and freezes over my soul. It helps me become the cold, hard, dominant bitch I have to be to protect myself.

I nod at him as he holds out a chair two seats away from me for Olivia. Then he sits beside her, in the chair just to my left.

"That seat belongs to Renata," he says matter-of-factly.

"I guess it belongs to me now," I reply.

Lorenzo raises an eyebrow and smirks, amused. "If you say so."

He turns his body sideways toward Olivia, grabbing her face in his hands and catching her off-guard with a passionate kiss.

My iced-over heart thumps an extra beat in jealousy.

Will I see Ezra tonight?

Is he okay?

When will I kiss him again?

I don't have much time to let my mind wander as more people enter the room. There's an older man Lorenzo introduces to me as his father and he immediately questions who I am and why I'm sitting in Renata's chair. Lorenzo speaks to him in Italian, saying something that seems to calm him enough to sit without saying another word. Two others are introduced as cousins.

I'm taken by surprise when Kostya enters. He looks like he's been through hell. Obviously, he's recovering from the gunshot wound to his shoulder, and that's partly why I'm surprised to see him tonight. But he also has a black eye, stitches along a gash in his cheek, and he's limping. He looks as though he's been mauled.

I push to my feet, somehow feeling compelled to go and help him to the table, but his eyes widen and he practically shouts when I do. "Stay." The insistence in his tone is jarring and it freezes me in place. I give him a nod as he hobbles in my direction.

When he reaches me, he leans in close, whispering in Russian. He tells me to stay in my seat and refuse to give it up if asked. He tells me to be headstrong with Renata, to show the extended family my assertiveness and demonstrate my authority. He tells me to keep my head held high, and when he pulls back to look at me, he taps two fingers beneath his chin with a small smile.

Chin up.

I watch him as he moves to sit along the long edge of the table. Strangely, I feel comforted by his presence.

Soon after, the room begins to fill with family. Too many of them come in at once for introductions, one filing in after the other. In moments, the table is full—except for one seat directly opposite mine—but the deluge of people continues to flood the room.

Within minutes, the open space around the table is nearly filled as members of the family crowd into the room. They came here for the Vittori family's talent show and reception, but they stayed because of Vigo's death. I glance around the room and see faces filled with sadness, anger, and confusion. Their questions are about to be answered, and I don't think they'll be pleased to learn the truth.

I grow more uncomfortable as moments pass, as familiar family chatter continues, mostly in Italian. It's a fight to control my breathing, to keep from hyperventilating when I feel like a fish out of water.

I'm an impostor.

I don't belong here.

I can't pull this off.

Why did I sit here?

My racing pulse hisses through my veins and I feel my heart slam against my ribcage with every pounding beat. I twist the rings on my finger with my hands on my lap, hidden beneath the table. My fear climbs a mountain and reaches the peak.

But then the currents of anxiety that ripple from my chest come to a sudden, stomach grinding halt. My hands still and I press my palms against my thighs. My hissing pulse slows to a steady thrum. Awareness makes my heart skip a beat before forcing the insistent thrashing to dull into a calm, steady rhythm. A gentle prickle at the back of my neck sends a pleasant shiver down my spine.

Ezra.

I know he's near before he appears in the doorway beside Renata.

His eyes immediately land on mine without the need to glance around the crowded room for me. He felt the familiar tug and pull of our souls before he rounded the corner, just as I had.

Neither of us react; we just allow our eyes to connect, and in that connection, strength builds. He feeds me the power I need in his gaze, just like he always has. I want to touch him, kiss him, hold him more than anything else in the world right now, but I'll have to settle for this brief connection.

Our gaze is interrupted when Renata sees me. She puts her hand on the center of his chest—his bare chest—and crosses in front of him, charging toward me with a graceful but fierce walk. But my attention is still on Ezra, distracted by his naked chest and the black leather collar around his neck.

She really has made him her slave.

Oh, God.

My stomach flips with nausea, but then anger burns my skin. I know I should be grateful she hasn't killed him, but I feel sorely indignant that she thinks she can take what's mine and make it hers.

I don't care who she is, Ezra is *mine.*

She smiles at me as she comes closer and I turn my head, lifting my chin to look up at her from the seat I refuse to vacate. She slips her arm around my shoulders and bends, making it look as though she's merely greeting me as she bends to kiss my cheek. She lingers there, whispering into my ear so quietly, I have to strain to hear her. "You can have my seat. I have your lover."

My head ticks, jerking toward her as she straightens to look at me with a smug expression. I let a smile spread across my face. There are so many things I want to say to her in response, a million retorts scrambling across my mind.

But I breathe deeply and hold them all inside, deciding that my silence is more powerful than any words I could ever give her. I hold her stare, smiling up at her until her cheeks twitch from her faltering resolve and she walks away.

I try not to make it obvious when I blow out the breath I was holding.

Renata moves around the table and sits at the opposite end, facing me. Her family has gone quiet when she lowers regally into her seat and all eyes fall upon her. She snaps her fingers and Ezra moves to her side. I can see the tension rippling through every beautiful, bare muscle in his body, the familiar battle against himself to control his impulses to fight and run.

My mouth drops open when he lowers to his knees at Renata's side and bows his head, and I force myself to clamp it shut.

She knows.

She knows how much this hurts me.

She knows how much it hurts him.

But what did she tell him to make him bow so easily? It's not right...

My eyes are on Ezra, though his eyes fall to the floor. I want to kneel in front of him, lift his chin, kiss him like I've never kissed him before, and bring him back to life with me. But I can't do any of that.

Not here.

Not now.

The whole family looks at Renata expectantly. She looks directly at Lorenzo, says his name, and tells him something in Italian.

He nods and glances at me and Olivia on either side of

him, then at Kostya across the table. "She's going to speak in Italian for the family. I will translate in English for you."

I give a single nod of understanding. Lorenzo may translate her words, but I'll be watching Renata—cataloging every twitch of her features, every flicker of her eyes, every movement of her body. She begins to speak slowly and clearly in her native language, and Lorenzo speaks quietly after her, translating in English.

"The events surrounding Vigo's death have been settled with the four families," Lorenzo begins. "There will be some changes to leadership." Renata pauses, as does Lorenzo, and quiet settles over the room for a few brief, tense moments. She begins again and Lorenzo's translations follow. "Lorenzo and I will serve together as Vittori Head of House to maintain our status and continue our business as one of the four families."

Someone I don't recognize shouts out something in Italian, and though I don't understand all the words, I clearly hear the name Nikolai Mikhailov.

I tense immediately.

Renata nods, then continues, as does Lorenzo. "Yes, it's true. Nikolai Mikhailov is dead. His former talent slave will be taking his place. As it turns out, she is his wife." The crowd breaks into a murmur of chatter.

Renata holds up a hand to silence the group, then gestures toward me. Lorenzo doesn't need to translate when she says my name. "Anya Mikhailov."

"Kostya Federov and Anya will serve together as Mikhailov Head of House. The Vittori and Mikhailov Heads of House will operate as a joint family board to make business decisions on behalf of both of our families. I know this is unexpected, but it has already been decided and it cannot be questioned. Anya is pregnant and the child may be of Vittori or Mikhailov blood."

More chatter comes with the thick tension in the room, all directed at me—as if I had any choice or say in what has happened to me in this life. I feel like shrinking, melting into the seat, dripping like liquid onto the floor and pooling safely beneath the table.

"Anya is to remain unharmed and treated with the same respect you would treat any Mikhailov with. I will hear no arguments to the contrary. Things will continue this way until we learn the paternity of the baby—the board will reconvene and evaluate the situation at our next quarterly meeting." Renata pauses, taking a beat too long to take in a steadying breath. "Funeral arrangements for Vigo are being made and I'll share that with you shortly. But first, I think some happy news is in order. Something our family can look forward to as we face these difficult challenges ahead."

Renata looks at Lorenzo and he nods, pushing to his feet. He speaks to the room in Italian, a genuine smile spreading across his face. Then, he gestures for Olivia to stand and she does.

What's happening?

Olivia smiles, looks at Lorenzo, then at Renata, who nods and smiles at her. Lorenzo snakes his arm around her waist and excitedly, Olivia announces, "We're having a baby!"

Lorenzo quickly translates to the room and there's an eruption of happiness—cheers and claps and overdramatic expressions of joy. I want to scream, puke, run from the room. My chest aches for the hypocrisy; the happiness over one former talent slave's pregnancy but not over another's.

Why should Olivia find happiness while I'm met with eternal dismay?

I recognize the jealousy and how it feeds my anger and I know I can't let it. I know it will only diminish my power.

Olivia glances at me with a sheepish grin and I force

myself to grant her a small smile. I nod in acknowledgment of her…happy news. I don't care to interpret the pitying look she throws my way. I can't afford to give away any more of my power.

Lorenzo translates as Renata begins to share the details of the funeral arrangements being made for Vigo—a vigil and mass that will be held in his honor. I breathe deeply through it, struggling to swallow the bile that rises in my throat from the thought of him being honored.

Fuck Vigo Vittori and his fucking family.

I feel the way my lips pull into a hard line across my face, my cheeks pulling and tugging my features into a look of disgust as I listen. I know how my face is twisting and contorting in hatred and agony. But I also know I can't let my feelings show. Somehow, I manage to force calm indifference to my expression.

Before Lorenzo translates Renata's final sentence, people break into chatter and those not at the table filter out of the room.

Lorenzo leans in close so I can hear him over the noise. "She's sending them away to fill their plates in the kitchen. Only the immediate family is served here."

Quietly, I ask him, "Do they all know what the four families do?"

"They only know of the hierarchy. They know that our family's wealth is generated by the business. I think most of them have figured it out for themselves, but it's a precious secret. Our extended family would have nothing without the work of the four families. No one questions it."

"Won't the secret find its way to the authorities? These people don't all live here, do they?"

"No, most of them have their own homes. There's never a concern for the authorities, Anya. You should know that by now. The four families own everything that's important in the world. We're unstoppable." He says it with pride.

I glance at Olivia, who suddenly looks upset. She tucks a strand of golden-blond hair behind her ear as her gaze darts uncomfortably around the room.

She *should* feel uncomfortable. Her happiness is traitorous to all the other talent slaves who have served the four families, just like her. She got lucky, fucking *lucky* that Lorenzo fell for her—even luckier that the family accepted it, embraced it even, and are allowing her to become one of them. I shouldn't be angry at Olivia—it's not her fault—but I am angry.

Suddenly, Lorenzo's face falls and he pushes to his feet angrily. "Bianca!" he yells across the room at my former cell mate, who is still sitting behind the harp. "You should be playing right now. Why aren't you playing?" His anger switched on so quickly, it's jarring.

Bianca jumps, straightening her spine and nodding before reaching forward to tickle the strings of the instrument. She creates a beautiful melody that drifts around the room and a cloud of music covers us with her haunting tune.

Olivia bites her fingernail, her eyes flickering up to watch Lorenzo's anger-shrouded face before he finally settles back into his seat. She stiffens with tension, but then she smiles, relaxing a little when he returns his lavish attention to her, petting her, kissing her, holding her hand.

Calm to anger to calm with the flip of a switch.

Does Olivia worry that someday he'll treat her like a slave again? She should.

Luca suddenly appears with a tray of salads. Renata bends to whisper something to Ezra, who is still kneeling beside her, and I shiver when he nods and stands. I watch as he meets Luca where he stands and the two of them begin to serve the family plates from the tray.

Ezra lays a plate and an empty wine glass in front of Renata first. She snatches his wrist and yanks him down before he can move to the next. She forces him to bend sideways as she presses her lips to his ear and whispers something I desperately wish I could hear. His cheeks redden with anger and his fingers clench to form a tight fist.

She releases his wrist.

I watch in horror as he places both his hands on her cheeks, bends deeper over her, and slams his lips to hers.

He's kissing her.

Ezra is kissing Renata.

And I can't do a goddamn thing about it.

CHAPTER 13

Ezra

RENATA TASTES LIKE sin and sadness and everything that I hate. She holds me captive to her kiss with her hand around the back of my head, her claw-like fingernails digging into my scalp. I only kiss her because she's threatened Anya again.

I hate the sharp pang of guilt I feel knowing that Anya is watching this. I can feel her eyes on me, and it burns. The moment Renata lets up on her grip, I jerk away and step back. I quickly grab another plate from the tray Luca carries and rush around the table to where Anya sits. She, Lorenzo, and Kostya get served after Renata and before everyone else.

I set a plate and empty wine glass in front of Lorenzo, then grab another and move to Anya. She sucks in a quick, subtle breath as I step up to her side, and I move in close, intentionally close. I slowly place her plate and glass in front of her and I feel the buzz of electricity before she moves.

Her voice is a soft whisper. "I'm so sorry if this gets you in trouble, but I have to." Her hands land on my cheeks, grabbing my face, and turning me toward her before slamming her lips roughly against mine.

Fuck.

One kiss from my girl makes the world fall away. Her

boldness scares me, but fuck, does it excite me, too.

I have to open for her. My lips refuse to stay shut when her tongue runs along the seam, asking me to taste her. I let my tongue slip inside her mouth, and I lap at her eagerly, licking away the taste of Renata and letting Anya's sweetness replace it.

The kiss only lasts for a moment before she snaps her head away and sits up taller in her seat. I stand looking down at her with my chest heaving and I see the twitch of her lips as she hides a celebratory smile for feeding Renata her own medicine.

I swipe my lips with the back of my hand to hide my own smile as I steal a quick glance at Renata. Her eyes burn into Anya, but my blue-eyed girl is strong, holding Renata's gaze just as fiercely.

Somehow, I manage to move on, serving the rest of the table, then Luca opens a bottle of red wine. He pours for the table as I stand waiting by Renata's side.

"What happened to Kostya?" Anya asks as they all begin to eat. "How did he get the black eye and the cut on his cheek?"

Everyone at the table steals glances at Anya as they try to figure her out. Renata hesitates and Kostya looks over at her with quiet disdain. He really does look like shit.

"Your dead husband caused quite a bit of chaos when he took you," Renata finally replies. "Kostya had to be subdued, but as you can see, he's fine. He's recovering." She takes a sip from her glass of wine, then looks at Anya discerningly, cocking her head to the side. "Are you concerned that he's being mistreated?"

Anya scoffs, "Of course, I am."

"Despite your prior experiences here, I assure you that I'm a rather exceptional hostess for our guests…particularly those that serve the four families. I suggest you watch yourself and avoid insulting me at my own dinner table."

I'm bristling with the urge to knock Renata off her damn

chair as I'm forced to listen to her.

But Anya lets it roll from her shoulders, lifting her fork and stabbing at her salad. "I'm not entirely certain that an exceptional hostess would make a Mikhailov wife sleep in the bedroom of her former tormentor."

Renata drops her fork and it clangs against her plate, the unexpected sound causing several guests' shoulders to jolt at the surprise. But not Anya. No, she's as cool as fucking ice.

"Your *tormentor* was my brother. And many would argue that I've given you the best room in our home. But I suppose if you're too weak-minded to handle the accommodation of a Head of House, I could find you another room. Perhaps something smaller, more befitting for your stature and general cowardice."

Anya's jaw sets. Her frame remains rigid and still. Her expression and body language give away nothing, but the flicker across her bright blue eyes is obvious—at least, it is to me. It's a flicker of fear, a look that only someone who's been through what she's been through could express in their eyes alone. I know she would've been happy to have a smaller room—anything to get her out of the room she almost died in. But now that Renata has challenged her strength and resiliency, I know she's gonna be stubborn as fuck about sticking it out there.

Anya swallows, lifting her chin a little higher. "I'm no coward, Renata. But you don't really know me all that well yet. You'll learn everything you need to know in time."

A flicker of a fake fucking smile tugs at the corners of Renata's lips, but falters just as quickly. She's pissed. She snaps her fingers at me again and I bend to take whatever order she's decided to give me.

As the table returns to side conversations and general chatter, Renata whispers to me, "Go remove the glass of wine from Anya's setting. She shouldn't be drinking in her condition. Take Olivia's glass, too."

Hmm. A request that's actually reasonable.

I stand to obey, but Renata latches her fingers around my wrist before I can straighten, yanking me closer to add a little something extra to her request.

"Spill both glasses down the front of Anya's blouse. That particular shade of ivory makes her look sallow, don't you think? Give her some red to bring out the pink of embarrassment in her cheeks."

"What? No."

"I'm not asking, Ezra. You know the consequences of your choices, so I suggest you do as I ask."

She is so fucking petty.

Spill red wine on her?

What the fuck is that supposed to accomplish?

Renata is acting like a petulant child and sure, I could give her leniency for the fact that she's just lost her brother at my girl's hand—which would make anyone want retribution—but this is just fucking dumb.

I shake my head as she releases my arm and I stand. I know I have to do it. I know I don't have a choice. Anya's life is reliant on my absolute obedience—Renata has made that crystal fucking clear.

I sigh, already feeling shitty about what I'm about to do as I move along the side of the table. I want to dump out both glasses on Renata's head and smash the glass into her face. I reach between Lorenzo and Olivia, removing her wine glass from the table. She's sweet, giving me a quick smile of gratitude for my service, and I can't help but feel sorry for her. This girl, marrying Lorenzo, would be like Anya marrying Nikolai—her captor, her tormentor, her master.

Fuck.

She did marry Nikolai.

My hands shake from the frustrated fury building inside me as I make my way to Anya's seat. She doesn't look up at me as I approach but continues eating silently. She looks restrained, like she wants to shovel the whole damn plate into her mouth but refuses for appearance's sake. She's stronger than I think she's ever been given credit for.

I admire her.

I adore her.

And that's why I feel like the biggest asshole in the world when I reach across the table in front of her and pick up her glass. I'm not able to catch her eyes before I do it, but I know I have her attention. I stand back up, one glass in each hand now.

Fuck, I hate this.

This is so childish and I fucking hate it.

"I have to, I'm sorry," I mutter quickly under my breath.

Anya turns her head to look up at me just at the moment I turn the half full wine glasses upside-down over her lap. I spill the liquid down the front of her shirt, and it pools onto her tight black skirt. She drops her fork and jerks backward in her chair, her hands raising in surprise as liquid tumbles from her lap, dripping down the chair and landing on the carpet beneath her.

I turn the empty glasses upright again. "I'm so sorry," I whisper before forcing myself to stride away while everything inside me screams to go back to my girl and help her get cleaned up.

I scowl at Renata's pleased grin as I return to her side.

Goddammit.

I fucking hate Renata Vittori.

Anya pushes her chair back and stands as silence falls in the room and everyone waits for something to happen. They're watching her, wanting to see her reaction—and I know how important it is that she reacts to this the right way in front of these fiends.

But who the fuck knows what way is the right way to act?

I took her completely off-guard by my malicious act, which was exactly why Renata asked *me* to do it. She could've had Luca do it, but the bitch wishes to torture me as much as she wants to torture Anya. But Anya is too strong to let it knock her down.

She brushes her hands down her front and shields her true feelings in her eyes behind a layer of icy blue. She pulls her shoulders back and steels herself. But as she opens her mouth to say something, Lorenzo slaps his palm on the table and leans forward, craning his neck around to look pointedly and severely at Renata.

"Will you *stop* it?" he practically shouts at her. "Is it really so much to ask for a peaceful family meal in Vigo's honor?"

Renata chuckles sourly. "In his honor with *her* at the table? His *murderer?*"

"There's nothing you can do about that!" Lorenzo says with anger edging his tone. "She's a Mikhailov, and she's one-quarter of our joint family board." He laughs a little, darkly. "This, *this* is why women aren't given the responsibility of being Heads of House. I suggest you keep yourself in check unless you want me to have a serious talk with Murphy and Leo about your emotional instability."

"Lorenzo…" Olivia carefully lays a hand on his on the table, but he jerks it back, pointing a finger at the poor girl as if he's going to start in on her now. But somehow, he softens when he looks at her, then settles back in his chair. He leans over to kiss Olivia on the cheek as he gradually calms, though the room still ripples with tension.

"Excuse me," Anya says quietly before she rushes with harsh strides from the room.

I'm itching to chase after her, grab her in the hallway, wrap my arms around her and tell her I'm sorry that I have to play Renata's wicked game with her.

I want to *be* there for her, and I can't be.

I have to be here at Renata's side.

I have to serve her to save Anya.

My blue-eyed girl comes striding back into the dining room about ten minutes later. She's always fierce and determined, but I don't think I've ever seen such cold hatred in her eyes. I hope all her hatred is directed toward Renata and not toward me, but I don't think I could blame her if it is.

Anya changed her clothes while she was gone and she looks so smoking hot, charging into the room with furious confidence, that I want to fall to my knees for her and worship her with my undying love. I don't know where she got these clothes I've never seen her in before, but she's come back daringly in a little red dress.

It's form-fitting, though it hangs a little loosely on her. Still, it has the same effect as if it were skintight. It stops just above her knees and the open neckline leaves little to the imagination. Her breasts are full and perky, and the low neckline gives her ample cleavage that makes me want to rip the dress right off her.

She struts across the room, heading right back to her chair—which Luca wiped clean—and she catches my eyes on her as she slowly sits. She blinks, giving me a brief glimpse of her understanding—a tiny, subtle smile—before she takes her position as the one and only Queen Mikhailov.

Anya takes her cloth napkin off the table, shaking it out and setting it on her lap just as Luca brings in a tray with the main course. "Thank you for the suggestion that I wear red, Renata. This dress does seem to better suit my small…What word did you use? Stature? It's more my style, wouldn't you agree?"

Renata's fingers are steepled in front of her chin as she waits for the next course to be served. "You look like a whore."

"Hmm. Your brother thought that, too. But let me remind you that this *whore* is now positioned to vote on business decisions for your family. It might be in your best interest to consider the way you treat me. Now, can't we just enjoy our family dinner? "

Anya is…She's just…She's fucking amazing.

I stare at her until she looks at me and she smiles before straightening her spine, leaning back casually in her seat, as if she owns the place.

She *could* own the place.

She has power now. She could rule and we could win.

For the first time I think we might actually have a shot at getting out of this alive.

CHAPTER 14
Anya

I COUNT THE nights by the number of times I pass Ezra in the hallway leaving Renata's room. After that first family dinner and the red wine incident, I was desperate to get to him, to find out how Renata was treating him, and most importantly, to tell him that I wasn't upset with him. He did what I'd helped him learn to do—keep his mouth shut and do as he's told to survive.

It was difficult to watch his movements during that first week leading up to Vigo's funeral weekend. The home was such chaos until that was over. I vomited during the eulogy Renata gave at his funeral mass. It was lucky that I was pregnant because I could blame my sickness on that. But really, it had only to do with the picture they painted of Vigo Vittori.

They said he was a strong and ferocious leader. A family man devoted to protecting and caring for his loved ones at all costs. A shrewd businessman whose savvy amassed a fortune that safeguarded the future of their entire extended family. An adoring cousin who loved playing with children.

That was the line that did me in.

But it was good to see for myself that he was well and truly dead. It brought me some semblance of peace and comfort, though it wasn't much. After the funeral weekend, the extended family began to depart in small groups. The mansion became less and less chaotic over the week that followed, and soon, I was able to see a routine develop.

I started to watch Ezra, tracking the routine Renata created for him. I made a point of cataloging when and where I ran into him, the times when he was with Renata, when he was with Luca, and when he was alone.

Renata had padlocked the collar to his neck, and I learned by asking Lorenzo that it kept him confined within the house. Every time I caught a glimpse of him—shirtless, wearing jeans that hugged his hips just right—I wanted two things more desperately than freedom. First, I wanted to find a strong pair of scissors and cut that fucking collar off him. Second, I wanted to... Well, there were actually a lot of things I wanted to do to him.

Initially, it had been only by sheer luck that I'd run into him, but I started to see the patterns in his days and nights. I kept quiet, watched, learned, waited until I knew with confidence when I could catch him alone without Renata noticing if he was gone for more than five minutes.

That time is now—just past midnight on our third Tuesday at the Vittori mansion.

I'm desperate for what we've both been denied for far too long—a touch, a breath, a kiss—just a moment of connection, if that's all that can be spared. I come out of my bedroom— Vigo's old bedroom that I stubbornly refused to leave after Renata's challenging remarks—and turn left, just as I always would to walk toward the staircase. But instead of descending, I keep walking to the opposite hallway. Renata's bedroom is at the far end.

I pause by the staircase, checking the watch I asked to have purchased for me. Ezra will exit Renata's room within the next five minutes or so. I'm going to walk down the hallway when he does, reach out for him, touch his hand, take what I can get for that brief moment.

Hardly a minute passes before I hear the sound of a door opening at the far end of the hall.

It's him.

I watch as he closes the door behind him. He pauses for a beat, looking down at the floor, his body riddled with tension that I wish I could release for him.

Oh, God.

I can't let my mind wander too far on such thoughts. I no longer feel sick all the time from these pregnancy hormones. Instead, they've turned me into a lust-filled, sex-starved woman who can't seem to keep her mind out of the gutter.

My mouth suddenly feels dry and I lick my lips as I watch Ezra rise to his full height and turn toward me. I step forward, directly in his path, only six doors separating us from meeting.

We see each other and there's a pause—a perfect pause of peaceful nothingness that I always get with him when we steal glances this way.

It's not that the pause is filled with nothing.

It's filled with everything.

But it's everything that's good and right and beautiful about the world—even if it's a world we're not given the privilege of living in.

His chest rises heavy and falls the same and I see his cheek twitch, curling one side of his mouth into a smirk. I gasp noiselessly, the way he looks at me sending shameless need straight through my core.

I stride forward confidently, wearing the same form-fitting, knit black dress I've been wearing all day—I've been wearing it all day for *him*. My breasts are growing along with my stomach, not to say my pregnancy bump has grown all that much. In fact, if I weren't wearing such a tight dress, you would hardly notice I was pregnant at all, even at nearly four months.

Doctor Lombardi assures me it's nothing to worry about, often reminding me that pregnant bodies come in all different shapes and sizes. By all accounts it's true. Olivia is only three months along, though her stomach looks much bigger than mine.

Regardless, I feel confident in this dress, confident that Ezra will like to see me in it with the way the V-neck cuts down between my full-cup-size-larger breasts.

God, this feels so strange.

By all accounts, I should be ashamed of myself for wanting what I want from him.

How can I be so goddamn horny after all I've been through?

But the way he looks at me now as we walk toward each other in the empty hallway; he looks as needy as I feel. My heart flutters inside my chest, wings flapping desire through my body, making me feel lightheaded from lust. I feel like I can't catch my breath and I don't know what's come over me.

His eyes flick over my body and I see his chest rise and fall as his pace quickens. He needs me as much as I need him, and that makes me want him all the more.

I want more.

More than a touch.

I think we're going to collide as he aligns himself directly with the path I walk. He's not moving aside to brush past me. He's walking straight toward me. He moves with such determination to get to me, that I actually stop and take a step backward as he moves unexpectedly into my space.

We have to be careful that no one sees us—Renata would lose her mind.

"What are you—" I start, lifting my head to look up at him as he pushes me back.

"Come with me."

Ezra flashes me a perfect, white smile and I feel every organ inside my body liquefy. I'm a useless puddle for this man and I don't want it any other way. He drags me sideways, opening a bedroom door that's close to the staircase—the farthest from Renata's room. He pushes me inside.

I whirl around to face him as he slips in behind me, pushing the door shut and turning a deadbolt lock from the inside. I open my mouth to tell him I love him, but he swallows my words as he crashes into me, his lips landing on mine, bruising and desperate.

I'm stiff with shock for a moment, but when my brain catches up to what's happening, I sink into his hold. I grab his face as his arms curl around my waist, pulling me tight against him.

He doesn't kiss me so much as he devours me, tasting my tongue with hungry licks and groaning from his enjoyment. The way he kisses me makes me feel like a delicacy he's been starved from. He walks me backward until I hit a wall and he presses me to it, rough and demanding.

My breath catches as a brief jolt of unease threads through my mind. I pull back, breaking the kiss and resting my head against the wall behind me as I look up into his green eyes. With a single look, my unease at his roughness instantly fades.

He pants as he watches me, his body so close, I can feel him grow hard with need. His eyes study mine for a beat. "Too rough?"

"No," I say on a breath. "Only for a second. I just needed to see your eyes."

He smiles with such light that I swear the room brightens behind him. With a deep inhale, he presses his forehead to mine. "I've been watching you. I knew you'd be here tonight."

I bite my lip. "I've been watching you, too." My back arches off the wall, my body swelling with need and my breasts seeking his touch as I push against him. "Are we safe in here? How much time do we have?"

He nods, then rubs his nose against mine. "We're safe here. My absence won't be noticed for another forty-five minutes or so." He tilts his hips forward, grinding his ever-growing erection against me. "An hour if we feel like pushing our luck."

I can't help my smile as he moves his head to nuzzle against my neck, his perfect lips spotting kisses down to my chest. "I know I should be the voice of reason here," I say.

I feel his grin as his teeth playfully nip across my collarbone. "Nah. Don't do that, baby."

"I just…" I moan when he licks across the hollow of my throat. "God. I want to push my luck with you. I need you, Ezra."

When he lifts his head to look at me, his eyes filled with desire, I feel my body slip down the wall as need clenches low in my belly and wetness puddles between my legs.

He pulls me closer with one hand gripping my waist as the other comes up to catch my cheek. The touch of his hand on my face feels like I'm home. I let my head fall into it naturally as his fingers reach back to flick across my earlobe.

"Anya." He kisses my lips once. "I'm shaking with need for you."

I turn my head to kiss his palm and desire takes over, directing me to stick out my tongue and lick his hand. He groans, shrinks a little, and presses me harder against the wall as he grinds his cock against my belly. I watch the way his eyes change as his need grows, a shadow falling across the green that makes them look darker and lighter all at once, though I don't even know how that's possible.

I like the way he looks at me.

I like the way he makes me feel when he needs me this way.

I could only ever feel this way with Ezra.

"Are you still mine?" I whisper.

I turn my head, dragging my tongue across the back of his index finger, and suck it into my mouth. I don't think I've ever been this way with a man.

Raw and wanton.

Seductive.

Attempting to draw out his need to take me.

"Fuck," he mutters as I wrap my fingers around his wrist, pulling his hand back so I can release his finger from my mouth with a *pop* before sucking on his middle finger. "I'm always fucking yours. Jesus, what's gotten into you?" He grins.

I smile at him as I *pop* out his middle finger. "I'm pregnant and hormonal and sex-starved in a way I never thought possible."

He groans. "I wanna make you come."

I let go of his wrist and he drags his hand down my chest, wetness from where I sucked his fingers dragging along my exposed skin. He cups my breast over my dress, and I gasp as my suddenly filthy mind screams at him.

Touch me.

Don't tease me.

Oh, God, I already need to come.

"Put your mouth on me."

He leans in to kiss the corner of my lips, wet and languid. "Where, exactly, do you want me to put my mouth?"

I hook one finger through the metal loop at the front of his collar and yank his head down, holding his face close to mine. "Everywhere."

I kiss him, pushing off the wall, feeling an incessant need to mold my body to his. I reach between us, fumbling to grasp his cock through his jeans before I even make a conscious decision to do it. He shoves me back hard, forcing me against the wall again, pinning me in place as he squeezes my breast.

He only breaks the kiss to whisper against my ear, "Lift your skirt, slip off your panties, and spread your legs for me, blue-eyed girl."

I gasp at the command. I turn my head to meet his eyes, searching. I have to find my safety net there before I do what he asks. In truth, hearing him tell me what to do, knowing how much he wants me, makes my stomach clench and my clit throb with desire to be touched. Against reason, against all the life lessons I've learned in being a slave, I'm actually turned on by his command, by the fact that he has some plan to use my body and I'm not privy to it. This should have me running scared, even from Ezra. But when I look into his eyes, all I see is the way he wants to worship me. And if that weren't enough, he knows me enough to reassure me. That makes me want him even more.

"I just want to make you come, baby. You're in control. Always in control. Do you trust me?"

I don't say yes.

I just reach for the hem of my dress and shimmy it up over my hips. I slide my panties down next, and just as I let them go to drop to the floor, Ezra lowers to his knees. He takes my panties from around my ankles, guiding me to step out of them one foot at a time.

He looks up at me as he fists my underwear in one hand, rolling some of the fabric between his fingers.

"Jesus Christ. These are soaked," he says and I blush. "Fuck, I wish I could keep these."

Ezra brings the bunched-up underwear to his nose and inhales, long and deep. I shudder, my spine literally quaking at the sight of it. It's sinful the way he desires me—dirty, raw, completely, and utterly without shame—and I like it.

I want more like this.

I need this with him.

The confident, sexual woman I used to be before I met Nikolai claws her way to the surface to see Ezra like this. He makes me feel like the only woman in the world.

I spread my legs apart. "Don't make me wait. Please."

He pushes out a heavy breath that has a hint of a growl to it as he drops my panties on the floor, his hands splaying over my thighs. I slump against the wall with a whimper as he scoots in close and his hands wrap around to the backs of my legs. I feel another pulse of desire and a gush of wetness flow when his hands cup my ass cheeks, digging his fingers into my flesh, showing me how much he wants me.

He drags my hips forward and my body starts to come off the wall.

"Lean your back against the wall," he practically snarls at me, his eyes burning dark green with reckless lust. "I'll put your ass where I need it."

"Oh," I breathe out, "Ezra."

I need this.

I need this so much, I might die without it.

I lean back though he keeps my hips thrust forward toward him and my neck still cranes downward to look at him. Ezra wedges in between my open legs as he nudges my hem with his nose, pushing it higher so he can press his lips to my belly button. He licks his tongue over my lower stomach, the skin just above my dark curls, before kissing his way down.

I nearly cry out when his head dips and his lips and tongue attack my pussy—as if it's my mouth and he's kissing me for the last time. I clamp my hand over my mouth to keep quiet as he sweeps his tongue inside me, swirling, licking, curling all the way around my inner walls and leaving nothing untouched.

His hands shift, grasping my hips, holding me up as my knees tremble. I let my head fall back against the wall and my eyes fall shut as he moves his tongue along my folds, seeking and finding my clit.

I moan and his fingers clench me tighter.

I've never felt so *wet*.

Between my arousal and the saliva from his mouth as he consumes me, I'm a sloppy, wet mess and I actually love it. It's dirty and it feels so good that I don't ever want to feel clean again.

Ezra tastes me everywhere, leaving no part of my pussy untouched. I'm panting as his hand sneaks in behind his lips and I feel a jolt of naughty electricity when his fingers explore the area between my holes.

He plays with me, dipping his fingers inside with a teasing sort of touch. He gathers my wetness and spreads it back, almost all the way to my back entrance. It feels so good in such a bad way, but it also freezes me with tension. I want to give every part of myself to Ezra, but that part of me…It has been used as a punishment so many times before, and I don't think I can do it.

Not now.

I dig my fingers into his hair and pull his head back. When he looks up at me, it softens the tension immediately. His eyes are hooded and he pants. His face glistens from my slick arousal, and when he licks around his lips to taste it with a look of pure hunger on his face, I remember that he isn't one of them. I remember that he wants to please me, not punish me.

His chest heaves and I can see how his erection strains against his jeans. I see it in his eyes how he struggles to speak through his arousal, but the fact that he struggles and speaks anyway comforts me.

"Too much?" he finally asks between deep breaths

He let me stop him.

He asked if it was too much

He cares what I want.

I know for most normal women that's a minimum requirement, but for me, it means as much as if he were to give me the moon and stars.

"No," I tell him, holding him, not just with my hands, but with my gaze.

He grins up at me, rubbing his hands over my hips as he waits for me to release him. But as amazing as it feels to have his tongue between my legs—and it does feel unbelievably amazing—locking in on his stare like this is more erotic to me than any physical touch he could give me.

Gradually, I lower, sliding my back down the wall until I'm kneeling in front of him. I let my hands fall to his shoulders as I do, slowly drifting down to land on his bare chest.

His large hands reach out to grip my face, fingers reaching back and combing into my hair. His eyes flicker as they watch mine, seeing everything that I see reflected back at him. I lean in and press a soft kiss to his lips.

"I want you on top of me, inside me," I whisper. "I need to feel you come inside me."

One of his hands slips around to hold the back of my head, the other to my lower back, and as Ezra dips to kiss me, he takes me gently down to the floor. I uncurl my legs and spread my knees, waiting for him to settle between my legs before I squeeze them tight to his hips. I reach between us as he bends to kiss me. I taste myself on his tongue while I work his zipper, stretching my small arms down as far as they can reach to push off the barriers of his clothing and free his hard cock.

As soon as it's free, I find myself desperate for it, straddling the line drawn between sane lust and depraved lunacy. I buck my hips up, wiggling around with frenzied urgency to feel him inside me.

I nibble at his lower lip and he grins as he moves his mouth to my neck, lavishing my skin with his kisses and licks and nibbles.

"Now," I whisper. "Please. *Now.*"

He reaches down, grabs his shaft, and moves the tip to tease against my folds as he finds just the perfect angle to—

"*Oh...*"

"Fucking..." he trails off on whatever crass language he was beginning to speak.

I would mourn the loss of those dirty words if it weren't for the way he moves inside me, driving his hips forward to press all the way in. He holds me in that sweet, unmoving torture until I'm wriggling beneath him, practically writhing to get him to move.

"There are so many ways I want to fuck you, Anya." He licks a long line straight up the side of my neck, then his nose runs over the skin just behind my ear. He inhales deeply, taking in the scent of my hair. "A lifetime of ways to fuck you. I could make you come every hour of your life and it would never be enough."

"Just stay inside me forever."

He runs a hand over my hip, down to my knee, pressing and holding my leg against his side as he pulls out slowly, then pushes in again to the hilt. I moan at the delicious intrusion, the way his cock stretches my inner walls. He's so thick when he's hard, the perfect size to fill me completely.

"Forever, baby," he whispers into my ear. "You and me."

I smile as he sits up. He shuffles his knees in closer as he pumps in and out of me again. There's a little extra roughness at the end of his stroke and it shakes me from my core all the way through my skull. A sound escapes me—something like a moan, but more feral and raw. My eyes take in the sight of Ezra's sculpted body, his flexing ab muscles and strong shoulders, watching him fuck me slow but hard as he reaches for my left hand.

He pulls it to his lips, kissing the tops of my fingers, starting from the index, until he reaches my ring finger—the ring finger where I wear the diamonds Nikolai purchased for me. I shiver as he runs his tongue from the base of my palm, over the backs of the rings, all the way to the tip of that very finger.

"Mine?" he asks, taking the very question I always ask him and using it to claim me.

I refuse to belong to anyone else by force ever again. But I choose to belong to Ezra, *only* to Ezra, for the rest of my life. And it's okay for me to belong to him because he belongs to me, too.

Neither of us is slave to the other.

If anything, we serve together as slaves to our connection, our bond, our chemistry, our love. But neither of us will ever be less than to the other. We belong to each other and we belong together.

Always.

That's why it doesn't even give me pause when I tell him, "I'm yours. Always yours."

A low, guttural noise indicates his need to cement that vow from where our bodies join. He laces his fingers between mine, holding onto my left hand. His other hand pushes my knee down sideways to the floor, holding it down with his weight as he leans on it. And then, he fucks me, with rolling thrusts of his hips that drive his cock upward, forcing himself to rub against the perfect spot.

My eyes squeeze shut as that beautiful tension builds, twisting and dragging all the good feelings down low in my core. He thrusts and thrusts, bending to push our laced fingers to the floor just beside my head. He pushes down on my hand

and my opposite knee so hard—bones-grinding-down-into-the-floor hard—that it causes the most incredible ache in my muscles. It doesn't hurt and it doesn't scare me, which surprises me.

It feels *good.*

I feel him everywhere.

I feel consumed by him.

I never want it to stop.

I'm shaking, literally trembling from the good feelings he gives me. He overwhelms my mind and takes control of my senses. I feel his eyes on me as he fucks me. I feel him pick up his pace when my muscles start to clench, when my fingers grip his harder, when I'm softly chanting, telling him of my frantic need for release with a single repeated syllable.

"Oh, oh, oh."

"Fuck. *Fuck.* Come for me, baby."

I feel his cock swelling, pulsing, nearing his own release. The extra tension as he grows inside me ignites a soul-searing fire—a flash fire that instantly consumes every part of my body.

It burns me, twists me, rumbles through me. I feel the explosion of it from deep within, bursting through my core. My pussy clenches and releases through a mind-numbing orgasm, tugging Ezra into coming hard inside me. His mouth drops open and somehow, I just know he won't be able to hold back a primal roar from his release.

I untangle my fingers from his as he pushes his cock inside me deep with his final thrust. I reach around, grabbing the back of his head with both of my hands. I yank him down to me and cover his mouth with mine, swallowing his groan, his shout of pleasure as he spills the last of his seed inside me.

As our orgasms fade into satiated calmness, we kiss. We kiss like it's the first time and the last time, like it's the *only* time. We kiss like we might never kiss again.

My heart thumps, and though I'm probably just being crazy, I swear I can feel Ezra's heart thump right along with mine, with the same rhythm and tempo.

This can't be the last.

"I can't live like this," I say bluntly, breaking our kiss.

He studies my expression, brushing the hair from my eyes with his hand and stroking down the side of my face. He doesn't say anything. He's just quiet, watching me, waiting for me to go on.

His silence reminds me of the first night we kissed in my bedroom at Mikhailov Manor—the night Nikolai raped me with Ezra's involvement. Ezra gave me silence when I needed it, allowing me quiet to process my thoughts before telling him what I was really thinking. He's doing the same now—one of the many things I love about him—giving me pause and letting me think. It makes me feel as though my thoughts are valued…wanted.

I press up onto my elbows and he moves as I do, sitting up and sitting back on his heels. "Ezra…we have to escape."

A neutral expression washes over his features and for the first time, I feel like I don't really know what he's thinking. He takes a breath, rises on his knees to pull his pants back up and buttons them, then lowers to sit back on his heels. "Do you mean it?"

I start to sit up, but it's a little challenging with my position; even with such a small bump, my movements have begun to feel awkward and clumsy. Ezra reaches down to help me, grabbing me easily from my armpits and practically lifting me off the floor toward him. He pulls me up onto his lap where he kneels, my knees spread on either side of him. Immediately, I look down between us as I feel the evidence of our encounter drip out from between my legs, right onto the crotch of his jeans.

"I'll leave a wet spot," I warn him.

But he only wraps his arms around me tightly, holding me

close to him. "I don't give a fuck, Anya. Are you serious about escaping?"

I wrap one of my arms around his neck, but let the other fall between us, landing on my belly. "I've never thought it was possible. And I suppose I still believe that's true."

Hearing myself say that out loud makes me feel flutters in my belly like tiny butterfly wings that fan an anxious, urgent feeling through my body. It could be the baby moving for the first time—Doctor Lombardi said it would feel like tiny flutters at first, but likely not for several more weeks. More likely it's a feeling of instinct.

"This probably doesn't make any sense, but…I feel like I have to attempt the impossible. Like I'll regret it forever if I don't try. If *we* don't try." I lift my hand to join the other around his neck as I lean forward and place my forehead against his. "I know this baby is yours, Ezra. I just…I just know it. It has to be. I won't accept anything else. And even if he's not, the thought of him being raised among the four families?" I blow out a breath as the idea of it spikes anxiety and Ezra rubs my back. "It's unthinkable."

"It's absolutely unthinkable." He sighs. "Wait. You said *he?*"

I lift my head to look at him better. "I don't know for sure yet. But I had a dream. I have dreams all the time actually. Nightmares. But he's always a boy. Maybe it's just wishful thinking because I don't know what they'll do if the baby is a girl." They might kill her and probably me with her—not that I'd want to live if my baby died.

Ezra nods. "You know I've had dreams, too."

My cheeks twitch, tugging a smile from my lips. "Yeah?"

"Always a boy. A little blond-haired boy with my eyes."

My shoulders relax at that. "Always green eyes."

"I know it doesn't mean anything," Ezra says. "It's just a

dream. But it feels real sometimes."

I kiss him, just a peck at first, but it turns into a slow burning fusion of my mouth with his. We stay that way for minutes, holding each other, kissing each other, loving each other to spite all the ways we've been denied that privilege.

"I do mean it," I tell him when we come to a stopping point. "I want to escape this life. I've been talking to Kostya."

"Yeah?"

"I think he's…Well, I feel like he's on our side. And with Nikolai gone, it almost feels like I'm the only family he has left. I think he might help us if I foster a friendship with him. I have to try. I *want* to try."

He seems relieved, as if he's been waiting for me to say something, as if it would be so easy to just up and leave.

It won't be anything resembling easy.

"Then I'll find a way for us, baby. I will."

"We'll do it together. Because we're better together?" For some reason, it comes out of me as a question.

His hands slide up from my back and he grabs hold of my face, leveling his eyes with mine. "Listen to me. You and me, together? We can do anything."

I nod and he kisses me. Then we wrap our arms around each other tight, and he hugs me in a way that warms my soul and positively melts me.

The icy cold exterior that's kept me shielded for all these years melts away, drop by drop, the permafrost threatening to fade away for good.

And I hope it does.

I want the tundra to become a desert.

I want to spark a fire in the dry heat, explode into flames, and burn down the four families with Ezra by my side.

CHAPTER 15
Ezra

"IT'S NOT TOO late to change your mind. You don't have to be punished this way." Renata runs her fingers down my bare chest.

The feel of her touch still makes my skin crawl, but sadly, I'm growing used to it. "Do your worst," I tell her through gritted teeth. "I'm not fucking you."

Her face slips from seductress to villainess as she takes a step back. "Have it your way, then. If I can't have your cum, then I'll take your blood."

"Drain me like the vampire you are. I'm. Not. Fucking. You."

She claims I have a choice, but it's no goddamn choice at all. Fuck her or let her hurt me. My blood is her retribution for her brother's death. I'd let her bleed me dry before ever letting her have my cock.

Her eyes narrow to slits and she snaps at Luca. The three of us are alone in her bedroom, as has often been the case over these past few weeks. He rushes to her side and begins to wrap the familiar coarse rope around my wrists. He's good at tying escape-proof knots, and I have a feeling Renata is the one who taught him how to do that.

I used to fight him, but that got me into trouble. It's not

that I care if I get in trouble—it's just that I know if I'm causing problems, it comes down on Anya. Aside from the singular fact that I would do anything to keep them from hurting her, we need her to keep what little status and authority she's attained—which means keeping the inane dealings of an unruly slave far from her concern. Anya has to be a master in this realm as long as it takes for us to figure out how to escape together. So, while I do it with a sour attitude, I comply.

"Stand here, raise your arms." Renata guides me to the foot of the bed, positioning me to face it, and I lift my arms above my head.

She and Luca work to tie the ropes to the canopy, one knotted around each of my wrists. My arms stretch wide above my head, pulling apart into a V as they tie me. The wooden frame that forms the canopy is solid and I know the knots are, too. It doesn't stop me from giving a good yank to test them, though.

I'm locked down.

My heartbeat spikes.

I take in a slow breath and blow it out to steady myself.

"What'll it be tonight?" I ask. "More of the knife? Add a few more knicks and scars?" It's not pleasant when she punctures my skin and marks me with tiny scars, but it's not unbearable, either.

Somewhere behind me I hear a drawer open and shut, and I turn my head to look over my shoulder. It's not until Renata comes up to my side before I can see what she's holding in her hand.

"I think a good whipping is in order for you. Twenty lashes? Thirty? What do you think you deserve for denying me, Ezra?"

I laugh, though a ripple of anxious adrenaline pulses through my veins. "Make it fifty. I don't give a fuck."

"*Fifty?* Hmm. Have you ever been struck with a cat o' nine tails before?"

"No."

But I've been struck with a cane by my blue-eyed girl.

Anya struck me the first day I met her, when Nikolai brought me to her. She had me strung up in the dance studio and struck me eight times with the cane. That was when her only choice was to break me to save herself.

That was before we fell in love.

"I'll give you twenty lashes to start. If you're not begging for me to fuck you by then instead, then I'll give you thirty more and call it a night."

"Just get on with it. I'm tired of hearing you talk."

There's a sudden slicing through the air and then a crack before fire licks across my skin, just to the right of my spine. I groan as my body sways forward from the unexpected hit, my shoulders straining against the ropes.

"Fuck," I hiss.

"Oh, did that hurt?"

"Nah, I'm good," I lie.

Fire flashes again, only this time it's brighter, lashing in nearly the same spot as the first strike. I clench my hands into fists and swallow the shout that claws up my throat. I won't give her the satisfaction.

Renata's fingers trail from the base of my neck, slowly down my spine. She intentionally strays from the path to trace over the line of flames—the way they flare against her touch tells me I'll have welts before this is over.

"Wouldn't it feel better to sink inside me?" she whispers.

I drop my head and my jaw ticks as I hold back my anger. "I can't think of anything that would feel worse."

"Fuck you!" she screams and strikes me again.

I grunt as I sway, but there's no time for me to take a breath, to calm myself, to prepare for the next lashing. I stripped her façade of control with my insult and I know I'm fucked now. She strikes, again and again, and fucking again.

She hits me with fury until my skin is ablaze.

She hits me until I shout for her to stop.

She hits me until my body slumps and the ropes hold my weight through my arms, until my head droops in surrender, and my heart is pounding.

She's given me fifty lashes, just as I asked for, and I already know this pain will last for days. I feel blood trickling down my back, and I can only imagine the scars this will leave on my body.

But those scars would be nothing compared to the emotional scars that would mar my heart if I had sex with anyone other than my girl.

I'm left to hang there in my physical pain—with my back bleeding and burning—as Renata and Luca move onto the bed. I close my eyes with my head hung as Luca removes her clothes and fucks her in front of me.

I hate it more than the pain when they do this. I'm ashamed of it, but I'm a fucking human man, and there's a porn movie playing out in front of me. It makes me hard—though I don't want it to—and being hard makes me think about my blue-eyed girl.

I'd prefer to keep her out of my mind when I'm here with Renata and her little fuck boy, but sex and Anya are permanently linked inside my mind. Especially, since we've been seeing each other in secret and making love in all the intense and passionate ways we were meant to. I can't keep her out of my mind, but I can protect the sanctity of our connection.

I don't let myself think about fucking Anya, touching her, making love to her. I let myself imagine her caring for me, nursing these burning wounds, showing me how much she loves me. It's what she's done with all the wounds Renata has given me over the past several weeks. Anya's love for me is stronger than Renata's hate.

I smile to myself.

Renata can hurt me, do whatever the fuck she wants to do to me, but she'll never break me down. I'll meet with Anya again in that secret room in two nights and she'll build me back up again.

Renata can't fucking win.

CHAPTER 16
Anya

EVERY OTHER TUESDAY night, Ezra and I meet for a secret rendezvous in that same bedroom on the east end of the second floor. Every other week, we kiss and touch and hold each other. I tend to his wounds inflicted by Renata, covering the would-be scars with ointment and showering him with attentive care. We survive the in-between times with stolen glances and our own daydreams.

But we won't get to sneak away together this week. Three months have passed since everything changed—since the night Ezra saved me, since I killed Vigo, since Nikolai died, and since I discovered I had become a Mikhailov.

This week we'll be attending the quarterly meeting of the four families at the O'Shea's mansion in Ireland. For the first time, I'm not here as a slave, I'm here as a member of the board.

Kostya has been helping me prepare for tonight's quarterly board meeting. He seems more human now that we've been spending more time together. My initial intent was to foster a relationship in the name of gaining trust, knowing he might be useful to me and Ezra in planning some sort of escape. But I've been surprised to find that Kostya's company has become a comforting presence—entirely different than when he followed me around as a slave to ensure I did what I was supposed to do.

He's nearby as I enter the O'Shea's recently refurbished theater-turned-opera house with my spine straight and my chin up, though I feel anything but regal or strong. My stomach is constantly growing and it's obvious that I'm six months pregnant.

Ezra loves how it looks.

Just thinking of the way he grins at me, rubs my belly, and tells me I'm a "cute little mama" every time he sees me makes my heart flutter and a smile threaten to undo my carefully crafted expression of stone-cold indifference.

I don't feel confident with this body, not in the way I used to be. I don't move the way I used to. And I certainly can't dress the way I used to. I was granted the privilege of selecting my own attire for this evening, but the options were scarce.

The gown I chose is a soft, blush pink with an empire waist. The top is made of lace that fits as closely as a second skin but has a low-cut V that dips between my newly ample breasts. It has long lacy sleeves that hug my arms. A metallic, rose gold belt without a buckle wraps around my waist, cinching me just beneath my breasts. The skirt flares out from there, all the way to my feet, with layers of fluffy chiffon that drape elegantly to the ground.

Though I tried as long as I could to wear high heels so I could at least match Renata's height, it simply isn't possible anymore. My feet are swollen—even after all the years of abuse my feet took dancing ballet, this particular ache is a torture I just can't stand. Doctor Lombardi has asked me to stop wearing heels anyway—he's afraid I might fall over and snap in two. According to him, I need to gain more weight, though I don't know where I'd put it. I feel bloated and swollen everywhere.

As I enter the new opera house, I feel the eyes of every member of the four families upon me. It's as though a thousand daggers are being shot from their eyes, stabbing me all at once, threatening to make me feel small, effectively cut down to size.

But I steel myself, remembering that tonight, I am one of them—a Mikhailov—and I have to demand to be treated as such. I glance over my shoulder to see Kostya somewhere behind me and he taps two fingers beneath his chin—a familiar, gentle nudge reminding me to display my strength and dignified grace.

Chin up.

I give him a grateful nod, then lift my chin a little higher, forcing myself to ignore the judgmental eyes and simply take in the beauty of my surroundings.

The opera house looks as though it belongs to kings, and in a way, I suppose it does. The O'Sheas are currently the only remaining family of the four who haven't been undone by all the upheaval from the past year. So, I suppose if anyone is king among these masters, it's Murphy O'Shea. Of course, he looks nothing like a king with his trimmed, but unruly-looking beard, and so many tattoos upon his arms that they creep out from beneath his suit jacket, tracing outward onto his hands.

Murphy stands in front of the first row of seats at the bottom of the house, looking outward and greeting those who feel compelled to say hello to the king of masters. I push out a breath, knowing I will have to greet him likewise.

I make my way down the aisle on the left, trudging down the dark-purple carpet that softens my steps along the lane. Rows of refinished wooden seats on either side of me are upholstered with a matching purple- and gold-embossed fabric. Everything in the theater is opulent, all shades of purple and gold and dark wood.

A massive crystal chandelier hangs from the center of the theater, casting light on the intricate wooden carvings along the rows of balcony seats on either side of the room. My heart thumps in a familiar rhythm as I approach the stage, feeling a tug from the performance space that calls to me still.

It's been nine months since Nikolai injured my ankle and sold me to Vigo. Nine months since I've really, truly danced, and the desire for it makes my entire body ache. Momentarily, I'm illogically jealous of the O'Shea talent slave because she will get to perform.

I glance behind me again, looking once more to Kostya for moral support, but he's stopped to greet someone nearby. I rub my sweaty palms on my skirt and move forward to greet Murphy on my own.

I plaster a fake smile to my face as I approach him and we greet each other with a kiss to the cheek, his hand landing on my elbow momentarily as he leans in. He's only doing what he's supposed to—I know he still considers me a lowly slave.

"You look well," he says with a tilt of his head. "How are things with the lady Vittori?"

"If you're asking me whether she's doing as she was told to do, then things are going as expected. My care has been managed."

He nods. "Good. I look forward to hearing from your joint family board at the meeting tonight. For your sake, I do hope profits are climbing."

I hate that I know anything about our profits from the sales of innocent human lives, but I am able to tell him with accuracy. "Yes. Unfortunately for the lives that were stolen, our profits are up."

I hear a snort of amusement behind me and turn to see a young woman sitting in the front row. "I like her," the girl says, pointing a finger from her crossed arms at me.

Her long, black hair dangles over her crossed arms and

the scowl she wears indicates that she'd rather be anywhere but here. She might be my age, maybe a couple of years younger. I've never seen her before and wonder if she is their talent slave—though I can't imagine her getting away with speaking up like that if she is.

Murphy's lips purse together with a forced smile. "Anya, this is my new bride, Stella. She doesn't quite understand her place yet as an O'Shea wife. Perhaps I should develop a training program." He looks around me to raise his eyebrows threateningly at her and I turn my head to look back at her as she straightens in her seat.

"Maybe I'll develop a training program for *you* on the health risks associated with trying to mansplain your way through marriage." Her fingers come up to make air quotes on the word *marriage*.

I step aside because I fully expect Murphy to haul off, grab her from the chair, and take her from the room by force—I don't need to get knocked over in the midst. But Kostya appears at my side, stepping between Murphy and Stella, and greets the Head of House cordially, defusing their tension for a moment.

Once the social niceties have been observed, I take Kostya's arm and dismiss us away, allowing him to lead me back a few rows. I never thought I'd be thankful to have him around, especially since I distrusted him so much before Ezra came along and everything changed. But he's quickly become a true ally—it sets my hopes high that maybe one day soon, he'll help me and Ezra.

My nerves buzz with a prickling energy beneath my skin as we sit and wait. Movement from the aisle beside us catches my attention and I turn my head to see Renata striding forward along the aisleway toward Murphy. I see Ezra pass by our row, behind Luca, as Renata, Lorenzo, and Olivia greet our host.

Ezra's wearing a navy-blue suit, his white button-down shirt open at the neck to allow space for his collar to show. He turns his head and winks at me as he follows the others and my heart skips a beat. I fight every muscle in my face to hide my grin and surely flushing cheeks.

I will get to spend some time with him tonight. Renata is his keeper, but he's still my talent, and I'm allowed to have my talent as an escort at the reception. That's how it's always been, for no reason other than tradition—I don't mind the tradition when it grants me time with my love without fear or secrecy.

The Vittori/Fiore crew soon fill in half the row beside us, sitting next to Kostya and leaving me happily at the end. I lean forward, look down the row, and gaze in Ezra's direction, staring until he sees me. When he does, he gives me a secret grin, briefly putting his hand over his heart, as if he needs to hold it inside for the way it beats for me. I put a hand on my stomach, and though I can't smile at him right now, I tell him with my eyes how much I love him.

Murphy greets his audience and introduces their recently-acquired talent slave, a singer whose been with them just shy of a year. I feel a stab of pain in my gut and I know it's nothing to do with the baby—it's just a pang of knowing for this talent slave. Knowing what she is, what she is forced to do, how she was forced into captivity; it's an ache of compassion for her.

The lights in the house dim, chattering fades slowly into expectant silence, and the curtain begins to rise. The young talent slave appears on stage, her long, strawberry-blond hair sweeping in waves nearly to her waist, blending into her sparkling gold sequin gown. With her porcelain complexion and ginger-colored hair, she almost looks like she could be a younger version of Cordelia O'Shea.

The young woman entertains us by singing several

beautiful melodies with impressive talent. She's a gorgeous young girl, a truly talented singer who had her whole life ahead of her. Her story is the same as my story. Funded by the O'Sheas' to develop her talent over the years, she's only recently been stolen away and made a slave. She'll likely serve them for years, possibly decades, missing out on every opportunity to live a full and happy life the way she wishes to. I wonder if Murphy and his family are as brutal with her as Nikolai and Vigo were with me.

Of course, they are.

Murphy is the ruthless king of masters.

We're all siphoned out of the theater following the performance. Renata and her clan exit fairly quickly, but Kostya stays behind with me as I sit and wait for the crowd to thin out a bit. My feet already hurt and I'm tired, so I don't feel in a major rush to wobble out of my seat and get to socializing with monsters any sooner than I have to. It's the same old routine at every quarterly meeting—talent show, reception, board meeting.

When Kostya and I finally exit the theater, I approach Renata where she stands with Luca and Ezra, waiting right by the door as was previously agreed upon. My eyes land on Ezra, inadvertently skimming down his body and taking in the absolutely perfect sight of him in a perfectly tailored suit.

My hormonal heart beats double time. "I'll take my escort off your hands now," I tell Renata.

My escort.

Just as I always was for Nikolai.

My left hand feels suddenly heavy at my side and I fight the urge to twirl my rings, averse to drawing attention to them.

Renata's scowl tells me how much she hates that I get to have Ezra on my arm for just a little while tonight. I have to fight my smile at that thought. This experience must be proving to be so eye-opening for her, to realize that it's these twisted traditions that oppress her so. If it weren't for tradition, she would be the sole leader of the Vittoris. But that's not the case and she'll just have to follow the damn rules like the rest of us.

Serves her right.

"There will be eyes on both of you this evening," she says as she nudges Ezra forward from the small of his back. "Don't try anything stupid."

"Stupid?" I say. "I wouldn't dream of it. I've always followed the rules." I tilt my head to the side. "Always."

"Come," she snaps at Luca and turns on her pointy heels.

I can't help but grin as Ezra holds out his arm for me and I take it. Kostya is in tow, following us into the reception space just outside the theater. I spare him a quick glance and a friendly smile over my shoulder.

Renata leads the way with Luca at her side and re-introduces me to practically every person at the reception. She does so begrudgingly, but it has to be someone's responsibility to do this—I thought it would be Murphy, as he's hosting, but he pawned off the task on Renata, much to her dismay. By the time I've been presented as Nikolai's bereaved wife to what feels like a thousand demons who I only vaguely remember, my feet and calves are aching and I'm desperate to get off my feet.

Olivia—a full month less pregnant than me—has already found a place to perch and put her feet up on Lorenzo's lap. He's taken off her shoes and is rubbing her feet.

They look happy.

I feel painfully jealous.

My mind flashes in envy and for a terrible moment, I see myself as Olivia—a happy girl with a smile on my face—and my feet on Nikolai's lap. It's a split-second vision and my heart drops into my stomach because that's not a vision I want.

I never wanted that…not with Nikolai.

Why doesn't my mind understand that my heart never wanted him?

Ezra taps my elbow and nods his head toward an ornate, traditional-looking loveseat in front of the fireplace—just big enough for two. I nod at him and we move to take the seat before someone else beats us to it. I plop down and Ezra tells me he'll be right back. I don't want him to leave me alone, but I'm not alone, really.

I'm surrounded by people.

I glance around the room as I wait and spot Kostya nearby, standing alone in the far corner, and I suddenly feel sad for him. He really has been all alone in his role, and I never stopped to think how lonely he might've been all these years. I smile at him and he nods at me graciously. His expression softens at my acknowledgment and that warms my heart.

Ezra returns with refreshments for me and I realize just how hungry I really am. "I can feed you if you want. I am your slave after all," he says with a joking smile as he sits beside me.

Our hips touch and I feel safe for the moment. We may be in a room full of trafficking, murderous criminals, but with Ezra by my side, I'm trapped in his sunshine, protected behind a thin layer of false normalcy. I give myself permission to enjoy it for the moment, because moments are all he and I have.

"I'll feed myself, thanks." I return his smile and take the small plate of hors d'oeuvres from him.

"I can't stop looking at you," Ezra tells me quietly as I eat.

I'm certain I'm blushing five different shades of pink. I wish he could crush my lips with a kiss right now. It's hard to breathe this close to him, knowing I can't touch him in a romantic way.

I glance around the room after popping another morsel

into my mouth. I chew and swallow before speaking. "Do you notice how distracted they all are?"

"Who?"

"All of them. Renata, Murphy, Leo. They're all so busy socializing that they're not paying attention to us."

"Renata has eyes on us, though." Ezra turns his head and looks behind us, then jabs his thumb over his shoulder. "See? Luca's watching."

I follow where he indicates with my eyes and see that he's right. I also notice that Lorenzo isn't entirely distracted by Olivia. He glances over at us, and his brows lift when our eyes catch, giving me an expression that tells me he is, in fact, watching us. "Lorenzo, too," I tell him.

"Why do you mention it? What are you thinking?" he asks as I turn my attention back to him.

"I don't know. I guess I'm thinking that if there were ever a time to attempt escape, perhaps it would be during a reception. There's access to transportation—"

"Security is focused on guests more than perimeter guarding. We might be able to slip out unnoticed," Ezra finishes my train of thought.

I nod. "We know how to do it now. We got away from the Vittoris with Nikolai's help."

"Right," Ezra turns his body sideways to face me and lowers his voice. "And we could escape from Mikhailov Manor with Kostya's help. There's nothing stopping us now. No one's trailing Lidia and Emma. And Kostya promised Nikolai he'd keep your heart beating, right? He wanted to keep that promise to Nikolai, and even gave us those cell phones in hopes it would keep you from…" *Committing suicide* is what he means to say, but I know it's hard for him to say those words. "Even Nikolai didn't know about the cell phones. And Kostya put his life on the line when we fled the Vittoris. Got himself shot for us so we could escape."

"Three months," I start in a whisper, looking straight ahead rather than at Ezra. "The next quarterly meeting is supposed to be hosted by the Mikhailovs. Renata thinks we should host it jointly at the Vittori mansion, but if I can convince the board to let me host it at Mikhailov Manor—"

He sits up straighter with a burst of energy. "Yes. And if I perform, we'll have access to Nobility Hall. We could escape from there, even before the reception starts. They wouldn't notice we haven't shown up for thirty minutes, maybe as much as an hour if we're lucky."

I inhale a breath of hopeful longing. "You're right. They'll expect me to give you time to change before heading down to the reception…"

"Anya. It could work. We could escape from Mikhailov Manor with Kostya's help."

I put my hand over my heart, willing my racing pulse to slow. "It could work," I repeat and turn my head to give him a small smile.

He looks at my mouth and licks his lips, sending a pleasant shiver down my spine. "You look so fucking beautiful."

I melt, wishing I could kiss him, but I settle for briefly brushing my fingertips over his knee. He tenses at my touch and I know he wants more.

"What about your due date? Won't that be cutting it close? It's only a week before the next meeting, right? "

"It doesn't matter. It *can't* matter. It's our best chance. Maybe our only chance," I tell him with a confident tone, though a twinge of fear strikes within me about the timing.

The timing does cut it close, fearfully close. But I know that it doesn't matter to me. Whether I'm still pregnant, in labor, or have my baby in my arms, I'll take him with me in this fight to be free.

We could finally be free.

"We'll make a plan," I tell him. "We can do this. We can survive three more months of this…right?"

He nods, leaning in just a little. "Yes. We can and we will."

CHAPTER 17
Anya

AS THE RECEPTION hours pass us by and the time for the board meeting approaches, anxiety weighs heavily on my shoulders. I'm separated from Ezra for the night, and because I have no reason to return to my bedroom before the meeting, I don't. Instead, I use the restroom for the third time over the last hour—baby enjoys kicking my bladder—and I pace outside the boardroom.

I pace until my lower back starts to ache and my swollen feet demand to sit. Kostya is still with me and he suggests I return to the reception area to sit and wait until it's time. But thankfully—or perhaps, not so thankfully—Cordelia O'Shea makes her way toward us just then, moving past me to unlock the boardroom.

She forces herself to greet me with a simple, "Hello," though I see the way her hands shake in rage as she turns the key.

She's enraged because I killed Vigo—because, apparently, she had some sort of affection for the monster who almost killed me. I don't feel an ounce of remorse for the fact that I took her lover's life. I don't know much about Cordelia, but I do know that anyone who would willingly have a relationship with Vigo Vittori is either evil or a moron.

And she's probably both.

In any case, my nerves send a ripple of unease through my limbs as I cross the threshold of the boardroom. Kostya graciously shows me where to sit, leading me to the spot where Nikolai would sit.

Nikolai.

Fucking Nikolai.

Each reminder of him is like a wrecking ball of pain slamming into my chest, stealing my breath away at the reminder of everything he put me through and worse with the reminder that he's gone now. He chose my fate—*this* fate— before he died, and he left me to navigate this nightmare with the four families alone.

I'm happy that my seat isn't near either head of the long, rectangular table. In the middle, on the side, I can blend in and feel less like I'm on display. Still, I know I need to assert myself. Somehow, I think that will be easier from this position.

Board members file into the room and settle into their seats. Murphy enters last, moving around behind the chair at the head of the table and he begins to speak before he sits.

"Welcome. I think it's best that we avoid the pomp and circumstance and get right down to handling business, shall we? The changes we've seen in the organizational structure of the four families over the past year have been unprecedented and dramatic. We have some major decisions to make tonight and we're going to dive right in. The finalized agenda is in your folder." The others open the black leather folio placed in front of them, one at each spot around the table, and I follow suit to open mine. "Any changes, additions, or objections?" Murphy asks the room.

"I object to *all* of this." Every head in the room snaps to look at the sassy girl I met in the theater—Murphy's new wife, Stella.

She still looks surly with her arms wrapped tightly across her chest. She has an interesting appearance, though she doesn't quite look like she fits in with the four families. She wears a tight, deep burgundy dress that cuts low between her average-sized breasts, revealing a tattoo along her collarbone—a scribbling of words I can't make out—and more artwork appears on the side of her arm. Her nose is pierced and there's an unnaturally bright red streak of hair peeking out from behind her ear. Not to say there's anything wrong with her appearance—I like it on her—she just seems out of place here.

Murphy finally snaps, bending over the corner of the table and reaching out to wrap his hand around Stella's throat. "Be quiet, lass, or I'll make certain you won't speak again."

She looks up at him with surprise in her eyes, but I'm not exactly sure she looks as fearful as she should be. Honestly, I'm surprised with Murphy's restraint. He forces a strained smile as he removes his hand from her neck, one finger at a time. No one bats an eye at the fact that this poor girl was just publicly throttled by her husband.

Fucking monsters.

Murphy straightens, smooths his waistcoat, and continues, "Changes, additions, or objections?" His eyes fall on Stella beside him with an intent glare.

She meets his eyes with unwavering contact and there's an almost palpable crackle between them—a sizzle of heat and chemistry. It makes my pulse quicken and it sends my thoughts spiraling to Ezra.

No.

Pay attention.

I glance down at my agenda for the first time, only just realizing I should have looked at it before he called for changes or objections.

Focus.

Breathe and focus.

Item one is listed as:

Family M: Gender & DNA Result

My head snaps up more dramatically than it should, and I find myself glancing around the room—to look at what or whom, I really don't know.

Murphy's commanding voice demands my attention and I whip my head toward the sound, finding he's already lowered into his seat. "First item of business is the matter of Anya Mikhailov, the gender of her unborn child, and the DNA result which determines family placement."

"You know the gender and the father?" I ask with too much nervous energy.

I'd been given an ultrasound a month and a half ago where Doctor Lombardi was able to see the gender of the baby, but no one would tell me. Now I understand why—the four families are nothing if not dramatic. And revealing this information here and now—determining the fate of my baby and my future as a board decision—was about as dramatic as they could get.

Murphy flips through his folio and produces a single white sealed envelope. He places it on the table and gives it a push, sliding it across the smooth surface so it glides toward me. Kostya grabs it to spare me the embarrassment of attempting to reach over my protruding belly for it and hands it to me. My name is scribbled on the front.

Anya Mikhailov.

I swallow, looking at Murphy for direction.

"Open it," he urges. "Read it out loud for the board. This letter was sent to me directly by Doctor Lombardi. This first letter should contain the gender of your baby as determined via your twenty-week ultrasound. Depending on what this letter states, we may or may not need to open the second."

"Why?" I run my fingers along the edges of the envelope.

"If your baby is a girl, the paternity result doesn't really matter, now does it?"

My eyes immediately fall on Renata across the table from me. "Does she know?" I ask Murphy.

"No one knows. The result is in that envelope and in Doctor Lombardi's personal notes. We're all finding out together. For your sake, let's hope it's a boy. Now open it."

I open my mouth to ask what will happen if it's a girl, but I close it again, realizing I don't really want to know.

They might kill her.

They might let her live and kill me.

They might raise her as one of them.

They might sell her for profit.

My fingers tear open the envelope before I even make a conscious decision to do it. I can't bear not knowing. The baby *has* to be a boy and I need to prove it now. I need to know right now that he's a boy and that he'll be okay.

I need to know we'll be alive in three months to escape with Ezra.

I tug the single sheet of white paper free from the envelope and unfold it with trembling fingers. But before I can read what it says, I squeeze my eyes shut.

I can't bring myself to look.

I place it on the table and push it toward Kostya.

"What does it say?" I ask him.

I suck in a breath and hold it through a pause, a painful beat of not knowing. I hear the quiet rush of air as he sighs…a sound of relief.

"Boy," Kostya says, angling the paper toward me to see it

before sliding it back across the table to Murphy.

I struggle to hold my cold, regal expression when I feel the rush of relief wash over my body.

I knew it.

I knew he was a boy.

My baby has always been precious to me, but because he's a boy, he's now precious to the four families as well—a direct heir of the Mikhailov or Vittori Head of House. Both my hands cover my belly as an instinctive urge to protect him takes hold of me.

They'll want him to become one of them. They'll raise him to be the next Head of House. They'll groom him for the role the same way they groomed Nikolai and Vigo. They'll prime him for violence and brutality. They'll strip him of his empathy and compassion.

Over my dead fucking body—and I will be dead if the results show he belongs to neither of them.

I inhale slowly and look at Murphy.

"Alright," he says, glancing over the paper before slapping it on the table in front of him. "Well done, lass. You've created the next Head of House." He flips through his pages and produces another white envelope, the sight of which makes my heart flip. "Now to find out if he's a Vittori or a Mikhailov."

Oh, God.

I feel sick.

He waves the envelope at me, but then he sets it on the table and pushes it to Renata on the opposite side. My mouth drops open in surprise that he's letting her open it. Those paternity results have *nothing* to do with her. I don't care if one of the fathers in question is her brother.

She tears into it and pulls the page out of the envelope, her eyes scanning it quickly to find the information she's seeking.

Her face falls and my heart beats harder. I don't know which would upset her more—if my baby is her nephew or if he's not. I don't know if she's hopeful that he will be the last bit of Vigo she might find to hang onto now that he's gone, or if the idea of her nephew belonging to me makes her cry into her pillow at night.

She forces out a heavy breath and her nostrils flare as she pushes the paper back to Murphy. "He's not a Vittori."

He's not a Vittori.

I want to leap on the table and cheer.

The four most beautiful words I never thought I'd be so happy to hear.

He's not a Vittori.

But is he a Mikhailov?

"Hmm." Murphy's brow furrows as he looks over the page and I sit up a little higher. "Apparently, the DNA result from Nikolai was inconclusive."

Inconclusive?

Perhaps it was because they took his blood sample after he'd already been dead for hours. I don't know. I have no idea how DNA testing works or what would make it *inconclusive.* I'm not even sure I understand what *inconclusive* means.

But I don't feel upset.

In my heart, I know the truth. I know that this baby boy is Ezra's and I convince myself that's the reason why the results were inconclusive. Really, it's the best result I could've asked for. If they'd determined with certainty that the baby wasn't Nikolai's, then they might work out that it's Ezra's. But only Leo Leblanc knows that Ezra and I were left alone in his dungeon the night I would've fallen pregnant. And thank God, he hasn't said a word about it.

I look expectantly at Murphy. "So, what does this mean for me?"

His eyes narrow and his jaw sets as he runs a hand over his beard. "Leo?"

All eyes turn toward Leo at the other head of the table. He's the only other Head of House, but he's young and new. I remember thinking how out of place he seemed the first time I met him. But now he looks almost cold, like he's been hardened by the business in such a short time. His face holds an expression of indifference and apathy.

"So, we assume the child is a Mikhailov since we know it isn't a Vittori." His eyes dare a quick glance in my direction and my heart hammers an extra beat at his secretive look. "I say, let her remain in the care of the Vittoris. She seems to be doing well there now and it makes sense for her to stay given that the Mikhailovs and Vittoris are making joint business decisions. Let her stay for a year and if she proves herself trustworthy," Leo leans back in his chair crossing his arms over his chest, "then she and Kostya can move back to Mikhailov Manor to run the business."

Murphy leans forward on his elbows, his eyes narrowed in consideration as he nods.

I swallow. "What about the next quarterly meeting? It's the Mikhailovs—it's *our* turn to host." We *have* to host at Mikhailov Manor. We can only escape from there with Kostya's help, and I can't wait another year for that to happen. "I'd like to host it in my home."

"No," Murphy says plainly. "It's too close to your due date in January."

"But I'm due a week before the meeting—"

"And will be in no condition to travel to Russia with a newborn," he says with his eyebrows knitting together. "You'll host from the Vittoris' home. That's final."

I stare at him, willing him with my eyes to change his

answer, but after several beats of stone-cold silence and his stubbornly powerful glare, I can see that he's not changing his mind. Not right now. But I know I have to host the next quarterly meeting at the manor, so I'll find a way to get a yes from Murphy. I just need to wait for the right time.

Cordelia suddenly leans forward. "Why do we need to give her any time with the baby at all?" she asks. "I would gladly take over care of the child after Anya gives birth. We won't need her after that. She can be decommissioned like the slave whore she's proven to be."

Decommissioned.

A nice way of saying she wants me dead.

Murphy snaps his head to glare at her. "She's a Mikhailov *wife.* We've been through this, Cordelia. We can't just off her."

"Can't we?" Renata asks with her arms crossed and her eyes burning into mine.

I shift uncomfortably in my seat.

Murphy bangs his fist on the table. "No. We *can't.* That's final. You can't just kill a wife because her husband is dead. If *I* died and you pulled this shit with Stella—"

His head turns a little to steal a glance at Stella beside him. She uncrosses her arms slowly as her expression melts from defiance and frustration to concern and sympathy. The sympathy isn't for me though, it's for Murphy.

His face transforms from angry king to indulgent husband. It's more than a little shocking the way that a single look from Stella has softened him so quickly. He takes a deep, controlled breath, then blows it out harshly. "The matter is *settled,*" he says, gritting his teeth. "Renata will continue to coordinate Anya's care for another year. We'll reevaluate at the next O'Shea-hosted meeting."

Renata scoffs and it sparks a sudden fire in my belly. I'm

already frustrated that I don't have approval to host the next meeting in Russia, and having her here to react like a child with her derisive noises only fuels that angry flame.

It angers me enough to clap back at her, even though I know it's stupid to bite the hand that feeds me. "Don't be such a bitch about it. Honestly, Renata, the way you behave is so childish. Sometimes I think you need a keeper. Really, Murphy," I say, catching his eyes, "that woman is emotionally unstable. She's lucky she has Lorenzo to help make her decisions because otherwise, she wouldn't know what side of the bed to get out of in the morning."

The men in the room snicker, enjoying my apt assessment of Renata. She and Cordelia are the only ones fuming at me. But Renata's fury is enough to make my spine tingle in warning.

A slow smile spreads across her face and she tilts her head slowly to one side. I feel a chill as she reminds me of the reason why I don't tell her every time I think she's acting like a whiny, entitled jackass.

"Darling girl, your lover still belongs to me," she says.

Ezra is still her slave when he's not my talent.

And she'll use him to hurt me.

CHAPTER 18
Ezra

I SHAKE MY head as I jolt awake—the side of my head that was perched on my fist slipped off when I drifted to sleep. My elbow was on the armrest propping me up, but now that I'm conscious again, I slam my arms down on the rests, pushing myself back in the seat and straightening my spine.

I'm determined to stay awake.

I want to be aware when Renata returns from the board meeting. I want to see her face, study her body language, get a sense for whether things went better for her than they did for Anya. If she comes back happy, then I'll know things didn't go well for my blue-eyed girl.

So, I hope she comes back angry as fuck.

I blink against the darkness. Renata had shut off the lights before she left me and Luca—chained to the floor by a cuff around the ankle—and locked us inside this bedroom. She told us to get some sleep, seeing that these board meetings are held late into the night.

But as tired as I am, I'm not going to sleep.

Luckily, I don't have to wait too long. I hear the click of the lock and in moments, it flings open wide, slamming back against the wall behind it with a thud that makes me jump.

The lights flash on and the door slams shut again. Renata starts spewing out a string of Italian words as she locks the door behind her. Luca springs up out of bed where he was sleeping and moves toward her. I have no idea what the fuck she's saying as he moves to her, putting his hands on her shoulders, stroking her arms in a comforting way.

Internally, I fucking cheer.

Everything about her demeanor screams that she's furious and I'm happy for it—it means my girl owned her shit in that meeting.

I push to my feet and cross my arms over my chest, waiting for Renata to start barking orders at me. If I have to watch her fuck Luca one more damn time, I swear I'm gonna claw my eyes out. As pissed off as she looks, I can't imagine she'll have the interest tonight, though I've been wrong before.

Luca rubs his hand down her hair, stroking the side of her face as she spits out rage-filled words that I don't understand. The poor kid is hopelessly in love with her, but Renata is so hateful, so prideful that she insists on drawing me into their twisted relationship instead of just focusing on the guy who actually gives a damn about her.

Her eyes catch mine during her tirade. She gives Luca an order and he's down on his knees in a second. But he sits back on his heels and bows his head instead of pushing her dress up over her hips and taking off her underwear.

Fuck.

She's coming after me.

She strides across the room and I drop my hands to my sides, fists clenched, skin buzzing with warning.

"Take off your clothes, Ezra."

My chest heaves with a heavy breath. Everything within me begs to resist her order, but I know I can't. She'll hurt me with the electric shock on my collar, but that's not what I fear. If I don't follow her orders, she'll hurt Anya and I will do *anything* to keep that from happening.

I took off my jacket, tie, and shirt from the reception before she left and I'm only left standing before her in my pants. I look down at the metal cuff around my ankle. "Am I supposed to do a magic trick or are you gonna remove the cuff?"

"Luca," she calls him over and he comes.

She pulls a key from her handbag and hands it to him. He bends to unlock the ankle cuff which is attached to a long chain that's bolted to the floor. Luca stands and gives the key back to her. It would never even occur to this sad sap to unlock his own damn cuff because he's so in love with this bitch that he wouldn't dare do something without asking her permission first.

I know the drill and I don't see any point in stalling, so I strip until I'm standing naked in front of her. It's happened often enough now that I've gotten used to being ogled by her.

Used to it, but not fucking happy about it.

Renata tilts her head, glancing down at my crotch. A nasty smirk lifts the side of her mouth and I can feel my nostrils flare with a slow-burning rage as I hold out my hands and narrow my eyes at her.

"What do you want from me tonight? Foot massage? Back rub? Tie you to the bed for fuck boy to use you? Maybe add another scar so you can play with my blood?"

"I'm taking your cock tonight, Ezra." Her hand lands on my chest and her fingers blaze a trail of fire until she reaches my belly button.

I dig my fingernails into my palms, fighting every raging instinct within me to slap her hand away. "Don't fucking touch my cock," I seethe through gritted teeth. "It doesn't belong to you." She steps into me and slaps her palm around my dick, gripping and tugging down to the tip. "Get your hands off me!" My jaw sets as every muscle in my body clenches in tension at her unwanted touch.

I take a step back, but my knees hit the armchair behind me and I fall to sit. She pulls the little black remote from her handbag. "No, don't—" She presses the button that sends a lightning strike of a shock right through me. "Fuck!" I manage to say before seizing from the pain that rips through my neck.

When the shock lets go of its searing hold on me, I slump heavily into my seat. My body goes limp and my chest heaves as I fight to catch my breath. Before I can move, before I can fight, Renata drops to her knees. She grips me around the base of my shaft, licks her tongue across the tip, then sucks me into her mouth.

Shit.

Fuck.

No!

Luca appears beside me and grabs my arm that's as limp as my dick. He wraps rope around my wrist, tying it tight before connecting it to my other wrist until my hands are bound together in front of me.

My limbs are weak from the electric shock, slowly prickling back into awareness. I will feeling to come back to me quicker and I stare at my fingers as I fight against my body for control. It's almost the exact moment that Luca finishes binding my wrists together that my fingers wiggle with intention.

My movements are floppy and gradual, but I manage to get my hands on top of Renata's head to try to push her away. But Luca grasps the rope from where it loops between my wrists and lifts my arms high, pulling them over my head as he moves to stand behind me.

My legs tingle and my muscles come back to life. I thrash

in my seat, but fuck if that doesn't just slam my cock deeper into her warm, wet mouth. She moans and the vibration ripples through my shaft, sending an unwanted rush of pleasure through my spine.

Goddammit.

Do not get hard for this bitch.

Don't fucking do it!

Renata is insistent, stroking my base with her fingers, bobbing her head up and down with her warm lips and swirling tongue tugging me into tension that I don't want.

I try.

I really fucking try.

I fight it for as long as I can, but she's relentless.

My cock thickens against my will and I feel absolutely powerless—exactly the way she wants me to feel.

Her mouth finally comes off my cock with a crude popping sound and she looks up at me, her red lipstick smeared from her assault. I'm panting through fury and fear and depraved, forced lust. She smiles and though I want to thrust my knee up into her chin and break her damn jaw, I don't because I know what she's capable of doing to my girl.

She gives me her most serious look, the one that tells me she means business—the look that tells me she's deadly fucking serious and I'd be stupid to cross her. "You're going to fuck me tonight and you're going to come inside me. I've been patient enough with you, but I'm done being patient."

My molars grind together. "Good luck making me." My hands stay high above me, though I lean my head forward, my shoulders tugging backward as I attempt to get in her face. "I don't come for you."

"You only think that because I haven't fucked you yet. But you will come for me. You will come inside me." She pushes her hands up my thighs. "And you'll do it enthusiastically. Because if you don't, I'll hurt her. I'll make you bleed, and I'll make her suffer."

She pushes to stand and my breaths shorten and quicken, my chest heaving as my temper flares, and I fight to control it. She gathers the hem of her skirt, swaying her hips as if she could seduce me. Her fingers slip beneath the hem and she drops her underwear to the floor, stepping out and kicking it aside.

"You stay the *fuck* away from me!" I thrash, yanking my hands with all my might. But Luca is at least as strong as I am, pulling my arms farther behind me, higher above my head, and achingly stretching my shoulders back.

I slump in my seat, trying to sink away from Luca's grip, but I'm not quick enough. Renata climbs over me before I can get away, straddling my legs and squeezing my hips with her knees. She brushes the thin straps of her bright red gown off her shoulders, shoving at the neckline until her breasts are bare in front of my face.

"Shit. Fuck, *no,*" I push my ass back against the seat.

That was a bad move.

Her cunt drags across my swelling dick when I slide backward, and it makes blood rush to my groin.

It feels…good.

But it's only physical.

Emotionally, this is wrecking me.

"Ezra," she purrs, grasping my chin and lifting my head, "if you don't come inside me, things are going to go very badly for you. But if you let yourself enjoy me, then everything will be fine. We'll just keep this our…little…secret. Your precious Anya never has to know." She dips her head, kissing me as I purse my lips against it. "What will it be?" She licks her tongue across the crease of my lips, and I cringe.

"Do whatever the fuck you're gonna do. I don't believe for a second you won't tell her anyway. Your promises mean nothing to me."

"Hmm," she tilts her head, "you're probably right." A twitch forces a crooked smile to her face and she shifts her body, twisting her hips, brushing her cunt across my tip, and wiggling her way onto it. Once the tip is wedged inside her, she sits down hard on my cock and I lose my mind. I try to pull back, to get away, but moving my body only thrusts me within her, spurring her on.

"Get the *fuck* off me!" I scream at her, horrified. Completely unexpected tears well and glass over my vision. "I won't do this to her! Don't fucking do this—" My teeth grind and I tense up as she rocks back and forth with me deep inside her.

She moans as she uses me, nuzzling her cheek against mine. "All you have to do is enjoy it. That's all. Come while you're inside me and no one has to get hurt. No one needs to know."

I don't believe her.

I *can't* believe her.

She's full of shit, full of lies.

I want to throttle her. I want to choke the life out of her with my own two hands and break her in all the ways our lives have been broken by the four families.

This is a stupid plan on her part.

I can win this.

All I have to do is hate this. If I can just keep hating this, she'll get bored and she'll stop. I put all my attention and focus into thinking of things that are undeniably unsexy. It's not hard to do given everything we've been put through.

Renata raises and lowers, arching her back as she swirls her hips and plays the part of the seductress. She plays it well. She's a damn cougar—experienced and confident—and it makes me physically ill. It's like she's been trained to do this, to work unwilling men into a frenzy, turning them into begging, hopeless shells of their former selves. I don't want to be a begging, hopeless shell, but my balls feel tight and my cock is hard as a rock with the way she moves.

"Stop. Fucking. *Moving*," I hiss through gritted teeth as I try to yank my hands away from Luca—though the attempt is useless with the way my shoulders strain.

"No." Renata bends, pressing her lips to my throat and licking her tongue across the spot.

I groan, both from the unwanted feeling of pleasure it drives and from the strain of fighting pure physical, sexual need. It takes every ounce of my concentration to fight this. She injected my heart with black venom and it surges through my veins, infecting me with dark lust that poisons my senses. I squeeze my eyes shut, trying to imagine my heart pounding, reversing the venomous flow, the black liquid drawing back from the very ends of my veins and turning my heart black as night.

But Renata rises and falls. She moans and gasps and pants and makes sinful noises against my ear. She nibbles at my earlobe and tugs on it with her teeth and fuck, I see Anya in my mind doing the same fucking thing. It drives me crazy when she does that and now, she's in my head.

Get out of my head, Anya!

Shit, shit, shit.

The black poison gushes from my heart, pulsing through my veins, masking any color, and coating my blood in the pitch-black toxin of pure aching need. It's a lost cause from the moment Anya's face and her captivating blue eyes pop into my mind—the moment I see her, I'm lost, because the mere thought of her erases everything bad.

"You're gonna make me come, Ezra," Renata whispers and

her words twist in my gut.

"Stop it…*Stop!*" I demand and then I groan.

Fuck. I can't stop this train wreck.

My voice turns to a hopeless, aching beg for her to stop. "Renata, please…"

But she only hears my begging and interprets it as me wanting her to do this. She becomes a rutting, desperate animal, a true fucking cougar in the wild taking down her prey—*me.*

And she really is taking me down because I feel all the blackened, poisoned blood in my body rush to my groin. I feel the familiar tightness coiling low and deep, tugging through the base of my cock, and I know it's going to happen in seconds. She's going to win. These few seconds of knowing are the most painful because I'm about to come inside a woman who isn't Anya.

Renata squeezes everything—my hips with her knees, my cock with her pussy, my heart in her fucking hands—and she gets exactly what she wanted from me.

I come inside her with a groan filled with heartache. My body feels incredible but my soul tears in two. As Renata comes from the pulsing waves of my swelling cock as I orgasm, nausea sets in and my body trembles.

I feel sick.

I feel disgusting.

I feel shame and guilt like I've never felt before.

I feel violated in a way I never thought possible.

Is this what Anya felt every time she was raped?

As soon as I think about it, tears creep down my cheeks and a broken sob escapes me. This is vulnerability in its rawest form, and though I despise the way it makes me feel, my breakdown is because of what I feel for my blue-eyed girl.

Renata climbs off me when she's done. She smooths down her gown and covers her naked chest as she pulls the straps back onto her shoulders. She bends and grabs my boxer briefs from the floor, tossing them at me carelessly as she slinks across the room to straighten her appearance in the mirror.

My heart empties of substance and collapses in on itself, sinking inside me like a black hole. It feels like a void that all the best parts of me circle around, constantly in threat of being sucked inside it and lost forever.

Did Anya's heart hollow out like this every time they raped her?

My girl is the strongest person on the face of this Earth. She's survived against insurmountable odds. She's stared death in the face, and though she's been tempted to chase it, she's found a way to stay strong and endure the shitshow that was forced upon her. She survived through this awful feeling of rawness, brokenness, hopelessness—and still found a way to love me.

She loves me.

But I don't deserve it.

Luca drops my bound hands after Renata gives him a quick nod. I grab my underwear in my lap and stand, pulling it on as quickly as I can because I urgently need that barrier of protection. I never would've thought that underwear could be this damn important to me.

"I suppose you were right," Renata says, turning around to face me again. "I think I will tell Anya about what we've done. I'm sure she'll enjoy knowing you came inside another woman."

She chuckles and a burning rage rinses away my own pain in favor of delivering it to her. Before I can think about the consequences of my actions, I charge for her. I hear Luca shout at me, but I'm faster than he is. I barrel into Renata's back, shoving her down to the floor. She manages to roll from her stomach to her back before I slam to my knees, straddling her tiny waist.

My hands are still bound at the wrists, but that doesn't stop me from wrapping my fingers around her throat. I want to snap it in two. I squeeze hard in my rage, my thumbs finding the hollow of her throat and pressing down hard. I hope I collapse her fucking windpipe. She gasps and writhes beneath me, her eyes popping wide as her slender fingers scratch at mine, trying to claw me away.

I throttle her until I can't anymore, until Luca rips me away from her and slams me to the floor instead. I kick and swing my arms. My bound fists collide with the side of his face, knocking him sideways to the floor. I scramble to get up, to get to Renata in my blind rage.

But then lightning strikes through my neck, the shock of my collar seizing control of my limbs as Renata presses the button on the remote she got to just in the nick of time. She holds it down, longer than she ever has before, ensuring that my body is nice and limp so she can control me.

I'm still on my back on the floor, watching her huff and puff to catch her breath as she stands above me. I don't know if my face muscles are responding yet, but internally, I smile seeing the red marks on her throat and the spots that will turn into bruises before long.

She clears her throat. "Lorenzo," she says to herself. "Luca, take him in the hallway."

Shit.

She storms to the door, flinging it open wide, marching out of the room, screaming, "Lorenzo!" before pounding on his door, which I know to be three doors down the hall.

Luca grabs beneath my arms, dragging me along the carpet as he spits out a string of words in Italian—I don't have to know the words to know that he's cursing at me.

My limbs start to tingle as feeling slowly comes back as

I'm dragged out into the hallway to face Renata's wrath. The hallway quickly fills with people hearing the commotion and suddenly, I feel small.

Renata Vittori has stripped me of my pride, my self-worth, my confidence. And as my eyes lock on Anya's coming from the far end of the hallway with a look of shock and fear on her face, I feel utterly undeserving of her love.

CHAPTER 19

Ezra

"RENATA!" ANYA YELLS from down the hall as she charges forward with her hand on her stomach. She looks ethereal in that blush-colored gown which sweeps the floor as she comes toward us.

I can wiggle my fingers and toes now, and I'm slowly getting feeling back in my arms and legs.

Anya lifts her chin a little higher and pulls her shoulders back as she meets Renata in front of Lorenzo's closed door. "What are you doing with him?"

Renata's head whips to the side to look at her. "I don't answer to you, you self-righteous slut."

Adrenaline kicks up, urging my limbs to wake the fuck up so I can fight for my girl.

Anya's eyebrows draw together and she steps closer to Renata. "You have no right to talk to me like that. I am your equal now by name alone."

Renata turns toward Anya, stepping close enough to touch her baby bump. "My dear, you have never been anything but a slave and a whore. A warm body for Nikolai to fuck, one who happened to have a pretty face and a talent for dance."

It's a good thing I can't get up because I might beat the

shit out of Renata if I could. But Anya doesn't need me to defend her. She's strong enough on her own, stronger than me.

"If that were true, then why did Nikolai go through the trouble of arranging a secret marriage with me? You're just angry you've met your match in me, that you've taken on a new slave boy who prefers me to you." Anya cocks her head to the side.

"Ezra *is* mine when he's not your talent," Renata insists. "He is a slave that Murphy put in my care. I make his rules and you know that."

"Yes, you're right. You don't have the power of a Head of House, so you take your orders from an Irish man a decade your junior." Anya smiles. "Thank you for the reminder."

"Ezra's time here is over," Renata says with an eerie level of calm decisiveness.

My time here is over.

She pounds on Lorenzo's door again and he finally comes to answer, opening it wide. He and Renata argue in Italian as I start to move, slowly working to get myself up off the floor. Luca sees me moving and grabs beneath my arms again, hoisting me into position on my knees. He hisses in my ear, telling me to stay put. I do because I don't feel I have enough strength yet to get to my feet—it's not like I could do anything if I did as I'm quickly becoming outnumbered here.

Renata and Lorenzo's voices raise, and his girl Olivia appears beside him, asking in English about what's going on.

"Stay in the room," Lorenzo tells her as they both disappear from the doorway.

"Wait, what are you doing?" Olivia's voice sounds frantic out of sight and soon after, Lorenzo appears in the hallway with Renata.

Holding a *gun.*

"What are you doing?" Anya demands, rushing to stand in front of Lorenzo, bravely putting herself in his path toward me. "Stop! What are you doing?" She puts her hands on his chest to shove him back and my heart stops.

"He raped her," Lorenzo tells Anya, looking down at me with spitting fury. "He attacked them and *raped* her." Anya's mouth drops open in surprise.

"You lying, bitch," I utter under my breath, pissed but not surprised that Renata would pull a stunt like this to get me killed.

Lorenzo glances down with a furrowed brow at Anya's hands on his chest. "Get your hands off me."

"Give me the gun. I won't let you hurt him," Anya demands, shoving at his chest.

He whips his free hand around and snatches hold of her wrist, squeezing it tightly and holding it up between them. "I said, get your hands off me."

"Don't touch her!" I shout, my heart jumping into overdrive and fearful nausea rolling through my stomach.

Anya freezes in his grip and I know why—because I see what she sees. Lorenzo's face has shifted and suddenly, he looks like Vigo. He holds the same unraveled expression that shadows the features of his face—the same vicious fire that would burn in Vigo's eyes. It's the same violence, the same brutality, the same disengagement from his humanity.

Vigo still haunts her through the rage of his family.

Lorenzo tosses her hand aside and slips past her, coming after me. I flinch when he starts to raise his gun, but terror grips me as I watch Anya step after him again. I shake my head at her furiously. "Anya, don't—" I start to say as she lunges for Lorenzo.

She reaches and latches her fingers around his wrist—the hand that holds the gun he was just starting to lift. She pulls back on his arm viciously, but is forced to let go and jump back when he whips around, shaking her grip from his wrist, and aiming the gun at her head.

She screams, throwing her hands up in front of her face as she sinks at the knees. The memory of Nikolai holding her at gunpoint just before he sold her to Vigo flashes across my mind and my body trembles with a pulse of adrenaline. "No!" I shout.

But then Lorenzo swings the gun around aiming at my head. My eyes widen as I watch it all happen in a blur.

He presses the barrel to the center of my forehead.

He cocks it…and pulls the trigger.

.

.

.

.

.

A click, then silence.

Silence from everyone except for Anya's piercing scream.

I gasp for a breath. If it weren't for the authenticity of my blue-eyed girl's scream, I'd believe I'd died and gone to hell— the same hell I've been living with the four families.

But I'm not in literal hell. I'm alive because the gun misfired. A violent sob bursts from Anya with her eyes squeezed shut. But then I see her features soften as she realizes she didn't hear the gunfire, either. I stare her down, willing her to open her eyes and look at me because I can't stand to see her this broken.

I can't die. I can't leave her here alone.

Lorenzo swears and Renata yells at him. He pops open the chamber to check for rounds and in a flash, Anya is in front of me—she jumps in front of me as a human shield for the next round and my heart disintegrates into ash.

"Anya, move," I plead, gripping her skirt with my bound

hands, and tugging to get her attention. "Move, baby, *please*."

She only shakes her head. "He can't harm me," she whispers. "I'm a Mikhailov." She lifts her chin. Even from behind her, I can see the tracks of tears streaming down the side of her cheek, streaking black streams from her make-up.

Lorenzo pushes the chamber back in and points the gun at her. I can't breathe.

I can't breathe.

"Move," he tells her.

Anya's voice is quiet power as she speaks through gritted teeth. "If Renata wants him dead, you'll have to kill us both." Her hands clench into shaking fists at her sides.

"I'll happily arrange that," Renata says, moving to stand beside Lorenzo.

Lorenzo steps forward, pushing the tip of the gun to Anya's belly, threatening her, threatening me, but more urgently, threatening the baby.

Anya stiffens. A strange sort of fear grips me, and I know she feels it, too—except, hers morphs into a protective fury. She doesn't scream and cower. She snarls, steels herself, straightens her spine, and pulls her shoulders back.

"I dare you," she practically growls at Lorenzo. "Pull the trigger. Kill a Mikhailov and her son and see if that will put you any closer to taking over the family bloodline. We all know that's what you want—for your Fiore name to be the one associated with the four families. We all know that's why you serve Renata the way you do."

His eyebrows raise and lower in surprise.

Olivia defies her order to stay in the bedroom and suddenly rushes out. "Stop!" she cries. "Why are you doing this?" Bravely, she wedges herself between Anya and the gun. She pushes Lorenzo's hand away from her stomach by grabbing his wrist and shoving back on his chest. "Why are you *doing* this? She's pregnant! They're in love, Lorenzo…in love like you and me! Renata's a liar. Why would he rape her? *Stop* this!"

Lorenzo looks at Olivia with a tilt of his head and drops his gun to the floor. The thud of it landing on the carpet makes us all flinch in fear that it might somehow go off. I watch in shock as he shoves Olivia back against the wall by her shoulders, shifting his anger to her instead of toward us. Olivia's eyes pop wide as tears pour down her cheeks and she opens her mouth to defend herself.

"I'm sorry," she says quietly. "I just…Lorenzo…d-don't hurt them." She puts her hands on his chest and grips the lapels of his jacket. "Please. This is insane. I was one of them. They're no different than we are."

There are a few tense moments where all I can hear is the pounding beat of my heart and Anya's rapid breaths in front of me. I think Lorenzo might hurt Olivia—the woman he claims to love.

But then, he sighs, softening for her, melting to her plea. He lifts a rigid finger between them, pointing it at her with intention. "Don't *ever* come between me and my gun like that again. Do you hear me, *amore*? I could've killed you."

"I won't. I won't," she says. "I promise."

He leans forward and kisses her and that's when I snap back to reality. I look at the gun on the ground. I glance at it and when I look back up, I see Renata lock her stare on Anya.

"Get the gun," I hurriedly whisper to my girl.

She doesn't take a moment to think, she just *moves*.

Anya and Renata both lunge for it at the same time. I hold my breath as Anya drops to her knees. Unable to bend at the waist to grab for it, she clambers on her hands and knees to get it. Anya reaches out, and just before Renata gets there,

Anya grabs the gun. She raises it and cocks it, sitting back on her heels and aiming at Renata.

Her hands don't shake. She's as steady as steel. "I want Murphy O'Shea here. *Now*," she demands.

"Put the gun down, Anya," Renata says to her, backing away.

Anya's finger hovers over the trigger and I know she itches to pull it, to end Renata's life like she ended her brother's. I'd be proud of her if she did; I'd fucking cheer for her if she did. But I'm also terrified of the consequences if she does it. Her favor with the four families is—as it always has been—on razor-thin ice.

"Get. Him. Here. *Now*." Anya's teeth grind together as she insists.

Lorenzo could knock the gun from her hand with ease, wrestle it from her without much struggle at all. And I think Olivia being so close is the only reason he doesn't.

Thank God for her presence.

Renata sighs heavily. "Luca, go get Murphy." He turns and runs down the hall.

I want to climb to my feet and barrel into someone, join this attack on Anya's side, but I don't dare move. She's got the gun and she's got *this*. I trust her, now more than ever, and I sense that she has a plan to get us out of this.

Shit.

I'm fucking lucky that gun misfired the first time.

I could be dead right now.

Soon we hear Murphy's voice echo from down the long hallway from somewhere behind me. "There'd better be a damn good reason this slave boy disturbed me and my wife."

I look at my blue-eyed girl on her knees a few feet in front of me in her lace and tulle gown, her gorgeous dark hair tumbling in soft waves down to the middle of her back, pointing a fucking gun at Renata Vittori. She's never looked more powerful as she does right now.

I can only imagine what this scene looks like to Murphy as he comes closer to us. A pregnant Mikhailov wife holding a Vittori hostage in front of a slave with his hands bound in rope, kneeling in his underwear. It must be intriguing, at the very least.

"Anya demands to speak with you, Murphy," Renata says as he approaches.

I turn my head to see him just a few feet away. He stops abruptly beside me. "Are you fucking—" He groans. "What the fuck is going on here?"

Anya speaks to him but doesn't dare turn to look at him, still aiming the gun at Renata. "Renata has attempted to kill the Mikhailov talent slave. She claimed he attacked and raped her, and I know she's lying. I will *not* have it, Murphy. There is no replacement for his talent, and we will *not* break the tradition of the four families just before my turn to host the quarterly meeting because of her false accusation. It's..." She nearly falters, but I think I'm the only one who notices it—she speaks in half-truths, trying to explain her motivations within a context that these vile creatures would understand. "This is my chance to prove myself worthy of my name, and I will not have her taking the life of our talent slave over a lie. It's unacceptable."

"You're quite the princess, aren't you?" Murphy says with a frustrated huff.

"He raped me, Murphy. He attacked me and Luca and then he raped me! I want him *dead*," Renata says it to Murphy, but her eyes never leave Anya. This whole thing is about Anya because Renata wants to hurt her.

"Oh, fuck off," Murphy says with a look of incredulity.

"We both know that's not fucking true. This isn't the first time you've cried wolf to get a slave killed."

Renata looks insulted and I almost want to laugh. "I never—"

"Shut your mouth, Renata. Our family has been putting security cameras in Vittori family guest rooms for over a decade of meetings that we've hosted. Your family is always causing problems. Keep talking if you want me to go look at the footage from your room. Always fucking causing trouble, fucking Vittoris."

Her wide-open mouth clamps shut, and she turns her head away.

Murphy rubs his hand over his beard. "Well, fuck. This is going to end disastrously if I send you back home with her now."

I watch Anya's chest fall as she lets out a slow breath and though she tries to keep her tone even and her words steady, they come out hurried and insistently. "Let us stay here…under the care of the O'Sheas. I no longer feel safe with the Vittoris. If she puts Ezra's life at risk, the stress it causes me could be detrimental to the health of my baby. The four families can't afford to lose my child. Give me and Ezra shelter here and send the Vittoris home tonight. The safety of the Mikhailov heir has been threatened."

"I've made no such threat to your child's safety!" Renata charges forward, but Anya lifts her gun higher, with more confidence. "You're the one pointing a gun!"

"A gun you meant to have Ezra killed with! A gun Lorenzo nearly shot me in the stomach with because of your lies!"

"Ladies," Murphy interjects, pinching the bridge of his nose, "I'm not in the mood for this bullshit."

"*Please*, Murphy," Anya pleads gently. "I've been through enough. You wouldn't put Stella through what I've been through. Don't put me through more."

Murphy looks up, his eyes falling on the back of Anya's head. His face looks somehow kinder, but there's also a look of confusion, as if he's just figured something out that shouldn't make sense. "If I say yes, will you put the gun down?"

"If you say yes and arrange for Renata and Lorenzo to leave tonight, then I will put the gun down."

Renata points her finger in Murphy's direction. "I approved your bride as a favor, Murphy. Stella was never fit to be one of us, but I gave my approval because you asked me for it. You *owe* me." She turns her finger to me. "Kill Ezra and do it *now*."

I feel the shift in his energy from calm negotiator to all-powerful king. "I owe you *nothing*. We both know that giving you women first approval rights on brides is just a social nicety." He chuckles darkly. "Do you honestly believe I wouldn't have married her if you'd said no?"

Renata seethes, fury rippling from her in waves.

"This has gotten out of hand," Lorenzo finally says. "We'll leave now, but I want my gun back."

"Anya," Murphy starts, "give him his gun and go back to your room."

She shakes her head. "I'm not giving anyone this gun until my talent slave is away from here and his safety is assured."

"Christ." Murphy sighs. "Call your pilot to be ready for departure within the hour. I'll bring your gun when I have them settled." He shakes his head. "You Vittoris cause so much fucking drama."

Shock and rage clamber for control of Renata's features as I feel the burden of fear slowly lift from my shoulders.

Anya slowly, gradually lowers the gun, but she refuses to give it up.

CHAPTER 20
Anya

I HOLD MY position on my knees, gun in hand, aimed at Renata. At my insistence, she sends Luca to her room to get the key to remove the padlock and Ezra's collar. I wait until it falls free from his neck and lands heavily on the floor before I lower the gun. But I don't give it up. Not yet. I hold it tightly in my grip until Murphy has led Ezra and I back to my room and he shuts the door.

Murphy holds out his palm. "Hand it over, lass."

"Where will he be staying?" I'm not giving up this gun until I know Ezra will be behind a locked door that Renata and Lorenzo can't access before they leave.

Murphy sighs. "Am I going to regret it if he stays in your room?"

My pulse thrums with unexpected hope. "You would let him stay with me?"

"It's probably against my better judgment, but since my home is a fortress and there are extra security measures in place while my wife…adjusts to her new lot in life, I'll allow you to keep your talent slave for now. Do you have any plans to point a gun at my head?"

I swallow. "No." As a show of good faith, I hand him the gun.

He takes it with a sigh. "Fuck, I've gone soft. Listen," he points his finger in my face and I lean back from the intensity of it. "I'm only doing this for you because Renata is on my last fucking nerve. If you test me, you *will* regret it. If you behave yourselves, then we won't have a fucking problem. Understood? There is no escaping my home, so don't even think about trying."

I nod. "Understood."

Murphy turns and walks toward the door, then stops and spins back to us, looking at Ezra. "Do you understand what's at stake here, slave boy? You step out of line and try to cross me, and I will hurt you in ways you never imagined."

"Yeah, I get it," Ezra says.

Murphy gives him a once over. "I really hope you do." Then he looks at me pointedly. "Watch him. You're responsible for his behavior. He fucks up, *you've* fucked up. And you know I'll make you pay for it." He turns the knob and pulls the door open. "Lock this," he says before he slams the door shut behind him.

I practically run to the door, turning both the lock on the knob and the deadbolt above it. Then, I press my back to the door and take what feels like the first breath since I saw Ezra lying there on the floor, facing Renata's wrath in the hallway.

Our eyes meet and my heart aches at the look on his face, at the sight of him trembling and terrified.

Oh, God.

What did she do to him tonight?

He doesn't just seem frightened for me as he always has been—he looks tortured in his own right. We both move at the same time and meet in the middle of the space between us, nearly colliding. I reach for his bound wrists, my fingers instantly threading between the knots to free him.

"Are you okay?" I ask, my fingers working frantically to loosen the knots, but they're tied so tightly.

"No. No, I'm not fucking okay."

"I'm sorry," I tell him, though I don't know what I'm apologizing for.

"I didn't rape her."

"I know that, Ezra. I know. What did she do to you? God, what happened?"

"I need a fucking shower. Fuck. Are you okay?"

"I'm fine. I just…" my voice cracks, "he pulled the trigger on you and you would've died if it hadn't misfired." I manage to free one of the knots and focus my attention on pulling the long length of rope through the loop, rather than let the reality of that truth sink in.

A tense, terrified silence falls between us as I work quickly to undo the heavy knots. It feels like it takes me forever to pull them free. His wrists finally separate with the knot I've just undone, but the rope is still tied to his right wrist. As soon as he's able to pull his arms apart, he shoves my hands away and throws his arms around me. The dangling ends of rope whip around to lasso me to him.

"I thought I was dead," he whispers. "I thought I was dead, and I left you behind."

His words grip me and shake loose the tears I've been holding back. I press my face into his bare chest and let them fall free. "That was terrifying. I've never been more afraid in my life."

He half-sobs, half-chuckles as he kisses my hair. He pulls back to examine my face with his hands holding my cheeks. "Never? After all you've been through?"

I blink up at him and it's hard to see him clearly with the gloss of tears clouding my vision. "The thought of losing you, of living this life alone without you…it's the most frightening thing I can think of."

He bends and kisses my forehead before clutching me in

his arms. I feel him shake. I feel the heaving of his chest as he cries, though he tries to hide it from me, muffling the sounds with his face nuzzled into the side of my neck. It threatens to shatter my aching heart, but I find my strength in his sadness, too. He's been strong for me so many times before and I want to give him this, give him my strength so he can fall apart here with me.

For the moment, we're safe.

Safe and together—a rare, precious moment for us to find in this world.

A minute or so passes before I quietly ask, "What happened with Renata?"

His body goes rigid. He pulls back and slips from my grasp. "I need a shower." He spins away, heading for the attached bathroom through the open door behind us.

I follow him but stop in the doorway. He marches straight toward the glass-enclosed shower, pulls open the door, and steps inside, still in his underwear. He closes the door shut behind him and my breath catches in my chest at the immediate separation he creates between us.

I move forward—stopping in front of the glass door—and watch as he rips off his boxer briefs, turns on the water, and dips his head under the flow. The rope still wrapped around his wrist looks heavy the way it hangs as he lifts his palms to press against the tile in front of him. He looks so troubled, so conflicted, but worst of all, distant.

I can't stand it.

I can't stand to have a barrier between us after what just happened. When Lorenzo pulled the trigger on him, I thought I'd lost him forever. I don't even have words to describe the kind of primal, raw pain that tore through my soul as I stood by watching helplessly.

No.

No separation between us.

I kick off my shoes, tear open the glass door, and step inside the shower before he can protest.

I slip between him and the tiled wall where the waterfall spills down on me and soaks my dress. I flinch and tense up as the water rolls down my back—just as I always do anytime water touches me now—but I force my bravery for him because he needs me. I would jump into the ocean to save him if he were drowning.

"Don't shut me out," I tell him.

"Anya—"

"Don't. I don't know what she did to you. I don't know how she hurt you. But you can't avoid me. You *can't.* I need you to need me."

He stares down at me, his eyebrows slanting toward his nose as his eyes burn me with his mystical green flames. His voice is gruff and quiet and haunting. "She fucked me and made me come inside her and I've never felt so…"

Oh, God.

I don't know why that shocks me, but it does. I fall back, leaning against the wall behind me for support as I look up at him with the truest empathy.

I know what he feels.

I know there are no words fitting enough to describe it.

"Do you hate me?" he whispers with a tilt of his head.

"I *love* you." I can't get the words out fast enough. "Ezra, I love you, always. I'm so sorry."

He shakes his head, stepping in close, taking my face in his hands and pressing his forehead to mine. "I don't deserve you."

"Yes, you do. You *earned* me. You're mine. *Mine.* Not hers."

His hands slip down the sides of my neck, grazing my skin

and landing on my shoulders. "Yours," he says, though it lacks conviction.

Does he feel unworthy?

"Say it again but mean it this time."

He sighs. "I want to be yours."

"You are mine. You *are*. Tell me you're mine, Ezra."

His eyes press shut, his face pulling tight, revealing the pain he feels from what Renata did to him. "Did you hear me, Anya? I came for her...*inside* her. How can you still call me yours? I wasn't strong enough for you. I couldn't fight it...I couldn't control myself."

I slam my hands against his chest and shove him back, pushing hard enough that he hits the wall behind him. His mouth drops open in surprise as my eyes narrow on him.

"For all the times Nikolai raped me and made me come for him when the *only* man I ever wanted to come for was you. Was I not worthy of you then? Did you disown me in your mind because he made my body do things my heart didn't want? Did that make me weak? Should I have fought my body harder when he demanded I come just to avoid painful punishment?" I shove him again. "How *dare* you say that to me?"

I turn away, flinching as the water splashes onto my face and I instinctively gasp for air. My body suddenly feels heavy, weighted down as if I were surrounded by water, drowning in it.

Take off the stupid dress.

I reach behind me for the zipper, but in my agitation, my fingers struggle to find it. I fumble and the fumbling quickly turns to urgency to remove the weight of the soaked layers of tulle and lace.

Just as my anxiety ticks up and my nerves spark, threatening a full-body blaze, Ezra's fingers find mine. He gently pushes them aside as he pulls the zipper down to my waist. I start to step forward, away from him, but he stops me with hands on my shoulders. He tenderly guides the long, lacy sleeves to slip down my arms, his fingers trailing behind the fabric across my skin. My breaths quicken at his tender touch and I'm frozen in time as he steps in close, bending to kiss my shoulder lovingly. His touch washes away my anger and pain.

"You're right," he says. "I'm sorry. You have to know how strong you are in my eyes. I never once thought you weren't. I never once thought you didn't fight enough. You fight every goddamn day—for you, for me, for the baby." His lips sweep in closer to my neck and he nudges the dress down, urging it to slip free from my hips and tumble onto the tile beneath our feet. I'm left only in my strapless bra and panties. "When it was happening and I couldn't do anything to stop it...I felt defeated. I felt ashamed. Embarrassed. Broken. I felt things I couldn't even put words to. I'm in awe of you. You are the strongest woman alive."

"The courage it takes to let your body have control of you, to betray your own heart and soul because your master demands it of you. It's—"

"Fucking horrible."

"Tell me you're mine and *mean* it." I feel breathless waiting to hear it.

"Anya, let me prove it to you. I need..." He hesitates as his arms fold around me, hugging me closely from behind. "I can't stop thinking about it...about what she made me do. And the thought that I might've died tonight without one last chance to hold you, kiss you, make love to you—" his voice cracks and so does my heart. I can't bear to hear him in so much pain.

"Forget everything," I begin quietly, lifting my hands to grip his forearms draped across my breasts. "Forget where we are. Forget *who* we are. Forget about time and fear and death.

Forget it all and just love me tonight…worship me. Show me how much you love me in all the ways you need to and replace everything that happened to you tonight with our love. Forget it all and make these memories with me."

I'm panting by the time I finish and he is, too. It's hard to be patient with this much wanting between us—it's hard to wait for him to touch me, to kiss me, to lead me into the physical connection we both so desperately need.

But I wait.

I wait with nothing more than the sounds of the waterfall and our uneven, heavy breaths surrounding us.

It's peaceful here and that's strange for me.

Showers are anything but peaceful anymore—the sound of the running faucet usually brings chaos and anxiety into my mind. But the sound of it now, here in this moment where I can breathe, alone with the man I love and safe for now…It's nothing but peace.

I lean into his embrace, resting my head back against his shoulder. The steady rise and fall of his chest sways me into a tranquil calm that I don't think I've really felt in years. We've never been told we could be alone together. We've never been given that permission, that time, that space. There's never been a moment of our love that wasn't rushed and urgent and dangerous.

He kisses the side of my head over and over again, softly, chastely. I cherish the sweetness of it and a true, happy, genuine smile spreads across my face.

How can he make me so happy amidst such despair?

I'm torn between enjoying the feeling of him holding me like this and wanting to turn around to see his face. But my decision to stay put is made for me as his hands move to my stomach, gently rubbing across my stretched skin. I sigh, loving the feel of his hands on my aching belly. He could almost make this moment feel normal.

But then I'm pulled back with him as he slumps against the wall behind him. When he sighs, I feel it deep within me. He's troubled and disconnected and that hurts my heart.

His lips brush against the shell of my ear. "I want to forget it all and just be here with you. I'm so stuck in my fucking head and I hate it."

I spin, breaking his hold on me and turning to face him. I look up at him and see a new sadness in his soul that I've never seen before. It shadows the brilliant green of his normally bright eyes. I thought maybe he needed more from me tonight, but I see the exhaustion draining his essence. He needs rest and comfort and a single peaceful night amidst the nightmare we've been living.

I grasp his arms just above his elbows and tug, encouraging him to spin around and change positions with me so he's under the flow of water. I want to tell him that I know what he's feeling, that I understand feeling trapped inside your own mind because reality is too much to bear.

But I don't say a word because that's not what he needs.

The O'Sheas have stocked their guest rooms with hotel-style amenities, so there's a small, travel-sized bottle of body wash on a ledge built into the tiled wall beside us. I reach for it and flip open the cap, pouring the silky, white soap onto my palm. I rub my hands together, working it into a lather, and I lift my fingertips to my nose, testing the scent. Satisfied with the clean, unscented freshness of it—knowing it won't mask the natural scent of him that I need for my own sanity—I press my palms to his chest.

I cleanse him diligently, spreading the soap over his pecs, up to his shoulders, and down his arms. When my fingers reach his, he snatches my hands in both of his. I lift my head to look up at him and he's staring down at me with love so intense, it could knock me backward—and it nearly does.

His voice is quiet and steady. "You're the best thing that's ever happened to me."

The air is sucked out of my lungs.

I see the rawness and truth in his gaze. My skin tingles at his honesty, knowing that loving me means being a part of this hell. For the years of abuse and pain and torment I've suffered, his pure, unconditional love for me still strikes me every single time. It's a lightning bolt straight through my heart that shocks my senses.

He drops my hands, grabs my face, and kisses me hard, so hard that his fingers curl around the back of my head and dig into my skin, holding me in place as his lips bruise mine with force.

He holds me there in that aching kiss for beat after beat, drawing in a long breath through his nose—drawing *me* in and taking me from the world around us. My hands find his skin without conscious thought, my fingers curving around the sides of his waist. His skin is slick from the soap as it rinses down his body and my hands slip over it.

My intention was to care for him—to help him cleanse the way he cleansed me the night of our first kiss. He carried me to my room, put me in the shower, and cared for me after the first time Nikolai raped me with his involvement.

I still intend to care for Ezra, but I feel him coming back to life with our kiss and I want him to get lost in this.

We both need this.

I let my hands drift down his stomach and his abs clench at my touch. His lips part, he groans, and our tongues lash. His nails dig into my scalp and I feel completely consumed by him.

My fingers draw lower, gliding down his front, and easily find the base of his cock. I don't care whether he gets hard. I don't care whether he fucks me. I just feel some instinctive primal need to reclaim him as mine. I know it should be wrong to feel that way considering…well, everything.

But I feel it.

So, I wrap my hand around his girth and slowly stroke down. He jerks in my hold, slamming his right palm on the wall behind me and I hear the slap of it loudly against my ear. I pull back, breaking our kiss just so I can look at him. His eyes are half-hooded as he looks at me and I can see the spark of something bringing the light back to his eyes. I stroke again, my hand striking the match to ignite that flame and fuel his fire. I stroke him slow and long, running my thumb over the tip of his cock at the end, making him shiver.

He grows hard and thick in my hand and his arousal triggers mine. I let out a moan on my exhale and his eyes widen in need. He crowds me against the wall, and I stroke him a little faster, grip him a little tighter. We stay this way for minutes, minutes that pass as quickly as seconds, minutes that I wish would stretch on for hours.

His eyes drift shut when I know he's getting close, when his cock is thrumming its own pulse in my grip and a groan rumbles deep in his chest.

"Ezra," I moan to get his attention and when his eyes meet mine, I ask for him to let me reclaim him fully. "Mine?"

His chest rises and falls heavily as I keep stroking, keep dragging him closer to the edge. He bends, his forehead touching mine, his nose nuzzling the tip of mine. I stroke faster.

Just on the edge, his hips jerk forward, thrusting himself harder into my hand. With a gruff voice, raw and stripped bare, he replies, "Yours"

I feel his sincerity. I feel it in my heart, in my soul, in the palm of my hand. His cock swells and throbs in my grip and I gasp at the feel of him, at the look of ecstasy on his face, at the pulse of his soul giving strength to mine.

He cries out when he comes, spilling and dripping over my stomach. I smile, moaning at the feeling of power he gives me. It's a power I can't take from him—it's something he gives me freely and it's something I treasure.

Finally, he smiles, big and bright and entirely disarming.

"Ezra, I love you. No matter what."

He slams me with a bewildering kiss and I'm lost in him.

CHAPTER 21
Ezra

"I WANT TO have the baby back home, at Mikhailov Manor," Anya says.

I drop my fork on my plate unintentionally and the metal clangs loudly against the porcelain dish. Murphy shoots daggers at me with his eyes, clenching his fork with a fierce grip before pointing a finger at me. His eyes narrow at me and he speaks through gritted teeth, "Be *careful*. Those were my grandmother's."

Well, shit.

Who knew monsters could be sentimental?

I raise my palms in mock surrender before making a show of how carefully I'm minding Grandma O'Shea's porcelain dishes. Murphy sniffs and his nostrils flare, and he cuts himself another bite of his rare steak.

I knew Anya was going to bring this up soon, but I didn't know it was going to happen tonight. Kostya's been here with us at the O'Sheas' estate for the past month, and he and Anya have been plotting. I shouldn't say plotting. Anya's been building a friendship with him. She's been successful in that, too, and just within the past week she's been putting a bug in his ear about escaping.

Kostya's come to our side—as fed up with the four families' bullshit as any of the rest of us—and though we can never really know for sure if he's lying, we have no choice but to hope and trust that he's with us…because there is no escape plan without him.

Kostya opened up to Anya, telling her that he really did care about his cousin Nikolai. He told her they'd been close friends, though the context of their relationship had them behaving like employer and employee—and that's because they were. Still, Kostya feels a sense of pride to keep his promises to Nikolai as a friend, and one of those was to keep Anya's heart beating.

He felt betrayed by the four families when he was injured in the escape from the Vittoris last quarter. He told Anya that he was tortured by the Vittoris' extended family. It went on for hours when the board left to hunt us down at Mikhailov Manor after our escape with Nikolai. He said the board turned a blind eye to the torture because they thought he deserved it for helping Nikolai steal back Anya. But Kostya argued he should've been praised for doing his job and blindly following the orders of his leader, his family's Head of House—it's what he was trained to do, what he was *raised* to do.

But they didn't care, which is why he's now willing to help us escape to spite them, because he's ready to leave, too. At least, we have to trust that he is. I suppose we can't know for sure until we're gone from this nightmare. I have hope that he's truly on our side—with Nikolai and his family gone, he's got nothing and no one else except for the friendship Anya has so carefully curated with him.

And that makes us fucking lucky.

I glance furtively at Anya when I sense her eyes on me, her anxiety growing when Murphy doesn't respond to her. I tilt my head in his direction, urging her to speak up and try again.

"Murphy—"

"I heard you the first time, lass."

I feel the steeling breath she takes from where she sits beside me at the long rectangular table in the dining room. "Then I'd like to hear your response."

He sets his utensils down on his plate, folding his hands in front of him with his elbows on the table. It's unusually quiet in the dining room tonight. We're expected to be here for family dinners every Sunday and Wednesday night. But Murphy's parents are gone on an anniversary trip to their vacation home in Portugal and they took the O'Shea talent slave with them—and I honestly don't care to know why.

And today, it just so happened that his brothers needed to leave on important family business—a routine maintenance check at one of their factories. That sounds so innocent outside of context, but really, it means that they were popping in to do a surprise inspection of their *human assets* at one of the warehouses where they keep women they've kidnapped to sell. Kostya is off doing the same at one of the Mikhailov factories—factories that now belong to Anya. Thank fuck they don't expect her to do that. I'd surely have their blood on my hands if they tried to make her.

Murphy takes his time to chew and swallow. I see his wife Stella's annoyance with him tick as she leans back sullenly in her chair, crossing her arms over her chest. She sits on the far end so they each form bookends to the large dining table—they're as far apart as they can get. The dim lighting and crackling flames in the fireplace behind Murphy add to the uncomfortable ambience of this unusually quiet family dinner.

Murphy swallows and looks down the long expanse of table toward his wife and speaks slowly, almost strained. "Stella. Tell me your thoughts on this…as…a woman."

Stella's forehead wrinkles as she sits up taller in her seat, leaning forward on her elbows and clasping her hands, mimicking Murphy in every sense of the word. "You mean you'd like to hear my opinion as the only other child-bearing person in this room? Since that's all I'm good for?"

Christ, here we go again.

These two fight like fiends all the goddamn time. They're both temperamental as fuck. Anya thinks they both get off on the constant fighting. I think she's probably right.

"That horse is dead, *wife.* Put your damn stick down."

"Then it's a fucking zombie horse, Murphy, because it keeps getting up to rear its ugly fucking head."

"Watch your fucking foul-mouth. I'll wash it out with soap."

Stella tilts her head, a scowl spreading across her cheeks. "Promise?"

Murphy slams his fist on the table and both Anya and I jump but Stella doesn't. I guess she's had a little more time to get used to his temper. Her chest heaves as she takes in a breath and fire burns behind her eyes. It's her temper showing, but there's something else there, too. She feels something for Murphy. I wouldn't have recognized a look like that a year ago—not before I felt the inexplicable, bone-deep connection I found with Anya.

Then something unexpected happens.

Murphy laughs.

I stare at Anya because it's really fucking weird.

"Would you just speak your mind, woman?" he tells Stella.

But Stella's not giving up her fiery rage that easily. Her hands slam against the edge of the table and she pushes back hard, the chair legs squeaking as they scrape against the floor. She stands with ferocity and flips her middle finger with a flippant tilt of her head. "Go fuck yourself, you fucking misogynist pig." She side-steps and storms toward the door.

Murphy's on his feet in a flash, but she's quick, slipping through the exit before he can reach her. Still, he pursues, following her out, and the private dining room door swings shut behind them.

Anya and I look at each other in bewilderment. Then she smiles. "I love that girl."

My grin spreads wide. Anya's smile is like light from a star, burning hot and bright, always heating me and giving me life, even when I can't see it behind the torrential clouds of despair.

She stands and shuffles quickly to the door, standing beside it, leaning toward the frame as if she's straining to hear. She stands still, listening, and I watch her facial expressions shift as she does. She looks back at me, mouthing words I can't make out, but she looks so entertained that it keeps me amused.

I shake my head at her with a grin and she mouths something else, then jumps and rushes back to her seat beside me. She plants her ass in the chair at the exact moment Murphy comes back in through the door. He marches across the room and huffs as he takes his seat. Stella doesn't come back.

Murphy doesn't return to eating, but he looks at Anya pointedly. "I can't let the two of you and Kostya go back to Mikhailov Manor unchaperoned."

Anya perks up. "But you will let us go back? So, I can have my baby there?"

Murphy sighs, but he seems less agitated than before. "You're a lucky girl that I'm trying to win over my wife, who just so happens to think rather highly of you." He slaps his palm down on the table. "She does *not* make decisions on our behalf, let me be fucking clear about that." Anya nods and Murphy continues, "But she made a compelling argument in your favor. We'll leave in two weeks."

"*We?*"

"Stella and I will join you. Frankly, we could use a break from...family pressures. We'll consider it an extended vacation."

"In the middle of the forest?" Anya asks. "In Russia? In January? I'm not sure I'd call that a vacation."

Murphy's jaw ticks, but he maintains his composure. "I'm not explaining myself to you. And you should really think twice about passing judgment when I'm giving you exactly what you want."

Anya casts a furtive glance at me and I see humor in her eyes. "My apologies."

"As I was saying, you can have your baby at home, as you requested. If we leave in two weeks, that will allow you time to get settled in before the birth and give you additional time to prepare to host the quarterly meeting." Anya's due date is only a week before she's supposed to host, with me as her talent. "I think what I'm offering you is more than fair. It's more than I ever would've offered you if Stella didn't give a fuck. Understood?"

Anya glances at me, but I don't even look at her for fear I'll give something away. If our escape goes as planned, we'll be gone after I dance on the night of the quarterly meeting. We won't have to worry about what comes after that. We just need to get to Mikhailov Manor to ensure everything is in place. It's the only place Kostya can help us escape from.

"That's fair, Murphy," Anya tells him. "Thank you for your generosity."

Murphy O'Shea has been fair.

Fair and nearly reasonable in our time here with his family. It would be too easy for Anya and me to settle into our stay here, to become complacent in this new environment where violence has been minimal, and we've been granted the privilege of staying together as master and slave.

I'm a slave to that woman regardless of our place because she owns my heart and soul.

If it weren't for his wife, though, I think things would be different. I've seen how his parents treat the talent slave and obviously, Murphy is the product of their upbringing. But Murphy picked a firecracker of a bride, a woman who he's thankfully head over heels for because he bends to her wishes like a doting husband—even if he fights her every step of the way. Stella is smart, stubborn, and gives a shit about how other people are treated—a fucking lucky combination for us.

Miraculously lucky.

But for us to become content in this nearly safe environment would be stupid. Our fates are yet to be determined, and though the baby has bought us time, there will be another decision coming about Anya and what should be done with her.

We have to escape.

There is no complacent life here.

And our last opportunity is coming.

I'm not exactly thankful to be back at Mikhailov Manor, but I am thankful for this time in the dance studio. Not that I have any fondness for this space on its own. It's just that this studio is the place I first met Anya, the place where I first discovered a passionate hatred for her in her icy coldness, the place where I ultimately fell in love with the truth of her heart and the goodness of her soul.

The once pristinely clean floor now holds the faintest hint of staining that tells the tale of how I dragged Nikolai into this room to die—the brownish-red streaks pull across from the doorway into the center of the room. I didn't want to bring him in here—I wanted to let him die alone in the car at the time—but the human in me felt some tug toward fulfilling a dying man's last reasonable request, even if that dying man was a monster who destroyed our lives.

That was the difference between him and me. We may both have been reckless, impulsive men with flaring tempers, but I still had compassion, and I'd shown him that compassion in his final moments.

I'm struck still as the memory takes hold of me.

Everything changed that day.

Power and alliances had shifted. Anya had been thrust into a role she never wanted, but gratitude was due to Nikolai in some respect—in the fact that he had planned for her to have a future, even if it was without him. It didn't change that he was the fucking devil himself, but it was enough that it makes me feel compelled to spare a moment of reflection before I rehearse in this space where he bled and died.

It's strange, really.

It's strange to feel relief to be back here. After everything that we've been through and everything that's changed, this place is now granting us a small amount of peace. It's a reprieve from the fear and daily torment we suffered at Renata's hands and the uncertainty of continued harmony with the O'Sheas. But it's also comforting to be in a studio to dance again, to prepare a routine for the talent show at the next quarterly meeting, to have something other than overwhelming worry to focus my attention.

We're safe for the moment and a chance for us to escape is on the horizon.

Anya asked to select the music I'm going to perform to for the four families. I can sense some unease with her lately— aside from the constant battery of unease we experience being slaves to these families—and I think it has to do with how oddly the tables have turned.

For three years, she danced as the Mikhailov family's talent. Three different partners, all taken from her, until me. And now, she *is* a Mikhailov, pregnant, unable to dance, and instead, preparing for a dangerous, risky escape from this life that will surely keep us on the run for the rest of our lives.

She puts a song on the speaker, listens for a few counts of eight, then turns it off, scrolling through the playlist again.

"It doesn't have to be perfect," I tell her from where I stand in the center of the dance floor. "The stakes aren't as high as they were before."

She snaps her head around to look at me, the familiar, coldly professional look of our early times together twisting her face into an adorably serious look.

"It should always be perfect," she counters. "I want them to see you like I see you."

I smile, stretching with my fingers linked on top of my head. "Tell me how you see me."

The apples of her cheeks flush a perfect pink as she fights her smile as she looks back to her playlist. "Be quiet. No flirting. They'll hear you." She glances toward the doorway, knowing Murphy is wandering nearby and could pop in at any moment.

"I don't give a shit. Tell me anyway."

She hesitates, bringing her head back around slowly to look at me. "I see you always dancing. Vibrant, strong, *mine.*" She smiles more broadly before turning back to the playlist, finally selecting a song.

I grin. "Yours, baby."

She turns back around and walks toward me as the music she selected begins to play. "Listen to this one. I think it's perfect for you."

I reach my hands out for her as she comes to stand in front of me. She's reluctant, but a quick glance over her shoulder gives her enough comfort to see that Murphy isn't standing in the doorway watching us. She's still so afraid of being caught in the act of intimacy, and I can't blame her for all that has cost us before. But I'm *her* talent slave and she can do what she wants with me. She steps closer to take my hands and immediately, I drag her against me, wrapping my arms around her before she can protest.

I sigh with contentment as soon as I have her safe in my hold. "Do you remember when we danced here together in the moonlight?" I ask, spinning her to face away from me and placing my hands on her hips. I kiss her shoulder softly, chastely.

"Do you think I could ever forget? That night was a precious gift to me. The first time Nikolai had allowed me to keep a partner. That night I was happy, full of hope." Anya sighs.

"Look how far we've come. Look at all we've survived. We're going to survive this, too." I lean in close and whisper into her ear, "We're going to be free again. We'll be free from this life. We'll have our own family." I let my hands roam to rub her baby bump.

She spins in my hold to face me again, holding up her palms. I place mine on hers, remembering the time I told her to do this, to listen to the music and feel her movement, to help her break free from her rigidity and perfection to find her soul's expression through dance. We sway together, walking through a few easy steps that we improvise in the moment. She can't do a whole lot right now, but she can do some, and she's all the more beautiful like this.

The corners of her mouth lift with her cheeks in pure joy, the kind of joy we only ever feel when we're dancing together. "It's our own little *pas de trois.*"

A dance performed by three—me, my blue-eyed girl, and our baby.

"Do you think he'll dance?" Anya asks, rubbing a hand over her belly.

"He'll have to if he wants to keep up with us."

I see Murphy come in behind her and I spin her out of a turn away from me. She sees him and comes to a stop.

"Murphy," she acknowledges him.

"I came to watch. I need a break from my wife." Murphy moves across the room and sits on the piano bench, then looks at us expectedly. "So? Are you going to dance or just stand there?"

Anya turns and gives me a final frustrated smile before moving away, going back to the stereo system behind where Murphy sits to restart the song.

I listen to the music and feel and dance as it tells me to. That's the way I've always created my routines. I've always choreographed them myself. But shit, do I miss dancing with Anya. I kind of hated dancing with partners before the mess of this life forced upon us by Nikolai.

Not that I didn't have great partners, but really, it never felt quite right when I danced with them. I was never able to pinpoint why I felt so off about it before. When I danced with Anya for the first time, I knew why. It was because she was the only partner I was ever meant to dance with. There was never a second when dancing with her felt wrong or unnatural or uncomfortable. We'd clicked from the very first count of eight.

I try a few things, some of them work with the music and some don't. Anya guides me, helps me with my transitions from one move to the next. She's the only person whose ever been able to see my failings and help me correct them. I've never known a dancer quite like Anya; one so spectacular with technique and teaching while also being so beautiful on the floor herself.

I wish I could dance with her now.

We'll dance together again one day.

"That was cool, you're a really good dancer," Stella says as she suddenly appears in the doorway, arms folded. "They force you to dance, don't they? Like their singer?" She nods toward Murphy, referring to the O'Shea family's talent slave.

"Yeah," I reply simply as Murphy shoots to his feet and marches across the room to Stella.

Anya leans back against the mirrored wall behind her, crossing her arms and glancing down and away. She knows better than to get involved in a conversation like this with Murphy and Stella, but it's clear it bothers her to stay out of it.

Stella lets her arms fall to her sides as Murphy approaches her. She looks up at him, raising her eyebrows in challenge and cocking her head to the side. "What? Am I not allowed to talk to people? Ask questions?"

Murphy grabs her elbow, turning her, trying to nudge her out of the room. "I expect you to talk to the *right* people, not to a fucking talent slave. You're my *wife*. You're above him."

Stella jerks her arm away from his grip. "I might as well be a slave. You don't let me leave. I get scolded for talking to anyone or asking questions. You leave me alone half the time and won't tell me what you're off doing."

I lock my fingers together on top of my head and spin away, pacing the floor while I wait for Murphy to blow. When I turn back around, I see Murphy grab her chin, yanking her head up to look at him.

My hands smack against my sides and I stomp toward them. Anya pushes off the mirror and shuffles in front of my path, holding up a hand to catch me on the chest before I haul off and knock Murphy on his ass for manhandling his woman like that. Anya gives me an admonishing look before whipping around to face them.

"Murphy," Anya pulls her shoulders back and puts on the Queen Mikhailov voice she's adopted to cope with her current position, "you're in my home and I ask that you find a way to use your words to convey your intent with your wife rather than your hands."

She's so fucking perfect.

I couldn't be more proud of her, though I know Murphy frightens her.

His shoulders stiffen and he stretches his neck from side to side before slowly loosening his grip on Stella's jaw, letting his hand slip down her shoulder, her arm, before releasing her all together. He slowly turns and faces Anya behind him. "Apologies, lass. She tests my patience."

"Something for you to work on, then? I don't imagine your wife desires to be treated like a slave."

Murphy smirks and something strange slips in Stella's expression. "She might," Murphy muses. "We'll let you two get back to it." Murphy spins to face Stella, twirling his finger. She spins to leave and he slaps her butt, making her jump before ushering her out of the dance studio.

What a fucking pair.

A moment later, Kostya appears and there's a long, still moment where we all just look at each other. Then Anya moves, jerking her head to indicate she wants us to follow her, and we do, to the stereo in the corner.

"Are you still in this with us, Kostya?" she asks him in a hushed tone. "The quarterly meeting is right around the corner. I need to…*We* need to know. Do we really have a chance of escaping?"

Kostya glances behind him. "Yes, but it is risky."

Anya shrugs her shoulders. "It's riskier not to try. I can't risk my baby being raised as one of them, with or without me."

Kostya nods. "I know. I understand. I have a plan."

"You really think it will work?" I ask.

"No choice. It must work," Kostya says.

I reach out to grip his arm, making sure he has my attention. "Hey, your ass will be on the line if this fails. Are you sure about this?" I realize after I've said it that I'm giving him an out. I don't want to give him an out. We need him to make this work.

His eyes meet mine. "Yes. I made promise to Nikolai," he assures me in his broken English and thick Russian accent. "If you stay, they will kill her eventually. I hear things you don't. I owe Nikolai for our friendship."

Anya is a blur, lurching forward and throwing her arms around him. "Thank you. Thank you, thank you."

A tiny smile appears on Kostya's face, but it disappears just as quickly. He gently unwraps her and pushes her back. "There is a camera in here. This will look suspicious. I just came to tell you I have plan. We must leave after you dance, before the board meeting." He nods at me. "It is the only time we can leave without being followed."

Anya looks at me, then back to Kostya. "Then that's when we'll do it."

"You will have baby by then?" Kostya asks glancing at her ever-growing belly.

"I should. He's due the week before." Her eyes widen as she considers something. "Will they let me hold my baby while I'm hosting? Oh, God. Why didn't I think of that before? They wouldn't make me give him to someone else, would they? I couldn't. I won't. What if they want Renata or Cordelia to watch him?"

I press my palm to the small of her back as she rises to a panic.

"No worry," Kostya says in a hurry. His eyebrows furrow with concern and it's directed at her as he steps forward to touch her elbow softly. "They will let you keep him. Mother is important first year…they all know this. After that is what I worry about."

"What if he can't stay quiet when we try to leave?"

"It will be okay. It won't matter once we are off manor grounds."

She nods, his assurance seeming to calm her. Anya has come to trust Kostya, someone I never in a million years would've thought could be on our side. If Anya trusts him, then so do I. It's not like we have much choice.

Kostya quickly tells us his plan and then excuses himself, worried about what this looks like on the security cameras, though we don't really know if Murphy is keeping a watch on those. Regardless, it's not worth the risk of looking suspicious.

With a plan in motion, the only thing left for us to do is prepare for the performance. Everything must look as it normally would. I have to dance as I would if I were dancing for my life—the way that Anya had danced for Nikolai all these years. She'll never have to again, because she has me now and her turn to dance for them is over. Now it's my turn, and I will readily take that burden from her, now and forever more.

I'll dance for her.

I'll dance for the baby.

I'll dance for our future so that today's *pas de trois* with my girl and our boy won't be the last.

CHAPTER 22
Anya

It's happening tonight.

Oh, God.

It's happening tonight.

The escape plan is simple, and I can't help but worry that it almost seems too simple to work.

Our plan is to sneak out of Nobility Hall after Ezra's performance as my talent slave, just after the four families have moved back over to the grand entrance of Mikhailov Manor through the connected hallway. The reception will start without us, as it usually does—that's always been the case with Heads of House and their talent slaves after a performance. The guests will socialize, drink, and eat and generally be too distracted to notice when too much time has passed beyond our reasonably late arrival.

We will already have met Kostya just outside Nobility Hall where he has a car waiting for us. We'll already be driving off the manor grounds, heading for the helipad. And if we're truly lucky, we'll be on the helicopter with the pilot that Kostya has paid handsomely to arrive at the pre-arranged time before the four families realize we've gone.

The helicopter will take us all to the nearest public airport and then we'll part ways with Kostya. We've all decided it's best that neither of us know the other's plans from there.

Ezra and I have cash, fake passports for the both of us and for the baby, and a credit card in Kostya's name. It will be traceable, but it's the only option we have—we can't book a flight without it. Our only hope is that we'll gain enough lead time on the four families to fly back to the States, maybe bribe someone into using their credit card to rent us a car in exchange for cash, and drive until we can't drive anymore.

A simple plan, but still so much room for error and complications. There has been one unforeseen complication that has us all on edge because nature is unforgivably unpredictable.

I'm still pregnant.

It's a full week past my due date—and I'm in denial. I deny the true nature of the cramps that started early this morning. I deny that they've been coming more frequently, increasing in their intensity, and quickly reaching a point where I can no longer ignore them.

Somehow, I've managed to greet my guests and welcome them. And now I sit in Nobility Hall waiting for Ezra's performance to begin.

Nikolai has cursed me.

I can't think differently when my labor comes a week past due and on the very night we've planned our escape.

Why is this happening now?

Maybe his secrets have cursed this seat, too.

Nikolai always sat right here during my annual performances—the same seat every damn time while I was his talent slave. I always thought it was strange for him to be so fond of this particular spot as it wasn't even the best seat in the house, though I'd never given it much thought before.

But it all made sense the night he died. He'd kept a box of

secrets beneath this very seat, a box of secrets that brought me to be sitting here now as the woman who was not just his slave, but his unknowing wife.

Even though he's been dead and gone for months, I can still feel his presence here now. If there were such things as ghosts and Nikolai were one now, I believe he would haunt this place. There's an undeniable thickness in the air tonight and it's oppressive, overwhelming—just the way his living presence had been.

The four families have settled into their seats and it's time to begin. It's not just time to begin the performance, but time to begin our mental preparation for our risky escape from this life.

I wring my sweaty palms together, then place them on my huge belly as Ezra's music begins in Nobility Hall. My stomach feels stretched and tight and it makes me horribly uncomfortable to sit here.

I force my focus to Ezra as he comes out onto the stage, strong and masculine and the perfect specimen of a true performer. I could sit and watch him dance all day, every day, which I intend to make happen in our new reality.

This escape will work.

It has to.

Ezra's costume isn't really a costume at all. He's shirtless, which I'm not ashamed to admit is because of my encouragement, and he's wearing a pair of simple, black slacks that fit him loosely, like jogging pants.

Watching him perform feels like nothing short of a miracle. Ezra is power and grace, strength and agility, a mighty force that's perfectly balanced. My hand finds my heart as he dances, and I feel how it beats wildly beneath my palm. It beats for *him*, the same way he tells me his heart beats for me.

Shit.

Another one already.

I can't ignore the pain that creeps in from the lowest part of my stomach, radiating out across my taut skin, a pain that feels like stretching, pulling, kneading, punching. A muffled groan escapes me when it goes on for...

One. Two. Three. Four. Five. Six. Seven. Eight.

Seven full counts of eight.

No.

That contraction was longer and it came sooner than the last two. It was immeasurably more painful, and I don't know how no one around me seems to notice what's happening to me.

This can't be happening.

Not now, not now, not now!

I gasp for air when the pain recedes and grants me a break from the relentless ache and suddenly, Ezra's performance is over.

I didn't even see it because the pain was too great for me to focus. There's a standing ovation for him and I realize I'm the only one still sitting. I'm sure anyone could argue that it's because I'm so massively pregnant, but the last thing I want to do right now is draw attention to myself. Pushing through my hands on the armrests, I get to my feet and I feel a sudden trickle of fluid flow down the inside of my thigh.

What is that?

Am I bleeding?

What the fuck is happening?

Before the fluid reaches my knee, I side-step out of my end seat onto the red carpeted aisle, hoping that if I'm dripping blood—or whatever the hell this is—it will blend with the carpet and I can hide it with my long gown. I can't risk having the O'Sheas step in it and slip on the hardwood floor beneath the seats as they step out of the row after me.

No one can know.

No one can know what's happening right now.

I just have to wait for them all to leave, just like Nikolai always did to protect his secrets.

Everything will be okay.

One. Two. Three. Four. Five. Six. Seven. Eight.

I count as the four families move toward the exit. I hold my head up high, breathe intently through my nose, keep the coldly indifferent expression on my face, though inside I'm screaming and begging for help.

Only Ezra can help me.

Just wait.

Someone touches my elbow and I flinch, turning sideways as Renata moves to stand in front of me. "I look forward to catching up with you at the reception," she says coldly, dark shadows beneath her eyes and a sneer across her lips. She glances down at my stomach. "Olivia had her baby early…last week. Why do you think yours hasn't found his way out yet?"

Because I'm fucking cursed.

I force a condescending smile. "He'll come when he's ready. I don't think you and I need to do any catching up. I don't particularly care how your life has been since we saw each other last." My voice goes up on the last word as pain grips me again. I have to end this conversation quickly. "If you don't mind, I need some time alone with my talent slave. You can head back to the grand entrance with the others. Please, enjoy the reception."

"Don't think that you and Ezra have gotten away from me just because Murphy took pity on you. Your baby is one of us now, and I intend to make certain that's how he's raised."

I swallow hard as my face contorts in pain, though I mask it as barely controlled anger. It seems to work as she gives me a vile grin, satisfied that she thinks she's upset me. I let out a long breath when she finally turns and walks away, marching back up the aisle like she owns the goddamn place.

She can fucking have it.

As she walks away, my hand falls to my stomach as the contraction takes over and grips me entirely. I glance up to Ezra, who is still standing center stage, his chest heaving with his fists clenched at his sides. He's eager to get to me, but he has to wait until she's gone, too.

Somehow, I manage to hold on, to keep my posture, my expression, my composure, as an invisible boulder crushes my stomach. When the final person clears from the house, I reach down with one hand to grip the back of the chair in front of me, folding forward, breathing, and counting through the end of this god-awful fucking contraction. I hear Ezra's footsteps jogging after me as he rushes down from the stage and he sprints down a row of chairs to get to me.

"Shit," he says, "it can't be happening now."

"It is." Nearly a full minute goes by before the pain flows to a gradual stop and I'm able to stand upright. My fingers scramble to gather my layered tulle skirt, clawing it upward to peek beneath—it's the same blush-colored gown with long lacey sleeves that I wore to the O'Sheas' last quarter. "Something's happening. I'm leaking."

"Is it…Did your water break?"

"I don't know. I think it must have." Whatever is leaking from me is clear and I don't know what else it would be. It just keeps flowing in a continuous trickle down my legs.

"Okay." I sense the fear in Ezra's voice, and it makes me scared, too. "This is it, Anya. We have to go. Now. This is our only chance. All you have to do is get changed and get in the car, okay? Can you do that?"

"Yes," I rush out. "Yes, of course I can. I *will*. We have to leave tonight. There won't be another opportunity. I'll wait here. Go get the backpack."

Ezra takes off, jogging up the side steps onto the stage, then disappears behind the curtain. I wait, breathing through the pain, my eyes hyper-focused on the seat of Nikolai's chair beside me.

I'm cursed.

He's cursed me.

Will I ever be able to escape him?

Tears pool in the corners of my eyes as I wait.

All I can do is wait.

Wait for Ezra to return.

Wait for the next contraction.

Wait for success or failure.

Wait for life or death.

I'm terrified. There's no better word for it. It's all happening so fast and I have no control over any of it.

Ezra comes rushing back with a black backpack slung over one shoulder. We've packed our essentials in that single black bag—clothes to change into, cash and Kostya's credit card, our fake passports, some diapers and basics for the baby... just enough to get us through the airport.

That's all we're leaving with—that and hope.

"Hey." Ezra bends and meets my eyes, surely sensing my fear. "We're gonna make it, baby. We can do this together. I've got you."

I hold him there with my eyes for moments longer than we have to spare. But I need this—I need him connected with me. I need the power he always feeds me with his brilliant green gaze.

His cheeks lift as his signature disarming grin appears. "We've got this," he says.

With that and a deep, steadying breath, I find my courage.

I nod and rise from my bent position. "Okay. Just leave my change of clothes in the bag," I tell him, "I might have to…The baby might come and I'll just have to take my jeans off again. The dress is easier."

His eyebrows slant toward his nose, erasing his smile as he pulls his clothes from the backpack. "Okay. Yeah, but I need you to put your sneakers on, okay?"

He helps me into my shoes, throwing on a T-shirt for himself and shoes of his own. We didn't have enough room in the bag for winter jackets to fight the bitter January cold, but it doesn't matter. We won't be outside long.

Ezra slings the backpack over one shoulder and takes my arm, guiding me up the red-carpeted aisleway. As I look ahead, to the doors leading out into the foyer, the truth hits me square in the chest.

We're leaving.

We're escaping.

This is really happening.

I'll never have to see this stage and all the horrific ghosts of my past partners again.

At the top of the aisle, Ezra tells me to wait while he pulls open the door to peek into the foyer for Kostya and the all-clear. I turn back for a moment, for one last look at the stage that was built for me, at the place where I danced for Nikolai. I feel the tug of something, a sharp yank on my heartstrings that draws my attention back to Nikolai's seat. When my eyes fall upon that spot, my heart drops into my stomach. I swear I can feel him there—Nikolai.

Cursed.

I want my last look upon this place to be a goodbye and a good riddance, but I still hold that faint sense of gratitude that Nikolai arranged for our legal marriage. Ultimately, it saved me and Ezra and somehow, it led us to this moment where we're finally able to attempt freedom with hope for a future.

"Goodbye, Nikolai," I murmur into the empty space.

I don't feel lighter or heavier for saying farewell to the vacant theater.

Suddenly, there's a crash and then the sound of a door slamming shut coming from the foyer. The sound makes me jump and immediately, I move, rushing after Ezra. If we're caught before we can escape I…I don't know what will happen to us.

I push through the door to the foyer and see Ezra in a defensive position to my left. I look to my right and see Stella, standing with her back to the interior door that leads back to the grand entrance of the manor—the door where all the guests filtered through to avoid going out into the bitter cold.

Stella?

Her eyes are wide and worried. "Where's Kostya?" she asks. "He's coming. Murphy's coming."

At that exact moment, Kostya opens the exterior door from the outside and all of us startle. He looks at Stella and I see the immediate sense of urgency wash over his features.

"Go," Stella says to Kostya. "I can stall him. But you have to hustle." Then, she looks at me and Ezra. "Get the fuck going!"

It hits me hard in the chest when I realize that Stella's helping us. She's putting herself on the line for us to help us escape. I don't know what Murphy will do or how he'll react when he finds out, and he *will* find out. Even when we're long gone, if she stalls him now, gives him the attention he wants from her, he'll make the connection later that she did that to help us.

I want to tell her to think twice. I want to make her understand that she can't put herself in that position. But more pain is sneaking in and I can't. I can't help her. I have to save my baby from this world.

"Come," Kostya says, pushing the exterior door open and motioning for us to follow. "Hurry."

We don't hesitate, we *move*.

The cold spreads around us as we step out into the night, cloaking us in a bitter chill that I somehow find comforting.

Coldness has saved me before, kept me alive, if only in the metaphorical sense. Freezing my heart, shielding it in a thick layer of ice has always given me the power to get through my worst moments, and now is no different. I let the real coldness that swirls around me seep in through my pores and strengthen the icy fortress of my soul to get me through the moments to come.

We use the darkness to hide us as we sweep around the corner of the manor outside to the car Kostya has parked nearby. He opens the back door of the sedan, waving us forward. "Lay down. Cover with the blanket."

Ezra steps forward. "I'll get on the floor. You lay across the seat. It's just until we get past the gate."

"We have to hurry," Kostya urges.

I nod at Ezra and climb in, practically falling across the bench seat, barely able to hold myself upright as that pain that was creeping in before punches low in my stomach. Ezra gets in after me, squeezing himself in on the floorboards. It's a tight fit for him, but he manages.

I moan as the full force of this contraction swells and spreads. My fists clench as I curl up on my left side, facing the front of the car. My eyes pinch shut and nothing exists but pain, pain, *pain*. I push out heavy, long breaths as Ezra reaches up to grab one of my clenched fists and I'm only vaguely aware of his attempt to comfort me.

The agony peaks as Kostya shifts above us, laying a large, black blanket over our bodies to conceal us. Ezra tugs at it, making sure we're sufficiently covered. If a guard wanted to look in the back seat, they would only need to turn a flashlight on us to know there are stowaways here.

But the only thing I can worry about is the pain.

I want to scream.

And I nearly do.

I gasp for breath as it ebbs and Kostya slams our door shut before he climbs into the driver's seat and starts the engine.

"Hang on, baby," Ezra whispers and I want to cry. I wish I could see his face in the dark beneath this blanket. I need to see him. "Hang on just a little longer."

Tears slip from the corner of my eye and I clamp my mouth shut to hide the sob that hiccups from my chest. The car moves forward and I'm scared. I'm scared for our escape and that it will be foiled before we've even had a chance. But more urgently, I'm scared of this pain. I'm scared of how much it hurts and how much more I know it will hurt before the end. I've endured horrifying things as a slave, but this is a fear I never could've prepared my mind to endure. I'm in pain like I've never been in pain before and it's all I can think about.

Time passes and it feels slow, though I know it's only been half a minute or so. We must be approaching the gate about now, but the car isn't slowing. Kostya is speeding up.

He speaks loud enough for us to hear him clearly. "No guard at the gate. It's open." He sounds as cautiously excited as that makes me feel. "It's clear."

It's clear?

No guard?

Why isn't there a guard at the gate?

My mind starts to question it, but my body shuts down my conscious thinking, forcing me to focus on the agony that's taking over. I start shaking, trembling out of control, and I can't stop it.

I feel the car turn. "We're out," Kostya says, and I hear the surprise in his tone. "We're on the road."

We're on the road.

We made it out.

We made it out?

No security stop?

Gate open?

Once I've finally caught my breath from the last contraction, another clutches me in devastating misery.

"No, no, no," I pant as it tightens and pulls and stretches across my belly, wrapping around my midsection and throbbing. It's like being crushed in a vice.

I can't speak through it.

I can't think through it.

The car speeds forward down the road, but our escape plan is lost to me now.

I don't exist.

My conscious thought disintegrates to the torture my body suffers.

Nothing exists now except for pain.

CHAPTER 23
Ezra

WE'VE BEEN ON the road toward the helipad for over twenty minutes and Anya is in agony. Despite the fact that we never expected her to be pregnant for this, let alone in labor, there's a feeling in my gut that I can't ignore—a nagging feeling that everything is wrong.

Fucking wrong.

Anya is trembling out of control and having what seems like contraction after contraction. I feel helpless and I can only imagine how much she's suffering. It makes me sick to my stomach.

We're sitting side by side on the bench seat with seatbelts on because the dirt path cutting through the woods is ice-covered—we've hit a few slick spots along the way, one that spun the car nearly all the way around. Anya's in the middle seat beside me, leaning sideways against me for support as she struggles through her pain.

It was easy getting through the gate at Mikhailov Manor. *Too easy.*

There's a cadence of worry that's been continually running through my mind since we passed through and drove away from the manor grounds.

Too easy.

Though there's still the light of hope inside me, I can feel it slowly fade. It scares me because I can't make sense of this feeling, this unease. It's a heavy sense of foreboding weighing on my shoulders and I just can't seem to shake it.

Kostya follows a curve that opens into a straightaway. The car goes up an incline. Kostya reduces his speed as we crest over the peak of the hill, then lets the car roll down the long, gradual decline. I feel gravity tugging me forward in my seat and my grip around Anya's shoulders tightens.

I glance over at her to see her face contorted in absolute agony, her chin dropping toward her chest as she grits her teeth through another shattering contraction. A hiss and a moan escape her and morph into a piercing scream through the last seconds of her recurrent torture.

She gasps for a breath and I can see the sweat on her brow. "Hurry...*please*," she begs.

She *begs*, but there's nothing I can do. There's not a goddamn thing I can do for my blue-eyed girl.

The back tires screech as they catch and skid over ice, tugging the car toward the right. I tense, holding Anya tighter, probably only hurting her more, but I'm terrified to let go of her. I don't want her flung across the car. Kostya's able to correct and ease the car straight again and we continue down the never-ending decline.

Our path is lined with trees—rows and rows of them creating the dense forest surrounding us. The tree line begins only yards away from the car on either side. I look out of the window on my left and it's like looking out to see dark soldiers in the night, threatening to bring war upon us if we venture from our designated path.

The thick trunks are black in the night and they threaten

to catch us, stop us dead in our tracks every time the car skids—and every time I'm certain we'll skid off the road and take a beating by one of the monstrous soldier trees. I turn to look at Anya on my right and I see that she's also looking out at them, at the rapidly falling snow that's intent on smothering us from above.

I catch her gaze and even in the dark, her blue eyes are bewitching.

Tell her you love her.

Tell her now.

Tell her fast.

The voice inside me is insistent and urgent, and the instinctual tug of it makes my heart drop into my stomach. I open my mouth to speak, but then Kostya shouts something in Russian, something urgent.

Anya's head snaps forward and her forehead wrinkles in confusion. "Spike strip?"

My chest feels hollow, my heart burning in acid where its sunk deep in my gut. This is it. That feeling that it's too easy, that everything is wrong. It's all going to hell and it's happening right fucking now.

It's unavoidable.

We feel the bump when the front tires roll over something in the road.

Spike strip?

There's a loud blast, quickly followed by another—the car teeters down in the front, then in the back, rocking us as the tires blow. We fishtail.

A fucking spike strip.

"Fuck!" I pull Anya hard into my side with one arm, my other grasping the handle at the ceiling.

We hit a patch of ice after the tire blowout and we spin.

My body falls against Anya's, but I try to pull myself away with the handle, tugging her with me as the inertia threatens to throw her to the other side of the car. Her middle seat belt doesn't have a chest strap—only fitting across her lap under her belly—and I have instant regret for telling her to sit there where I could comfort her.

"Ezra!" she screams.

The blown-out tires snag on the edge of the road and the whole goddamn world shifts. Everything happens slowly and quickly all at once, and *fuck,* I think this might be the end of everything.

The car tilts.

It lifts.

It rolls.

It lands upside down and slides toward the dark warrior trees. One of their massive trunks is heading right for us—I can see it through the window on the opposite side of the car…like it's coming after Anya.

It slams into us, metal crumbling and crushing and closing in around us.

A sudden stop.

My head slams sideways against the doorframe.

And everything goes black.

I hear my name, but it's faraway.

A frantic voice is calling to me, but I'm struggling to wake from this darkness. I blink, hoping my eyes will open. It takes a few times, but when they finally do, I'm torn from this strange, dark slumber of nothingness. The voice is still calling to me, but my ears are ringing and it's not clear. I shake my head and though the ringing starts to fade, the movement makes me feel like I'm fucking falling.

I'm still in the car.

There was an accident.

Shit. Anya.

"Ezra! Ezra, *please!*" she says as I turn my head to look at her.

The world looks strange. Her hair stands up straight above her head and it takes me a minute to work out why. It's hard to make sense of things with the way my head throbs.

"We're…are we upside down?" I ask.

"Ezra," she cries. "Help me. I…I think the baby's coming…I feel like I need to push. Help me get out!"

She sounds frantic, unhinged, and desperate.

That wakes me right the fuck up.

My vision is fuzzy, but I act without thinking, ignoring how off-centered I feel. I fumble to find the latch of my belt buckle, but when my fingers find the button, I push and unhook myself without thought. I fall from my seat to the roof of the car and flinch from my landing. Thank God it didn't crush us when it rolled—a fucking miracle. Still, the space I have to work with is tight.

I maneuver myself around and realize right away that there's only one way out of the backseat. Anya's side of the car is curved around the trunk of a tree. The massive base is only a foot or so away from her and the sight of it spikes my adrenaline.

I've gotta get her out.

We have to go out the opposite side, through the door I sat beside. The window is blown out, and I know I can squeeze her out through it if I have to, though I'm hoping to God that the door will open. But first, I have to get her down.

"I've got you," I tell her, reaching up for the seat belt that comes across her lap.

I push the bright red button to unlatch it and she falls. I cradle her upper back and stretch out beneath her to guide her down, trying to ease her fall.

"Ahh," she whimpers, "mmm. I…need to push." I see the strain stretch her features as her body takes control of her.

She's pushing.

She's having the fucking baby.

"Fuck!"

I have to get her out of this car.

I shift her off me, turn, and crawl, reaching for the door latch. I lift it and push on the door, but it doesn't budge. "Shit." I find the lock mechanism and lift it up, praying there isn't some fucking child lock engaged, too. I lift the latch again and shove. It budges. I shove again, then again, and finally, the door slides open. "Thank fuck. Hang on, baby," I tell Anya, but she has no awareness of me or what I'm doing.

I crawl out through the small opening I've managed to create and scramble to my feet. I grab the outside edge of the door and pull back hard, dragging it open as far as it will go. I have to force it as it digs into the ground, hauling snow with it as it drags. I drop to my hands and knees and crawl back in just as Anya's head drops back and she screams.

"He's coming! Hurry, Ezra."

I have enough adrenaline rushing through me to flip the fucking car back over if I have to. I slip my arms beneath her back, grip her by the armpits, and fucking pull. I hear movement from the front of the car as I tug her out—Kostya groaning, the click of his buckle, and the rustle of him shifting from his seat. But I don't have time to worry about him.

Anya's backside runs over broken glass in the snow as I tug her free and I'm kicking myself for not brushing it out of the way first. Her soft pink gown snags on it, some of the tulle tearing away. As I pull her free, I see the left behind patches of fabric stuck to rough edges of the broken window in the snow. I move her to a small clearing between the overturned car and the dirt path we traveled, gently laying her on the fresh blanket of snow that covers the ground.

"Can…can you walk?" I ask, kneeling beside her. Unease rolls a wave of nausea through my stomach at the eerie silence of the forest around us. "We have to meet that helicopter, baby. We're *so* close."

She shakes her head furiously, sweat coating her forehead, though the temperature outside is below freezing. "No…no…I have to—" She presses up onto her elbows, bends her knees, and parts her legs. Her face strains and she drops her chin toward her chest as she squeezes her eyes shut.

She's pushing.

She's pushing and I'm…I'm frozen.

How does she even know what to do?

I'm literally shocked into stillness because I can't wrap my head around what the fuck is happening right now. She throws her head back and screams before gasping for a deep breath. She turns her head to look at me, just for a moment. Her eyes catch mine and she unknowingly feeds me her instinct, her strength, the depth of her courage. Suddenly, I know exactly what I need to do.

I dash back to the car and reach inside, pulling out the large black blanket we hid under to get past the gate. I rush back to Anya as I fold it in half, dropping to my knees at her feet. I wedge it between her legs and lay it on the ground, scooting in close and grasping the hem of her torn and tattered gown. I pull it up over her knees and tear her underwear down her legs, pulling them off and tossing them aside. That's when I get my first view of the nightmare that's happening to my blue-eyed girl.

I can see him.

I can see the baby's head.

How the fuck is she doing this?

"Oh, shit. Okay. Anya, I see his head. There's only one way out of this, baby, and you've just got to push, okay?"

"You can see him?" she pants.

I nod. "Yeah, he's…he's right there."

I watch as her face pinches tight and she groans with another contraction. She takes a deep breath and bears down with all her might.

She pushes for beat after beat, and then she *screams.*

It shakes through the trees and echoes in the dark forest and it completely stops my heart. There's nothing except for her scream and the darkness and the trees and the deafening silence. Large snowflakes drift to the ground all around us. The long beats of silence after her piercing scream reminds me just how alone we truly are. Kostya hasn't made an appearance and we're all alone in this now. All she has is me and all I have is her and the horror of this moment. We're stranded in this forest as she brings life into the world.

She takes another breath and pushes again, her strength and endurance bewildering. I beg my mind to switch away from the horror, to let adrenaline and instinct take over and help me help her—but fuck, this horror is so *real.* The baby's head is moving gradually, little by little, forcing his way out until she stops pushing to take another breath.

"Come on." I try to encourage her. "Come on, Anya. Don't stop. Push. It's almost done, he's coming."

Another breath.

Another push.

Then again.

And again.

His head slips out from the opening and I have no fucking clue how this is physically possible.

"Holy shit. Shit," I mutter, reaching for him, carefully wrapping my hands around his tiny head. "He's almost out. *Push.*"

I tug lightly and somehow, his shoulders slide free as Anya bears down one last time. With a final agony-filled scream, she's done what seems like the impossible. He's out. Her baby. Maybe *my* baby. Definitely *our* baby.

Beats pass in silence.

Silence, deafening stillness as Anya and I both hold our breath. But then a cry from our baby's quivering lips bursts into the night and I feel…I feel…fucking *everything*.

"Blanket," Anya pants out. "Cover him."

I set him down on the blanket between her legs and start to wrap him in it, shielding him from the frigid cold surrounding us. I lift him, wanting to show Anya, but the white snow that was hidden by the blanket instantly turns crimson. Blood rushes out of her, spilling fast and dark.

I look up at her just as her elbows slip out from beneath her and she falls onto her back, her knees slumping to the side as she instantly slips from consciousness.

"No!" I shout, shuffling to her side on my knees, still holding the baby in my arms. "Anya…"

She's still, silent, and I don't know what to do. The adrenaline in my veins spike again, but the frequent ebb and flow is draining me, making the chemical rush useless other than to agitate and cloud my senses.

I wait.

I watch.

I hope for something to happen.

Then she blinks and I gasp with relief.

Her eyes flutter and her head rolls lazily to the side, turning toward me. Her voice is unnervingly quiet. "I…I think something's…wrong." Her eyes roll back before jolting back into focus, but the focus is only there for a few moments at a time as she fights a terrifying sleep that threatens to steal her from me.

"Anya," my voice trembles, "you can't do this now. We're almost there. We've almost made it."

My breath catches in my lungs and my eyes threaten to shed tears that have no business being shed—we're *almost* there.

We were almost there.

"It's close," Anya whispers. She shuts her eyes and blinks out a lonely teardrop that rolls slowly down her cheek. She looks at me with a fierce determination when she opens her blue eyes again. "It's only another mile, maybe two," she gasps. "Cut the cord. Take him. And run."

Cut the cord.

Take him.

And run.

Take him and run.

"No, baby, no. I'm not leaving you here."

"I think you have to. Please. Go. If they catch you…they'll take him. They'll take him and…kill you…and they'll raise him as their own. Don't give them that. Don't let our baby have that fate. Please. *Go.* I can't go with you."

"You can't go with me? You have to. Anya, you *have* to." Agitation reaches my tone. "We're so *close,* so goddamn close!"

"I'm…losing a lot of blood, Ezra. Don't waste time."

"Baby, no, don't say that." My eyes are pulled away, trailing down her gown as I see the crimson life force pour from her, staining her gown, tainting it with gore, soaking the fabric, and spreading endlessly.

I meet her eyes again and her forehead wrinkles as her

brow furrows. "I love you, Ezra. You did everything you could."

My face scrunches in anger and my heart thumps wildly. "Don't fucking tell me goodbye!"

She smiles at me, though I scream at her. "Mine?"

I shake my head furiously, emotion building pressure behind my eyes. "No. Don't."

Her eyes beg me. "Please..."

How can I deny her?

My head drops and I look at the tiny baby boy in my arms. Only his face is visible peeking out through the blanket, his skin streaked with blood. His screaming has slowed to squeaks and brief shouts of protest against the cold. Just as I look at him, he starts to blink his eyes open. I wish I could see the color of them, but we only have the residual lighting from the headlights of the overturned car and the bit of moonlight shining from up above. Still, it's as though I can see his entire life there in his tiny baby eyes.

Anya is bleeding.

She's not okay.

She can't run with me and I can't carry her.

Fuck. I can't carry her.

Overwhelming sadness shakes me from deep within my chest and I sob. I sob over Anya as she fades away from me.

"Yours," I choke out the word. "Always."

She gives me a sad smile and her tears fall with mine. "No regrets, Ezra."

I lose myself.

Bending over her, with the baby in my arms, I cry. I cry like I've never cried before.

I cry until Anya is quiet.

Until I feel the essence of her fade.

Until she shuts her eyes and turns her head away.

Until she's still.

A disturbing silence wraps around me like a snake, gripping me in its hold. The snow continues to fall in large, soft flakes that drift leisurely to the ground and it's calm, quiet…as if the whole world has stopped.

Because it has.

But then I hear it…the helicopter nearing.

There's a snap inside my chest, right over my heart, and it shocks me into action. I can't save Anya, but I can save her baby. *Our* baby. I can still end this. I can still come back and seek retribution against the four families for what they've done to us.

I set the baby on the ground beside Anya and run to the driver's side door of the car. Kostya is lying awkwardly on the roof, unmoving. I don't know whether he's dead or alive, but there's no time for me to wonder. I feel a stab of regret in my gut that I might be leaving him to die, knowing I'll never get the chance to thank him.

I reach around him to the center console where I remember seeing him put his gun, a knife, and a stun gun. I pop it open and the items I'm searching for fall out onto the roof beside Kostya. I grab the knife.

The sound of the helicopter is drawing nearer. I spot the black backpack we brought with cash and Kostya's credit card lodged in the passenger seat. I stretch, reaching farther across the console as the baby starts to cry, his protests echoing loudly into the night. I grab the strap of the bag and yank until it falls free.

I take the backpack and the knife and hurry back to Anya's side. I swallow hard, steeling myself before I use the knife to slice into the thick umbilical cord. I cut the tether and it's like slicing through my own fucking soul and leaving half of it behind.

I don't want to look at her.

I'm afraid that if I look it her, I won't be able to leave. I'll stay here and wait to be found and killed. They'll take the baby and he'll become the future Mikhailov Head of House.

I can't let that happen.

I toss the knife inside the backpack, sling it snugly over both shoulders, and slip my hands beneath the baby, repositioning the blanket to ensure he's covered well and protected from the cold.

I start to push to my feet, but I feel rooted to the spot.

How can I leave her?

How can I leave my blue-eyed girl behind?

She's asleep, unconscious…no awareness of whether I'm here or gone. Blood continues to spread across her gown, a slowly creeping darkness telling the tragedy of the life she was forced to live, reminding me that I'm powerless to help her. But I don't know if I can pull hard enough, fast enough, to yank myself free of the hold she has on me. My breath hitches and I let myself sob, let myself have one last look at her.

My blue-eyed girl.

I bend over her, pressing a kiss to her lips that are somehow still soft and warm.

They did this to her.

They did this to us.

There is no more time to waste and I won't fail her—I'll escape and I'll save our baby. I won't let them take him, too.

I cradle him in my arms and head toward the road. I look back the way we came as the clouds part and moonlight glints off the metal. I strain my eyes to see. There really was a spike strip laid across the dirt road, at the bottom of the long decline.

It was put there intentionally.

It's why there was no guard at the gate.

They knew this would foil any escape attempt.

Well, fuck them.

I can't take my girl with me, but her baby and I…we're getting the fuck out of here. Anger bolsters my intent, punches another rush of adrenaline, and fuels my determination.

I turn.

I take a deep breath.

And I run.

CHAPTER 24
Anya

One. Two. Three. Four. Five. Six. Seven. Eight.

One…Two…Three…Four…Five…Six…Seven…Eight.

One.

Two.

Three.

Four.

Five.

Six.

Seven.

Eight.

"Not now." I hear Kostya's frantic voice say to me in Russian. "You were almost there."

My chest hurts. Rhythmic pain pulses over and over on my ribcage. An engine rumbles in the distance, the sound drawing nearer and nearer.

"I promised him," Kostya utters in his native language. "I promised I would keep your heart beating. Come on, Anya!"

I want to scream at him to stop whatever it is he's doing to me because it hurts. Everything hurts. I've never been in this much pain. But I can't open my mouth to scream at him.

Suddenly, the pounding on my chest stops. The sound of the engine peaks in volume and then shuts off. Kostya's voice grows more distant and he begins to speak in English. "Murphy, I'm sorry. I did not—"

"Save it," Murphy says with an edge to his voice. "I'm not the one who put that fucking spike strip across the road."

"Please, don't—"

"My wife told me everything, Kostya. I know every detail of your involvement in this attempted escape."

"Then kill us now," Kostya says and I wish I could shout at him to stop talking. "Kill us before they come for us."

"She's alive?" It's Stella's voice this time, and when she speaks again, her voice is closer, as if she's right beside me. "Oh, my God. Murphy. Please. We have to help her."

"You've already gotten me into enough fucking trouble with your involvement, Stella. And where the fuck is Ezra?"

Kostya replies, "He's gone. With the baby. On the helicopter that left ten minutes ago."

"She's bleeding," Stella says, sadness touching her voice. "Did she give birth? Out here? Oh, my God. Murphy…" Her voice moves away. "Please. You told me you could change. You told me you could be a better man for me. You told me you had enough power now to

make changes and be a better father than your own. I'm fucking begging you. Don't let this poor girl die. Not like this."

Am I dying?

"You don't understand, Stella—"

"No, you don't understand, Murphy. You find a way to save her life or I go to the board and tell them everything. I'll tell them how I helped Kostya plan her escape and you know what will happen to me then. Are you willing to let me suffer those consequences? Or can you step the fuck up right fucking now?"

There's silence.

It stretches for too long.

Maybe I've died.

Maybe this dark awareness is what it's like to be dead.

But I still feel pain.

"Well, fuck. Let's get her outta here before the rest of the four families come looking."

"Where are we taking her?" Stella asks. "And what about Kostya?"

"I have a plan. Go get my phone from the car so I can call our pilot. I can stall the rest of them from coming out here for maybe a half hour. We need to move quickly. I can't afford any suspicion on my head. We'll tell them they all got away on the first chopper and you and I went after them in the second. Understood?"

Stella sounds relieved. "Thank you. Really, thank you, Murphy."

But I'm still not so sure I'm actually alive. Maybe this is all a dream. Perhaps death is simply this state of awareness where only darkness exists without a physical being. Maybe I'll be trapped inside my own rotting corpse forever.

Purgatory.

But then, I feel fresh cold along my back, the familiar damp cold of fresh, powdery snow, and I realize my body is being moved. I'm hoisted from the ground and I feel Murphy's shoulder jab into my stomach and it fucking hurts.

I scream and the movement stops.

"Anya? It's…You're gonna be okay, just hang on," Stella says.

Could she hear my scream?

Did I make a sound?

"Jesus, why would they do this?" she murmurs. "Why would they put a spike strip in the road?"

"Fucking Vittoris."

"It's…it's vile."

"We're all vile, sweetheart," Murphy says, and I realize he's carrying my limp body over his shoulder. "It's in our blood. It's our business."

"If you're so vile, then why are you helping her?"

"For you, lass. You wanted proof I could be a good man and stand up for you? Well, here it is, sweetheart. I'm saving her to show you that I've…that I'm capable of being better. This poor girl has been through enough. Maybe I'm a little tired of it, too."

I want to laugh.

I wish I could.

Murphy O'Shea, of all people, ruthless king of masters, has come to my rescue.

Unless he's too late to save me.

Unless I'm already dead.

CHAPTER 25
Ezra

1 Year Later

I PLACE MY silver laptop on the small table in front of me, lifting the screen and powering it on. I bring up my video chat app and wait for Lidia's call. She promised she'd check in with me at noon, New York time. I'm not exactly sure what time zone I'm in right now crossing the Atlantic Ocean.

The private jet we fly on was chartered by the agents that I've finally convinced to help me. The FBI and CIA were no use to me—they outright denied the existence of the four families and any such operations they ran in their trafficking factories. No doubt they were corrupted from within. I knew I had to take matters into my own hands when they were insistent in their naïve denial.

It hasn't been an easy journey getting where I am today. In fact, this past year has been arguably the second worst of my life—the first, of course, was being a captive of the four families.

When I left Anya—dying alone on the side of the road—I'd had enough adrenaline to fuel me, to keep me going to run the mile and a half to the helipad. I'd gotten there just before the pilot was about to take off again. My timing had been nothing other than pure fucking luck.

The pilot wasn't going to let me on at first without Kostya, but I pleaded with them, showing them my baby boy, fresh from the womb. I tried to get them to help me, to go back to get Anya somehow, but they refused. They had orders to pick-up and drop-off and nothing more.

I seriously thought about putting our son on the helicopter and running back to be with Anya. The pull of my soul to hers was still so strong, still urgent and desperate, and there was a purely selfish part of me that wanted to be by her side—even if she was dying, even if it meant leaving our child's life to chance, even if it meant I'd be with her for mere moments before losing her and facing the wrath of the four families on my own.

But there was no way I could turn back when I realized that Anya would never forgive me for abandoning her child, *our* child. I would never forgive myself for doing something like that. By then, the baby's tiny lips were turning blue from the cold, even while he was wrapped and bundled in the blanket.

The thought of losing the baby and Anya all in one fell swoop was horrifying. I knew I couldn't save her, and he was all I had left of her.

I couldn't lose him, too.

It was the hardest fucking thing in the world to leave her.

But somehow, I climbed on board the helicopter, knowing that my last act of love for her would be to ensure a long, happy, healthy life for her son.

Fuck, it hurts to think about that night.

Things got complicated when the pilot dropped me and the kid off at the nearest public airport. I had the credit card and cash Kostya had given us—if it had just been me and Anya, I could've booked us on the next flight home. But with a newborn baby in my arms that desperately needed to be fed and cared for, I had to make a decision that scared me.

I had to take him to the nearest hospital.

We were still in Russia, too close for comfort to wherever the fuck Mikhailov Manor was tucked away. I had no clever cover story. I walked into a hospital with signs I couldn't read and people who spoke a language I didn't understand. I showed them the baby and had to have faith that they wouldn't take us from each other.

I thought I knew fear before then, but I didn't.

The thought of them taking him from me—separating us—that was true fear.

But I guess we got lucky. A kind woman, a nurse, held out her arms and waited for me to hand him over and it took every ounce of strength I had to do it. She cradled him in her arms, smiled at him, looked up at me, and asked me something in Russian that I couldn't understand. It took a few tries and some gesturing for me to figure it out, but eventually, I worked out that she was asking for his name.

I didn't have a name for him.

Anya never told me what she wanted to call him.

I worried I would pick the wrong name, but I had to decide in a split-second. So, I did the only thing I could do and that was to rely on my gut. I said the first name that came to mind.

I told her to call him Brandon.

It was the plainest, most American name I could think of, because I thought Anya would want that. She was Russian born, but she loved the American life she'd been living since she was eleven. And after all she'd been through, I couldn't imagine her wanting him to have anything resembling a Russian name.

So, just like that, he was Brandon Bell.

The nurse waved me along with her as she took Brandon back to an area of stretchers divided by nothing other than a simple curtain between. The vinyl floor tiles were cheap and peeling, and the place was buzzing with noise, overcrowded with people and doctors and nurses. There was an overwhelming stench of bleach and cleaning chemicals that gave me an instant headache. The place was a hot mess compared to any hospital I've been to in the States.

The nurse gestured for me to sit on one of the stretchers at the very end of the long hallway, and she handed Brandon back to me as soon as I did. I felt such a massive amount of relief, knowing I was doing the right thing—if not for me then for my *son*. Because regardless of whether he was fathered by me or Nikolai, I knew right then that this child was *mine* because I'd claimed him as such.

The nurse cleaned him up, checked him over, and did everything that needed to be done to ensure he was okay. She stayed by our side when a surly-looking doctor came back to check Brandon, and she doted on him while he did.

She gave us bottles of formula, diapers, swaddling blankets, basic onesies, and wipes—things I think she had to sneak away to give us because this hospital didn't seem like it was made of money. She made sure we had everything we needed before we left the hospital and she walked us out a back entrance—I thought it was odd that no one asked for payment, but I think she knew, somehow, that we needed this off the record.

I tried to give her some cash from the pile in my backpack, but she absolutely refused to take it. I had no other way to thank her, but she seemed happy to have been able to help Brandon.

We left and I took the risk of getting a hotel room for the night, thankful they let me pay cash for it. Brandon and I were exhausted, and I couldn't wrap my head around getting on a plane just yet.

That first night was the hardest.

Brandon cried.

He cried a lot.

And so did I.

I cried over the loss of Anya. I cried angry tears at how close we'd been to having the life we deserved as our own family—me, Anya, and the baby. I cried that the three of us would never dance a *pas de trois*. All I'd ever wanted was a family of my own because I never really had one as a foster kid. And the closest I'd ever come to having a family was brutally taken from me by a spike strip across the road, placed by the vilest monsters on Earth.

I went to a local store the next morning and got some basic supplies, using cash as much as I could. We hurried off to the airport and booked the next flight out of Russia—two fucking layovers along the way, but then we'd land in New York and I would at least have the advantage of being on my home turf, even if they did come after me. I had to use the credit card to book the flight, so naturally, I was jumpy, anxious as hell waiting for our plane to board. Every stop along the way, I expected someone from the four families to show up, kill me, and kidnap Brandon.

Thank fuck no one ever tried.

When we finally got back to New York almost two full days later, I went straight to Emma's apartment, my ex-girlfriend. I went to her partly because I wanted to make sure they hadn't gotten to her, but also because I had no one else to help me.

And she did exactly that.

She let me sleep on her couch for four months with Brandon beside me in a portable crib. He was a fussy little fucker, had me up all hours of the night, too. She was an angel to put up with that for as long as she had, but each day that passed, I knew we were getting closer and closer to an eviction. Not because she wasn't happy to help, but because her relationship with her boyfriend had turned serious and I knew they'd want to be living together before long.

And it was probably for the best because seeing them together and happy hurt like fucking hell. They had everything I was supposed to have with Anya, and it twisted painfully in my gut every time they smiled, laughed, hugged, or said goodbye at the door with a kiss.

Emma tried to help me grieve the loss of Anya, but whenever she brought it up, something about it just didn't feel right. It didn't feel right inside me to think of her as being gone. It didn't feel like she *was* gone, absent from the Earth…and I don't think it ever really had felt that way.

Twice before that night in the forest, I'd been nearby when Anya almost died, and I'd felt the snap of it breaking my heart, followed by a hollowness in my gut. But that hollowness was quickly filled when her breath returned. It was once before when Nikolai drowned her in the pool and again when Vigo tried to drown her in the bathtub.

I remember thinking she seemed invincible for all that she'd been through, and that word was rolling around in my head more persistently.

Though I'd been sad, though I'd cried a billion tears, though I'd cursed the four families for causing the death of my blue-eyed girl, I didn't feel empty…I didn't feel hollow in my gut. At first, I thought it was just because I had Brandon to fill the empty spaces. But more and more, I was feeling her absence as something that needed to be corrected, as something that *could* be corrected.

My heart insisted that she was invincible.

Four months into my stay with Emma, four months of conversations with local police, the FBI, the CIA, I decided that I needed to find her, with or without the help of law enforcement.

But first, I had to find her sister. I'd already waited four months too long and my only excuse was that Brandon took up all my time and attention.

It was almost too easy to find her. Lidia Antonov was on several social media sites that she posted to regularly and that was shocking to me. It was shocking because the four families could've tracked her down and taken her out after our departure, even though Nikolai had called off his goons who took weekly pictures of her with a scope measurement from the rifle they aimed at her.

Initially, I thought that must mean that Anya was, without a doubt, dead. Because they would have no reason to go after Lidia if Anya were dead. After all, I had no ties to Lidia in their eyes. If Anya was somehow still alive and in their care, they might've killed Lidia as punishment. They might've taken Lidia and sold her. But that just didn't feel right to me.

And then I thought, *What if Anya is alive, but the four families don't know? And if she is alive, where the fuck is she?*

I'd gone to Lidia then and told her everything.

She believed me, thank fuck.

She believed me because Brandon looked like Anya, except for the eyes.

His eyes were a light gray with flecks of green and brown when he was a newborn. But gradually, the brown faded and so did the gray, leaving him with stunning green eyes and a quickly growing mop of thick, blond hair.

He and I share the same eyes and hair, but the rest of him is undoubtedly all the best parts of Anya.

Lidia took to Brandon instantly, and suddenly, I had a family. Unfortunately, I never got to meet Anya's mother. Lidia told me that she died of a heart attack a couple of years ago—undoubtedly, the stress of not knowing what happened to her oldest daughter took a toll on her health.

But right away, I bonded with Lidia and she stood by me as I lost my fucking mind deciding to pursue a potentially useless search for Anya. We both felt that if there were any possibility that she was still alive, that we would leave no stone unturned to bring her back.

We got a small place together because she insisted that I needed her help with Brandon. I did, but really, she wanted to be close to him because just like me, he was all she had left of Anya. It turned out that the 5,000,000 Rubles of Russian currency Kostya had given us was about 70,000 American dollars. It was enough to get by on while I went crazy in my overseas search. Lidia stepped up to take care of her nephew when I had to be gone to chase a new lead.

I talked to some unsavory people and I did some things that I'm not proud of, but if I hadn't, I never would've stumbled upon the underground group of rogue agents who had been trying to bring an end to the four families for two decades. It took me a couple of months to convince them of my story, to feed them the information I'd gathered about the four families so they could compare it to their own intel. Once I introduced them to Brandon and Lidia, that was it.

We partnered.

Their intel, military training and expertise, their insiders… they gave me access to everything they had to help me find Anya. They had a stake in finding her because undoubtedly, she could give them even better information than I had since she'd been temporarily the sole leader of the Mikhailov family.

Things were starting to fall apart for the four families. It had started with the Leblancs, formerly the Campbells. The insiders knew of the changeover in family leadership from the moment it happened—when the Campbells were punished for their role in killing Nikolai's family.

The agents had someone on the inside—a girl named Callista Campbell, the granddaughter of Charles Campbell, niece of the murdered Head of House Chandler Campbell. She wanted out when Chandler was killed, fearing for her life, but I guess they had convinced her to stay, took her away for some time and trained her in the art of becoming a trusted confidante to the new Head of House, Leo Leblanc.

Apparently, Callista was making waves. Though Leo was her first cousin once removed—the son of her great aunt and uncle—he had a thing for her. And Callista was using it to her advantage.

With the Leblanc family slowly unraveling and intel that Murphy and Stella O'Shea have started decommissioning some of their factories, the time for this group to act was now. And that meant they were willing to help me find Anya, which is exactly what they did.

It's why I'm flying across the Atlantic right now.

Lidia's name appears on my video chat and I click to bring her up.

"Hey," she says, a little out of breath, "sorry I'm a few minutes late. Brandon figured out how to get out of his diaper and took a shit behind the couch before I realized it."

We both laugh.

"Where is my precious little fucker?"

"Hang on," Lidia says, stepping away from the camera for a few seconds, returning with my boy, plopping him down on her lap. "Say hi to daddy."

I wave at my little buddy. "Hey, baby. I miss you."

Brandon babbles something incoherent at the screen and my grin makes my cheeks ache. Anya is the only other person I've loved as much as I love Brandon.

Lidia's face turns serious. "How long before you land in Oslo?"

"About twenty minutes."

"And how long before you reach the warehouse…the factory…whatever they call it?"

"It's a warehouse, but they call it a factory. It'll be at least another hour before we get there, but it'll be longer than that before we have her. If she's actually there."

"She *has* to be there. I know it, Ezra. She's my sister. I know she's not dead, I would *feel* it."

I nod a little. "I know. I promise you, the moment we know more, I'll call you."

The rogues have been watching Murphy O'Shea's movements for months. They noticed him spending a lot more time away from his factories and a lot more time at home with his wife. He's closed two factories over the course of the year. But they expected to have seen bodies moving—dead or alive—and being shipped to other factories. They hadn't seen any such movement. It was like the girls they kidnapped and kept just disappeared.

I think Stella had something to do with it all. I think Murphy fell hard for her, and because she's such a force to be reckoned with, something in him changed and shifted his perspective. I can only hope that's why. Falling in love with a good woman can take a weak man and make him stronger… can take a worse man and make him better.

Whatever the case, the agents spotted a girl who matched Anya's description living in the Oslo factory for the last six months or so, with no other signs of life there.

And we're on our way there now.

"Ezra, let's brief," one of the group members calls to me from the back of the private jet.

"I've gotta go," I tell Lidia.

"Call us the moment she's safe. Make sure she's safe, Ezra."

I smile and nod, too terrified to get my hopes up that it might be Anya living in that warehouse, too terrified to let Lidia down and remind her not to hold her breath.

I wave goodbye to my son and close the laptop, pushing to stand, buttoning my navy jacket, and brushing the wrinkles down from my lapels. I step out from my seat and straighten my tie as I move toward the back of the plane where the group of almost twenty men gather around a table with maps and plans.

"We've got five SUVs waiting for us at the airport in Oslo," the leader of the crew says. "The moment we land, we're piling in and heading out." He holds up a picture of my blue-eyed girl—she was younger in the photo, before she was stolen by Nikolai, but it looks like her all the same. "This is Anya Mikhailov. She is our lead mission today. She is a victim who needs to be recovered. Prioritize finding her. Take out any man who is armed. We don't really know what to expect at this factory. Others we've raided have been used as a prison for the women they kidnap. They keep these victims here while they break them, preparing them to sell off, sometimes by the hundreds. Any victims found, we will recover and transport via plane to Stockholm for treatment. Local authorities in Oslo cannot be trusted. The four families pay them for their silence."

"How do we transport them by the hundreds?" one of the men asks.

The leader clears his throat. "We've never actually recovered any of their human assets in the factories we've raided. Somehow, they always seem to get a tip and have them cleared out before we arrive. But our intel has shown us the deplorable conditions inside." He lays out a few photos on the table showing women packed in a row of prison-like cells.

I shouldn't say women, because some of them are teenagers, *children.*

"What happens to these girls when the families clear out a factory on a tip?"

"They decommission them—their word, not ours. Normal people would call it murder. But that's why this mission is crucial. The four families are anything but normal." He holds up the picture of my girl again. "Anya Mikhailov is essential to our cause to end the four families once and for all. She has information that we need, and she needs to be recovered and protected. I want everyone clear-headed and focused on the mission. We land in fifteen, and I want silence on this flight until then. Take that time to focus, do what you need to do to switch from human to soldier, because that's all you are once we land. Understood?"

There's a murmur of agreement and the men disperse. I head back to my seat, drop my head, and press my eyes shut, wringing my sweaty palms together in front of me with my elbows on my knees. Behind my eyelids, there's a flash of sapphire blue and Anya's face comes brilliantly to the forefront of my mind.

I focus intently on her as my pulse kicks up and a steady rhythm of hope punches through my veins with each beat of my heart.

Hope. Hope. Hope.

If there is a God and he has any mercy at all, we'll find her, alive and well, and I'll have her safely in my arms before the sun sets on this day.

CHAPTER 26
Anya

JANUARY...NEW YEAR, NEW me.

It's been one year since I was left behind in the dark forest—one year since I danced across the line of death and somehow found my way back to the side of life.

It's taken me nearly the full year to get back to the level of health I maintained as Nikolai's slave while he owned me. Going through a pregnancy after the way Vigo ruined my body and my health had taken a toll on me.

By all accounts, I should be dead.

But there was one simple thing that kept me alive. It was the same thing that had kept me alive on three separate occasions since Ezra joined my captivity.

Hope.

Hope was something I'd long before lost, but Ezra brought it back to me. He brought hope back into my world and I fought for him because of it, fought for *us*.

Murphy and Stella had been the ones to find me that night in the forest with Kostya—unconscious, bleeding out, knocking on death's door. But instead of letting me die or taking us back to the four families, they had rescued us both.

They saved us.

They snuck us away into the night and flew us back to the four families' private airstrip via helicopter. Murphy pulled a cover-up for our escape out of thin air. He told the four families that we'd gotten away, that he and Stella were hunting us down, so they could carry on with business. He took off in one plane and headed straight for his Oslo factory that night. Stella and Kostya boarded a separate plane with me and took me to a local hospital in Moscow. I had a concussion, needed a blood transfusion, stitches where the baby tore me and for a gash in my side from the car accident.

The fact that I'm still standing is nothing short of miraculous.

Stella and Murphy stayed in close contact during my treatment. He insisted that they discharge me the moment I appeared even slightly stable because neither of us were safe there for long. When I found out he was arranging to take me to one of his factories, I was horrified. I thought I was about to enter a whole new nightmare, to become one of their human assets, to be sold as a slave to one of their clients.

But when we arrived in Oslo, Norway, the factory was inexplicably empty. Murphy had ordered it to be cleared out by his men in Oslo before we landed. I don't even know how they accomplished such a thing. Oslo wasn't their largest factory, but it was big enough to house dozens of girls in the basement.

It was horrifying to see the rows of cages in the wide-open rectangular space of the warehouse basement.

It was a prison.

The empty cages with metal bars, their doors now left open, reminded me of the box I lived in at Vigo's home. My cage held me in with plexiglass, but the women who'd been kept here were trapped by iron bars. I panicked when I saw them with Stella and Kostya, but Stella was surprisingly kind and gentle with me.

She made a promise to me that I didn't ask for and that I didn't believe she had any way of keeping. She promised she could end the O'Sheas' alliance with the four families. She promised that Murphy was a better man than even he knew. She told me that she intended to escape from him before, but seeing the realities of their sick work firsthand fueled her determination to change him.

It almost made me laugh when she said that, which was much needed at the time. I told her that men don't change and she either had to love him as a monster or leave him.

She wasn't convinced.

After a short visit from Murphy a week or so after that, Kostya and I were given burner cell phones, like the ones Kostya had given to me and Ezra when we were separated by Vigo and Nikolai. There were two contacts programmed in—one was Murphy and the other was one of his Oslo employees. That Oslo employee was ordered to ensure that Kostya and I didn't leave the city. But he was also to ensure that we had what we needed to survive comfortably in this warehouse until Murphy could figure a way around letting us go back to normal life.

Whatever *normal* is.

The first thing I asked Murphy's watchdog for was a laptop with internet access and new pointe shoes. Everything I asked for went through Murphy for approval. He approved the laptop, but he wouldn't allow internet access in the warehouse— he was afraid he could be tracked there. But there was a little coffee shop I was allowed to go to once a week with Kostya and the Oslo employee as our escort.

The first time I got on the internet, I did a Google search for Ezra Bell. I didn't know where he was, where my baby was, or whether they were okay. The first article that came up in the search was from over two years ago. It was a report that he was a dancer gone missing from a festival in Kyiv. I found his Instagram account, but nothing had been posted to it or updated since before he went missing.

I quickly realized that if he's alive and out there somewhere, he'd be in hiding, too. He couldn't have an online presence. The four families would find him and come after him, then they would kill him and take my son.

My heart split in two that day when I realized I had no way to find him. I was held hostage here in Oslo just as I was as a Mikhailov or Vittori slave. But what could I do? What choice did I have? I wouldn't give up on finding him. I just knew it in my gut that he was alive, out there in the world somewhere.

And that hope he gave me—hope that I used to think was terribly naïve—was burning bright inside me. I was incapable of freezing myself in an icy exterior of protection because Ezra's eternal sunshine still kept me warm.

So, I'd made Murphy a promise. I would stay there at the warehouse in Oslo. I wouldn't put up a fuss. I'd remain in hiding and I wouldn't try to run. I'd do all that if he promised me he would help me find Ezra. Murphy quickly realized that finding Ezra and giving me over to him would relinquish him of his and his wife's responsibility in this mess. If he gave me to Ezra, it would look as though we'd done just what Murphy had told the board had happened—that we had escaped on our own.

He agreed to search for Ezra and told me he would let me go with him, so long as I accepted that he couldn't keep me safe from the wrath of the four families if they found out we were alive and tracked us down.

I would happily choose to be on the run forever so long as I was running with Ezra. And so, I don't have much to complain about at the moment because I'm alive and there's *hope*.

PAS DE TROIS

Though I'm still captive in Oslo, I have Kostya to keep me company. I have an entire warehouse to myself. I've managed to make a nice little temporary home here. But the best part is that I have the space to dance—I was finally healthy enough to get back to it after a few months and it's how I spend most of my days.

I finish slipping on my broken-in, scuffed-up pointe shoes, wrapping and tying the ribbon securely around my ankle. I rise from the concrete floor of the main level of the warehouse and tug down a bit on my cotton shorts to adjust them.

It's late afternoon and the sun shines in from the row of square windows at the top of the high wall, near the ceiling. There are no ground-level windows, only the ones high up above, out of reach. The windows slice the orange sun glow so that it casts down across the concrete floor in stripes of alternating sunlight and gray stone.

I pull my long, dark hair up and away from the off-shoulder gray sweatshirt I have on, twisting and tying it into a messy bun on the top of my head. I place my wireless earbuds in my ears and bend down to my laptop on the floor, tapping play on the music I selected and turning the volume all the way up.

I only have one full-length mirror in the warehouse, which is to say that I don't have any mirrors to watch myself dance. But it doesn't matter to me now the way it used to. I don't care so much now about my movements being perfect and precise. I only want to dance what I feel, like Ezra taught me. I rise to my toes and bring my arms up high above my head, then bring them down the sides of my body, lowering them slowly as my feet begin to move.

I spin on the top of my toes in a pirouette, twirling around over and over before stepping out of the turn gracefully. I listen to the mood of the music and I follow it. The way I dance now is a fusion of ballet and contemporary style, the best of my world and the best of Ezra's. As I move, I find myself drifting, floating through movement with my eyes closed. Gradually, my movement morphs into the routine, *our* routine—the performance Ezra and I danced for Nikolai on stage in Nobility Hall.

As I move, I mark the leaps and lifts that required his hands on me. He would move me with such strength and effortless grace—each lift and spin that he would have been part of forces a bubble of sadness to rise in my chest. With the somber music playing through my earbuds, tears begin to fall.

But I don't stop dancing.

This is what Ezra taught me—how to move through the emotion, how to follow my feelings instead of the steps. My dancing becomes dramatic, wide sweeping arms and legs, erratic and desperate turning and falling and rising.

Thud.

The music crests and reaches a crescendo and I'm lost in it. I'm lost in the memory of his hands on me, his green eyes tracking my every move and feeding me fuel to live.

Thud.

Crash.

I spin and dip out of the turn, tumbling to the floor and rolling over, coming up on my knees—

I freeze.

Armed men burst through the front door while I was dancing and are coming toward me, guns raised. I rip my earbuds out and lift my hands, drawing back to sit on my heels as I look at the men dressed in all black with wide eyes.

"That's Anya," one of them shouts, and I hear the click of a man's dress shoes from behind the throng of at least a dozen men.

They've found me.

Oh, God…

The four families have found me, and they've come to kill me.

I'm a statue in my panic, dropping my terrified eyes to the floor.

"Clear the warehouse," someone says, and the crowd of men thins out as half of them sweep outward, away from the center of the clear open space where I kneel.

I focus on my breaths as terror grips me and I count.

One. Two. Three. Four. Five. Six. Seven. Eight.

One. Two. Three—

They lower their weapons.

The few men remaining part and my eyes lock onto a man's feet coming toward me from a distance, the click of his heels echoing in the warehouse. His footsteps stop in the center of the floor, but my eyes are glued to his feet.

Something in my soul pulses, causing my heart to skip a beat, and suddenly, I'm nervous. My hands tremble where I hold them above my bowed head, but it's not from fear, it's from…it's from a familiar, prickling awareness. My eyes draw a line up his pressed navy slacks, skimming across his tailored suit jacket, glancing over his white shirt and blue tie, his chin, his lips, his vibrant green eyes…

Oh, my God.

"Ezra?"

He sighs and then he brilliantly smiles and my heart beats wildly, beating furiously at the sight of him.

I rise from the floor and run to him.

He opens his arms for me and I leap. He catches me, pulling me close as I wrap my legs around his waist. I press my face into the crook of his neck and inhale the scent of him deeply.

Peaches and cream and sunshine.

He smells like him.

It's him.

Oh, God, it's really him!

I pull my head back to look at him, locking into his green gaze for only seconds before I let my mind truly believe that it's him, he's here, this is real.

This is real.

I kiss his face, his cheeks, his lips, his nose; every inch of skin, I cover with a kiss, tasting the salt of my own tears that drip from my eyes onto his skin.

I squeeze him tighter and press my face into his shoulder, sobbing into his nice, clean jacket. I say the only thing I can think to say. "Mine?"

I feel the tension in his body slump and fade and the sound of his voice as he responds sends a shiver down my spine. "Yours." He holds me tighter. "Forever, *forever* yours."

I kiss him.

I kiss him with my entire body because I can feel him everywhere. I don't ever, *ever* want to let him go.

"You found me," I say.

"I found you, baby. I found you and I'm taking you home."

Home.

Ezra found me and he's taking me home and all I can do is cry. But these tears aren't from sadness, or pain, or torment, or fear. These tears are an expression of pure joy that I welcome. These tears are cleansing my soul and for the first time in a long time, my soul is at peace.

I'm finally free and I'm going home.

CHAPTER 27
Anya

1 Week Later

"LIDIA?" I DROP my bag at the front door of the townhome Ezra rented just outside of Philadelphia. "Lidia!" I run to my little sister and throw my arms around her, knocking into her a little too hard.

We tumble to the floor in a fit of giggles and sobs as I hold her tight, stroking her hair as we lay on our sides. I pull my head back to look at her and fresh tears pool and fall.

"I've missed you *so* much," she tells me as she cries.

I press my forehead to hers. "I've missed you, too. So much."

"I'm just gonna—" Ezra literally steps over us to continue on past, and Kostya follows suit.

Lidia sits up, swiping beneath her eyes. "You're gonna make me mess up my mascara."

I sit up, reaching out to stroke her hair with a smile. "And you did such a nice job of putting it on, too. I remember the first time you did it when you were…maybe thirteen? You put on way too much and just when you finished—"

"I sneezed." She chuckles.

"Tiny little black lines all the way across your cheeks." I laugh. "You thought it was the end of the world."

"At the time, it was." Lidia laughs and the sound of it is so sweet. "I cried for an hour and all the black lines dripped down to my chin."

I smile at her. "And you're going to have them again if you don't stop crying now." I'm having a hard time seeing her as an adult. But it's been five years and she is one.

"Are you really okay?" she asks after a beat.

I nod. "Yes. I will be. Nothing's easy right now."

"I know. I just want you to be okay."

"I'm alive." I grin at her reassuringly. "And I'm here now. No one is ever going to take me away again. I won't let that happen."

A comfortable yet anticipatory silence falls.

"Do you want to…Are you ready to meet Brandon?" she finally asks.

I suck in a sharp breath as a bundle of nerves tugs tight in my gut. I got to see him on video chat every night this week while Ezra and I settled things and traveled back to the States. But this is my first time coming home.

Home.

Such a strange thought.

It's a happy one, but strange.

Ezra didn't want to live in New York anymore, not when he knew it would make us easier targets for the four families to track down, especially since we'd both lived there before we were taken. He'd lived in Philadelphia for a while with a foster family growing up and the foster father had a connection with a landlord here. He helped him rent a townhome for a steal, and Ezra created a life for us here.

Well, he created a life for him and Brandon and Lidia here. But he was clear with me before we came back that he wanted it to feel like my home, too.

I think it will just take time.

I climb to my feet and Lidia does the same. "I'm nervous," I admit as Ezra holds out his hand for me to take.

He grins at me and my heart melts. "Nothing to be nervous about."

"He won't know who I am," I remind him, looking nervously down at the space between us.

Ezra's fingers tickle beneath my chin with a spark of lightning that makes butterflies flap their wings in my stomach. "He'll learn who you are. You're his mom, the one and only."

My body sways toward him, the light in his eyes drawing me in like a moth to a flame. He releases my chin, catching me in his arms, pulling me closer. He's the same Ezra he always was, but somehow different. He's grown as a person, as a man. He's mature and responsible and so goddamn sexy it hurts.

"I love you," I tell him, pressing my cheek to his chest as he cradles me, rubbing a hand over my back.

"I love you, too." He pulls back and smiles. "Come on. I've been dreaming about seeing you with him and I can't wait anymore."

He takes my hand and pulls me along, leading me upstairs as Lidia shoos us away encouragingly. I realize I've completely forgotten about introducing Lidia and Kostya, and I turn my head back around to do it quickly.

Maybe it was stupid for us to let him come back with us. Maybe it makes us easier targets. But I've come to see him as my friend, and I couldn't leave him behind. It would've been hard for us to separate after the year we spent bonding in the Oslo factory.

Lidia surprises me with her confidence and maturity as she takes it upon herself to greet him without me. "You must be Kostya, it's good to meet you." She holds out her hand for him to shake and my heart thumps an extra beat—I've missed so much time with her and she's grown up so much.

Kostya smiles at her—a rare, happy, hopeful smile—and says hello.

Ezra tugs on my hand, drawing my attention back to him. "Come on," he says, grinning at me.

His townhouse—*our* townhouse—is humble, small but reasonably-sized for a family to live in comfortably. It's cozy and I feel immediately at ease, like I could actually relax and just exist here peacefully. There's a happy kind of energy in this space, like nothing I've ever felt before.

I stop again halfway up the staircase to look at the pictures hung neatly on the sky-blue wall.

Pictures of Brandon…of my son.

My son.

My heart skips a beat and I place my hand over my chest.

"Lidia put those up," Ezra tells me. "She decorated the nursery, too. Most of the place, really. She said it needed a woman's touch."

I give him a smile and squeeze his hand.

Did they seek comfort in each other when I was away, when they didn't know if I was dead or alive?

I swallow hard at the thought that came from nowhere.

It never even occurred to me to ask if he'd been involved with anyone in the year we were apart, least of all my sister. But realistically, they've been living together, raising Brandon together. He and Lidia are as close in age as Ezra and I are to each other.

A lump rises in my throat.

"What is it?" Ezra stops when we reach the landing, turning to face me, noticing my sudden introspection.

"I think I should ask you something, but not right now."

His eyebrows slant toward his nose. "Okay. Later tonight? After you spend some time with Brandon?"

I nod. I can feel the tension suddenly pulse out from my chest, poisoning the air between us. I don't like it. I don't like that this thought popped into my head. I don't like knowing that it could be true, though I hope it's not. I can see how my tension bothers him. He forces a half-smile and nods his head toward the end of the hallway before leading me forward.

We walk together to the second door on the left, at the end of the short hallway carpeted with brown shag. The hallway is dark and the door is shut. When we stop in front of it and he glances at me, I know this is the door to Brandon's nursery.

All conscious thought leaves me in a rush.

My heart stops and stutters, then thuds hard against my ribcage. I grip Ezra's hand tighter and he squeezes back.

"Ready?" he asks.

Am I?

I can't speak, so I just nod.

Slowly, he turns the knob. He steps forward as he cracks the door open gradually, blocking my view as he peeks in. I expect that we'll creep into the room and I'll see my baby for the first time, asleep in his crib.

But then Ezra speaks, and I feel nauseous. "Hey, bud, why aren't you sleeping?"

And then follows the sound I know I will treasure more than any other sound heard for the rest of my days…my baby, babbling back at Ezra.

Oh, God.

The sheer joyfulness of the sound is so intense that it sinks inside my gut and my body curls around my stomach. It's joy that grips me entirely, shooting like a burst of lightning from the pit of my stomach, like a starburst blasting its rays outward to the rest of my body. It forces tears to rise and spill and threatens to drop me to my knees.

But Ezra slips his arm around my waist and pulls me inside the room, shutting the door behind us. He lets me go with a quick rub over the small of my back and I slump against the wall behind me as I blink through the waterfall spilling from my eyes.

I have to concentrate. I have to focus to watch what's happening as my breath quickens toward hyperventilation. I don't want to miss a moment of this excruciating joy.

Brandon's standing in his crib, smiling a toothless grin that sets my world on fire. He reaches his tiny arms into the air, eagerly waiting for Ezra to pluck him from his bed, but he loses his balance when he lets go of the side, falling backward onto his butt. He pulls himself up again with his hands on the rail and his knees bounce with energy.

Ezra reaches for him, grips him beneath the armpits, and lifts him. He pulls Brandon close against his chest and that's when my knees buckle beneath me.

I fall to kneel on the floor.

Ezra crosses to me quickly, dropping to one knee, still holding Brandon tight to his side. "Are you okay?"

I nod through my tears. "I'm okay. It's just a lot."

His voice is soft and comforting. "I know. Just sit down there. Brandon will sit on your lap."

"He will?"

It feels so surreal.

"Yeah, of course." He looks at Brandon and smiles. "You'll sit with Mommy, won't you, buddy?"

Brandon coos.

Ezra sniffles and I see the sheen forming over his eyes.

If he cries, I don't stand a chance.

"This is your mommy," he says. "She's the best person you'll ever know." He moves to sit beside me as I sit with my back against the wall, both of us stretching our legs out.

I look over at Brandon and smile, quickly wiping away the tears from my cheeks with the backs of my hands. He looks at me with curiosity, blinking his bright green eyes. They're the same vibrant green as Ezra's and equally bewitching, actually more so. One look at him and I'm hopelessly in love. My smile for him brightens and after a few moments, he smiles back.

And then the most perfect thing happens.

Brandon reaches for me.

I gasp as the most unexplainable kind of happiness spreads warmth through my entire body. Ezra lifts him and shifts him over, sitting his bottom on my lap. I grip beneath his arms and hold him delicately with him facing me as his tiny legs spread across my thighs on either side.

"Hi, baby," I say quietly, afraid of my own voice. "I'm your mommy." My voice cracks and a joyful sob breaks through. I push a smile through my cheeks as Ezra's hand sneaks around my back and I lean into him.

Oh, God.

I've never felt this way before.

I feel like…

"I feel like I'm finally home."

Ezra turns his head and presses his lips to my cheek before a shallow sob hitches in his chest. He turns his head and nuzzles his face into the side of my neck.

"We're all finally home," he says.

CHAPTER 28
Ezra

I'VE NEVER BEEN happier in my life. Anya is alive and free and finally home with me where she belongs. It's probably silly to think this way, but it was almost like Brandon knew his mommy was coming home tonight. He's usually such a good sleeper, but tonight he was awake when I brought Anya in… like he was waiting up to see her.

Of course, it's an adjustment for everyone, and some things are going to take time and patience and care, but there was no sense of strangeness or discomfort between Anya and Brandon. There was intense and immediate love—the moment they met couldn't have been more perfect.

But as I shut the door to Brandon's room after we get him back down for the night and I lead Anya to my bedroom—*our* bedroom—I can tell something's weighing on her mind. She wanted to talk to me about something earlier, and I don't like the worry I feel pulsing from her as I show her our room.

Our master bedroom is a decent size with a connected bathroom. The carpet is an old, dark teal. There are hardwoods beneath that I want to restore someday, but for obvious reasons, that hasn't been a priority. We have a single dresser with an attached vanity mirror to the right of the queen-sized bed and there are two end tables on either side of that. There's a small closet, but that's pretty much it. It's nothing to write home about.

I close the door behind her after she enters and I stand there, watching her as she takes in her surroundings. She takes a few steps in, twirls around slowly and stills, her eyes falling on mine.

She grins. "So, this is it?"

I hold out my hands. "This is it."

She sighs, crossing her arms over her stomach. "Today has been a little overwhelming."

"Of course, it has. I can only imagine."

Anya lowers slowly to sit on the edge of the bed. Her ass only touches it for a moment before she pushes herself right back up to standing. "There's something I need to know, Ezra. I don't really know how to ask. And it's not really…I mean, I don't really have a reason to be upset if you did—"

"If I did what?" She crosses her arms again, looking down and away from me. She's nervous to ask, or maybe nervous for my answer, I don't know. But I don't like this. "Just ask me."

"It's been a year…" Words burst from her in a ramble. "And you were alone taking care of Brandon. You didn't know if I was dead or alive, and I can only imagine you had to go on living life as if I *had* actually died. My sister and I aren't all that dissimilar, and I know you've been living together for at least six months. I know I have no right to be upset if you and Lidia—" She shakes her head. "I just need to know. For my own peace of mind. Did you and Lidia…" She lets her unspoken, but crystal-clear question hang in the air.

My head tilts all the way to the side as I watch her squirm her way through her nervous words. Shit, it twists something painfully deep inside me to hear her ask me this. I get why she's asking; I get why she would think that Lidia and I had become something more than friends. I've wondered the same thing about her and Kostya having spent the past year together. But it kills me how it pains her to even think that could be true.

I charge across the room, rushing to stand in front of her, and I grip her face with both hands, turning her head to look at me. "No, we didn't. I never even thought about it, Anya. Lidia is as much a sister to me as she is to you. And you're not as similar as you think you are…you couldn't possibly be. There is no one, Anya, *no one* who could take your place in my heart, in my soul." I shuffle closer as her delicate hands land gently on my wrists and she blinks up at me with those perfect sapphire eyes. I lick my lips as I watch her mouth part to take in an uneven breath. "I have been achingly, *painfully* celibate since that last day I saw you in the forest. And I probably would've been forever if you hadn't survived. Something inside me knew I had to wait for you, knew that you were alive, knew that someday I would bring you back home."

I hardly get the last word out before Anya rises on her toes and slams her lips against mine with enough force that I have to take a step backward. She kisses me hard and pushes me back until my back hits the closed door behind me.

I drop my hands from her cheeks and grip her hips tightly, spinning her and pushing her against the door instead. I pull my head back to break our kiss, though my hips grind my cock against her lower stomach. "Are you sure you want this now?" We've only kissed since I've rescued her because she was struggling with something, struggling with herself, and she asked me to wait. "I'll wait for you. I'll wait years if that's what you want, but I need you so much right now. If we start this…"

Her shoulders relax as she drops her head back against the wall. "Everything feels right. Everything finally feels right. I want to start this, and I don't want to finish until the sun comes up."

I bring a hand up to stroke her cheek, tilting my head as I study the absolute beauty of her face. "This will never be finished."

She breathes out a sigh and as her lips part, I dive in. I kiss her and forget the world. Anya moans, her fingers tickling my skin as she slips them beneath the hem of my T-shirt. She lifts and tugs and our kiss breaks only for the time it takes to rip my shirt over my head and toss it to the floor.

I slam my hands to the wall on either side of her, bending to taste her again. This kiss is frantic, desperate, eager...it's fucking everything because I've been starving for this freedom with my blue-eyed girl since we met. I snake my hands around behind her, grip her ass tight, and lift her up along the door. She squeezes her legs around me and I groan, feeling her shift along my cock. I move one hand up to dig into her hair at the back of her head, tugging back on the strands ever so slightly to angle her face upward, just so I can bend over her and kiss her more deeply.

She is fucking everything.

I hold her close as I turn us and walk her to the dresser, setting her down on top of it, putting her ass level with my hips. She peels off her shirt, tossing it away as her eyes take me in, raking down my body and making me feel like the most desired man in the world. She reaches behind her and unhooks her black bra and my hips jut forward, pounding my cock against the edge of the dresser.

"Fuck," I groan.

Anya lets her bra fall from her shoulders and everything slows to the speed of the garment slipping so slowly down her arms. "Ezra..."

The way she breathes my name—as if I were the very air that filled her lungs—makes me fucking hard.

She reaches for me, her hands locking together around the back of my neck, and she pulls my head down to her, our foreheads touching. She pants and breathes as her knees squeeze my hips to hold me in place.

"I love you and I'll never stop," she says.

Christ.

That makes my whole goddamn body tingle for her.

"I need you *now*, baby." I'm panting, gasping for her like she's oxygen.

Her mouth drops open and her fingers find my buckle, working frantically to free me from my jeans. "I need you, too. Now."

I push her trembling hands away and take over, shoving my pants and boxer briefs down as soon as I get my jeans open. My dick is already hard and straining, springing free from my clothes and ready to be inside her.

I grab her leggings at her hips and tug, but the damn things are so tight that I pull her body down with them. Her covered pussy hits my stomach and she gasps. Holding her knees tight against my sides, she lifts her ass just enough for me to peel them off her and I toss them to the floor.

Then I stop.

I catch the reflection of her backside in the vanity mirror on the back of the dresser and I just have to pause to appreciate her perfectly imperfect figure. My eyes cast over her body, taking in the fullness of her curves—the stretch marks on her stomach where she carried our baby, the hint of extra weight she still carries there that reminds me she's a fucking warrior.

I revel at the contrast of her skin, smooth and supple in most places, but rough and weathered where she's been battered and abused and marked in her captivity. My thumb grazes over the scars at the top of her thigh, scars Nikolai put there with his switchblade.

She'll never be marked by them again.

This is the first time it's really hit me that it's true and relief washes over me. The literal weight of the world tumbles from my shoulders.

I *finally* feel free.

And it's because I'm with her.

I grab her face and kiss her hard, leaning her back against the mirror as her ass slips down to me at the edge of the dresser. I fist my cock, angle it against her pussy, and press inside her. I push in deep, probably too hard and too fast, but she's so goddamn warm and wet that it just slips right in.

"*Oh,*" she gasps as her heels dig into my ass, encouraging me to stay right there. "Oh, God."

She looks at me, her blue eyes sparkling, full of passion and life and love, more than I've *ever* seen before.

I pull out and shove back in and we both moan. Her eyes never leave mine; she never looks away, not for a second. I thrust again, starting to move in and out of her with long, hard thrusts. I fuck her recklessly while she makes love to me with her eyes.

When I start to feel her pussy clench around my cock, when she's shaking, tensing, trembling in my hold, gasping out those sweet little "*oh*" sounds that she makes for me, I put my thumb over her clit and press.

"Ezra!" Anya's arms whip around me and she squeezes me in her embrace, lifting her hips and changing our angle. "Yes… yes. Please, Ezra…I need you."

I need you.

"I'm yours, baby," I whisper against the shell of her ear, her hair tickling my face as I nip my teeth down the side of her neck.

When I lick behind her ear, it detonates her.

"Ezra!" She goes rigid and then she sinks, gasping through her orgasm, her arms losing their grip around me.

I grab onto her, hold her steady as I rut inside her, hard and fast. The edge of the dresser slams against the wall with a thud with each thrust.

Thud, thud, thud.

Her eyes drift shut while I fuck her and she smiles, looking sleepy, sated, happy. "Mine," she whispers and that's it for me.

I come inside her, hard and long, and I've never felt such a perfect release.

It feels like the first time.

It feels like the last time.

It feels like the only time.

And it's fucking *everything*.

It could be a dream, but I'm thankful it's not.

Anya and I are together in bed, in our cozy townhome in Philadelphia.

We lay on our sides, facing one another, only Anya has just pulled me from the only peaceful slumber I've had in months. I'm okay with it because reality is better than the dream of her.

We fell asleep naked, tangled in each other after an extended fuck session. It's still dark in the room and a quick glance at the bright red numbers on the digital clock behind her on the nightstand tells me its three o'clock in the morning.

I can't see her clearly in the dark, but I can see her well enough to make out the curved line of her smile. Her fingers softly trail up and down along my arm. Her coldness is gone. The icy exterior she used to shield herself as a slave has melted away, leaving her bare and exposed to me in her rawest, truest form.

I would move mountains for this woman.

She snuggles in close and presses her lips to mine, just a brush to test my interest. I'm tired, but I'm still fucking interested. I move a little closer and so does she, parting her lips and sliding her tongue along the seam of mine. I run my hand over her hip, slipping down to her knee, and I slowly lift her leg, encouraging her to wrap it over mine.

We kiss for minutes, slow and deep and relaxed. There's no rushing, no urgent need for release. Just the feel of us together without limits or fear. As my cock gradually thickens, I wedge it between her legs. I reach down between us to rub her clit, feeling how wet she already is for me. Without hurry, I angle and push my cock inside her, my hand on her lower back dragging her closer. She sighs into my mouth and I taste her love on my tongue.

We hold each other this way, kissing deeply, hips rocking slowly. I can't think of a better way to wake up. We rock and grind lazily, making love with our bodies connected deeply. The craziest thing is that I don't even need to come—and I don't think she needs it, either. This grinding is about our connection and the connection alone feels like heaven on Earth.

In fact, neither of us come this way.

We rock, we caress, we kiss, we moan.

And at some point along the way, we fall asleep like this, tangled up in each other.

Together.

In love.

Free and finally home.

EPILOGUE
Anya

3 Years Later

"ARE YOU READY for this?" Ezra grins as brightly as the sun.

My smile is no dimmer. I snatch his hand at my side and squeeze tight, the old, familiar bundle of nerves and excited energy pulsing from within me. I'm practically bouncing with excitement.

The smell of being in an open theater, a nearly full house in the audience, the thrill of the performance to come excites me in a way it never has before. Anxiety grips me, too, in a strange sort of way. I've been looking forward to this performance for months, but I never imagined I would be this nervous about it.

Ezra locks our fingers together and squeezes a little tighter. "Whatever happens on that stage, it's going to be perfect. You know it is."

I sigh, trying to blow out the anxiety. Ezra's touch helps to calm me, just as it always has.

The sounds of chattering fade into silence as the performance time nears, as they dim the lights and make the announcement to silence cell phones and enjoy the show. My heart kickstarts in a rush.

It's okay.

It's going to be okay.

It's going to be amazing.

When the curtains on the stage suddenly part down the middle, I gasp, my heart leaping into my throat and stifling my breath.

But it only lasts a moment.

Ezra shifts our two-year-old daughter, Faith, to a more comfortable position on his lap and she giggles in transit, reminding me that everything is okay as long as our family is together. I rub my hand over my pregnant belly, take a deep breath, and smile.

The music begins to play and Brandon's recital group walks onto the stage in a straight line—well, as straight as a line can be with ten four-year-olds—and their tiny fists are on their hips as they march out.

"There he is!" I whisper excitedly, spotting him at the end of the line.

Brandon looks out at the audience and I wave at him excitedly, knowing that I shouldn't because he is the most distracted child in history. He spots us sitting there together in the third row and doesn't see the line stop. He keeps walking and bumps into the little girl in front of him, bouncing back a step. He giggles and the audience does, too. The children perform the steps of their synchronized routine and it's all lovely and good, but then it's time for Brandon's solo. He moves in front of the line of children, now with their hands on their knees, bobbing up and down to the beat of the music, and he starts his routine.

I never could have imagined that the product of Ezra and I—a contemporary dancer and a ballerina—would turn out to be a tiny breakdancing prodigy. Prodigy may be too strong a word, but that's what he is in my eyes.

Watching him spin and kick and dance and move in his

own special way absolutely melts my heart. I remember when I first met Ezra, back when Nikolai wanted me to break him, and I'd mistakenly thought he might be a beat boy, a hip-hop dancer, judging by his clothing and the way he carried himself. But I'd been wrong. Looking at Brandon now, I almost have to wonder if that's what I had seen in Ezra at first—if I'd already seen the first hints of our future son that day when I looked into his bewitching green eyes.

Brandon and Ezra do look so much alike.

Brandon finishes his solo on the floor, lying on his side, elbow on the stage and his head propped in his hand. It's the most adorable, casually cool pose for this four-year-old charmer. He points a finger gun at the audience and winks and the house erupts into laughter and cheers. Ezra taught him that move, told him he'd have the audience in the palm of his hand if he did it.

And, of course, he was right.

Faith claps, her tiny little hands slamming together awkwardly as she sits on Ezra's lap.

This, right here, this moment…it's everything.

It's the life I thought I'd never have.

It's the life I'd been so sure was stolen from me forever.

But Ezra found me in my captivity and saved me. He kept his promise and now we have forever together.

I look at Kostya and Lidia to my right and it still amazes me how quickly and easily they connected—right from the start. He smiles at her, leaning over to whisper something into her ear, and she absolutely lights up. If someone had told me eight years ago that I'd someday be helping my little sister plan her wedding to the man who kept tabs on me for Nikolai, I would have laughed.

But I suppose stranger things have happened…and they have.

I became an advocate in my own case against the four families, working with the private team Ezra had hired to rescue me. It took years of diligent work and it took my open and honest bravery…it took coming out publicly and sharing what I knew. Going public was a huge risk, but Ezra and I knew we could face it together. We knew we would rather risk the danger of exposure for a chance at taking them down, rather than being on the run our entire lives.

But the risk was worth it.

It was worth it because we fucking took them down.

We found the Vittoris' island with the help of expert trackers, and Renata and Lorenzo were arrested. I don't know what happened to Olivia and their baby, but I hope they've found peace somewhere out there in the world.

Murphy disbanded his factories and worked with the authorities, earning himself some level of immunity from conviction. Part of me wanted him to spend the rest of his life in jail because he was one of them, too. But another part of me was okay with his immunity. He had saved my life and had given me a place to hide safely from the four families. I was grateful for that, and for Stella, too. They're still married, as far as I know.

Leo Leblanc disappeared, and no one knows if he's dead or alive.

According to the private team's intel, ninety percent of the factories they'd learned about had been swept and shut down by force. Hundreds of women and teenage girls were found alive and rescued, rehabilitated, and sent back home to their families.

There was still much work to be done. There are still extended family members out there in the world, some still running factories that the private team hasn't tracked locations for just yet. And furthermore, the four families certainly aren't the only traffickers that exist in the world. There are still victims being taken and sold.

If I hadn't gone public, the four families would've remained strong. As an international conglomerate that's been in successful operation for generations, I'm proud that the risk I took effectively disabled them.

I still dance daily for myself, but my career desires changed dramatically after my captivity. With Ezra's help, I started a non-profit group that seeks to support and rehabilitate trafficked survivors through dance therapy—the Encore Center for Survivors.

I didn't have a college degree or really any knowledge of my own at first, but going public about what I'd endured earned me both monetary and expert support—I heard from dozens of psychologists, sociologists, social workers, counselors, and dance and music therapists after our news special aired. I didn't have the therapy knowledge or the business knowledge when I started, but I learned. I learned a lot and I worked constantly, and I'm proud of the work I'm doing now.

I get to dance.

I get to teach.

I get to help survivors find their way back to a happy and healthy life.

But most important of all, I get to be with my family....a family Ezra and I created from the nothing we had when we were slaves. Brandon's life saved us in so many ways. If he hadn't existed, the events that led to our eventual escape would never have come to be, and Ezra and I both would likely be dead.

The fact that I'm able to watch him now, performing happily on stage, makes everything I've endured worth it.

He's a miracle.

After the show, we collect our little ray of sunshine from

backstage and I hold his hand as he bounces through the parking lot. I look over at Ezra, carrying Faith on his hip, and I smile with nothing but pure joy glowing from within.

Ezra turns his attention away from our beautiful baby girl in his arms to return my smile with a dazzling white grin of his own. "Whoever would've thought I'd have two beautiful blue-eyed girls?"

I catch Faith's eyes in my gaze and make a silly face at her, making her giggle. Looking into her eyes is like seeing my own reflected back at me. They're big and blue and bright and happy. If I could only do one thing for the rest of my life, it would be to fight for her to have a life that keeps the sparkle in her eyes, to fight to keep her blue eyes vibrant, innocent, and wondering.

I will fight to find and destroy the bad men and women in this world who seek to steal, abuse, and destroy human lives. I will fight for the rest of my life to ensure that my babies will know nothing but happiness and freedom.

We reach the car that we'll soon have to trade in for something larger when the third little Bell baby comes along. Ezra and I split on either side of the car and I buckle in Brandon while he does the same with Faith. We shut their doors at the same time and though I reach for the handle of the passenger seat to climb in, he walks around the back of the car and reaches out for me, pulling me into his arms.

"I'm so in love with you, you know that?" He kisses the corner of my lips on one side, then the other.

"I know." I smile at him, holding up my left hand to display the engagement ring and wedding band he bought for me soon after he brought me home to Philadelphia—we were married and had my name changed from Mikhailov to Bell as soon as we were able to make it legal. "You did promise me forever, so…"

His hips push against my protruding belly as he leans me back against the car. "I'd like to spend forever between your legs once we get these two adorable little shits down for the night."

"Oh, you would?" I tilt my head, biting my lip. "I think I'd be okay with that."

"I thought so." He kisses me once and heads back around the car and we both climb in.

He starts up the engine and we both look behind us before he backs out of the space—I've made a bad habit of double-checking when he drives because heaven forbid we should hit something with my babies in the car.

Brandon catches my eyes and gives me the biggest grin. He holds out his little arms like he wants a hug, and I'll give him a damn big one when we get home. "Mine?" he says in the sweetest little voice.

And at the same time, Ezra and I recognize our truth, declaring our loyalty to both our children—and the baby to come—that our hearts will always belong to them. We speak a single syllable in unison that expresses our absolute devotion to our family, to each other, now and forever.

"Yours."

PLAYLIST

Shallow by Lady Gaga & Bradley Cooper
Good Years by ZAYN
Take Me to Church by Hozier
Easy Way Out by Low Roar
Lost Without You by Freya Ridings
Dark Side by Bishop Briggs
Smile by Maisie Peters
War of Hearts by Ruelle
Dangerous Woman by Ariana Grande
Rewrite the Stars by Jess and Gabriel
Run For Your Life by K. Flay
Nothing's Gonna Stop Us Now by Chase Holfelder
Salvation by Gabrielle Aplin
There You Are by ZAYN
Dance Inside by The All-American Rejects

FINAL NOTE FROM THE AUTHOR

Anya and Ezra's story is a work of fiction—intended only for the purpose of entertainment—but human trafficking is a very real issue that demands our collective attention. While all aspects of the *Four Families* series is fictitious, it's important for us to acknowledge the experiences of real-life victims and bring attention to this serious issue.

If you or someone you know is a victim of human trafficking, there are resources that can help. One such resource in the United States is the National Human Trafficking Hotline.

NATIONAL HUMAN TRAFFICKING HOTLINE
1 (888) 373-7888
SMS: 233733 (Text "HELP" or "INFO")
Website: humantraffickinghotline.org

Everyone deserves a happy ending to their story.

Love,

Brynn

ACKNOWLEDGMENTS

I cannot believe that the *Four Families* trilogy is complete! I spent a little over a year lost in writing Anya and Ezra's story and I can't explain how hard it has been to say goodbye to these characters. But I could not have done what I needed to do to tell their story if it weren't for the help of some truly amazing people.

First and foremost, I have to thank my best friend, Sara. Though she's physically gone, her spirit has been with me throughout this entire series and I wouldn't have had the bravery to tell this story without her. I owe my boldness to her, and without that, this series would never have made it into your hands, readers. And to my ride or die crew that exist because of her, you have to know that I couldn't do this without your support. Rachel, Carrie, Kaylan—you girls are everything.

To my editor, Silvia. You are a godsend! I'm so happy I found you. My writing has improved so much as a result of your magnificent work and I'm so grateful for the time you've put into making this series shine!

Rachel, Danielle, Ashlee, Mary, and Maria—I'm so lucky to have you on my beta read team! You all give me confidence and inspire me to have faith in my work, especially when I'm struggling through rough rewrites and wondering if I should scrap the whole thing and start over. I can't think you enough for that. For all the promo you do for my books…I just have no words. You're all amazing and I love you!

Najla and Nada Qamber and their team over at Najla Qamber Designs have done such fabulous things to make my work sparkle and shine with gorgeous design work. You all are truly wonderful to work with and I'm so grateful I found you!

To my husband and children, thank you for letting me

have my time with my stories! I wouldn't be able to do this without your support and willingness to give me the time and space I need to write.

Anya and Ezra…you may just be characters on a page, but to me you are real, and I'm humbled to have been the one to tell your story. Thank you for letting me put you through hell and I wish you a happily ever after as you continue on in the minds of my readers!

And you, daring reader…I am beyond thankful that you picked up this series. To know that you've connected to this story or these characters in some way, however big or small, means more to me than you could ever possibly know. Thank you for reading this story. Your love and support mean everything to me.

ABOUT THE AUTHOR

Brynn Ford is a USA Today Bestselling Author of dark romance for daring readers. She writes emotionally heavy love stories that will twist your soul and shatter your heart before pulling you back together with a hopeful happily-ever-after.

Brynn's books are dark, sometimes disturbing, and often overwhelming. But they're always brightened by an insistent, spicy romance that will live rent-free in your head long after you've turned the final page.

When Brynn isn't obsessively writing, you may find her binge-watching favorite shows while eating far too much junk food or fanatically reading, always seeking to lose herself in the emotional roller coaster of a damn good story. She's a firm believer that her characters continue to live outside the pages in the minds of her readers. Stories don't end just because there aren't any more pages to turn.

CONNECT WITH BRYNN FORD

WEBSITE
Click "Newsletter"
to subscribe to my author newsletter!
www.brynnford.com

GOODREADS
www.goodreads.com/brynnfordauthor

AMAZON
www.amazon.com/author/brynnford

BOOKBUB
www.bookbub.com/profile/brynn-ford

INSTAGRAM
@brynnfordauthor
www.instagram.com/brynnfordauthor

FACEBOOK
www.facebook.com/brynnfordauthor

FACEBOOK GROUP
Brynn's Daring Darlings
bit.ly/brynnsdarlings